S
C

PROLOGUE

The paddocks around the Hopkinses' property were damp for eight months of the year. A smallholding nestled in the western shadow of the sprawling Forest of Dean, the wet came with the territory. But, on a fine, chilly November morning, one might have been excused for believing rain was a stranger to this place with the blue expanse of the heavens above and the ground beneath rock hard from the third consecutive night of frost.

Chris Hopkins blew pluming furls of steam from his mouth into the windless air, then smiled as he stepped out into the yard from the warm farmhouse kitchen. Despite his two sweaters and a waxed jacket, he shivered. He cupped both hands around the Thermos of coffee he'd just prepared, but it didn't help. How could it? Chris smiled and shook his head. Far too early for all this.

Five steps and his ears were already stinging; always had and always would in this weather, being the generous size they were. His smile widened into a grin that had won him some good friends and several lucrative contracts in the competitive animal feeds' market, which occupied his nine to five and a good slice of his remaining waking hours. He put the Thermos under one arm, curled his fingers into a soft clenched fist, and blew into both his hands before rubbing them together to get a little circulation flowing.

He had warned her, but as usual she'd insisted and got her own way. He shook his head and wondered again at his daughter's stubbornness, knowing it was glued onto a gene with more than its fair share of his wife, Sara's, DNA. OK, perhaps it was better that at sixteen Nia still wanted to sleep in her horse's stable with her best friend, rather than hang around outside pubs or stay up all night at some rave experimenting with God knows what, but she could have chosen a better night for it, for crying out loud. Well, maybe it would at least cure her of the habit for the winter. It hadn't been so bad during the summer but this was becoming ridiculous, hi-tech Arctic sleeping bag or no. Next thing you knew, Gwen would be wanting to do the same thing and Sara, still warm and cosy under the duvet upstairs, would throw a blue fit. She was not going to let a ten-year-old girl freeze to death in a stable, even if her big sister wanted to, and that was that. Gwen had yet to develop Nia's manipulative skills, but it would come. Chris secretly looked forward to it.

Jesus, it was cold. He shivered and hurried down the yard to the whitewashed stable that had been nothing but a rat-infested hen house when they'd bought the place five years before. He glanced about him as he walked, feasting his eyes on a Christmas card landscape of white. All around him the bare trees were wreathed in feathery hoar frost, and across the lower fields a surreal milky mist hung low, creeping stealthily upwards towards the tree-lined horizon. It was going to be a beautiful day. Crisp and clear and unpolluted; the sort of late-autumn day he loved.

'Wakey, wakey, girls!' he called as he pushed open the stable door. The musty odour of hay and horse greeted him, mixed with something else, something unusual: a sharp, unpleasant tang.

He heard no rustle of sleeping bags and so added a chastising, 'Come on, ladies. Don't tell me you're still asleep? I come bearing hot coffee!'

His eyes locked on to the horse. There was something wrong with Genevieve. The mare stood huddled in the corner of her stall, shivering and twitching, not offering her usual greeting nicker.

'Nia? Beckie?' He stepped in and looked over Genevieve's stall to the stall containing the camp beds, fan heater and rickety desk lamp Nia had collected into a makeshift bedroom. Everything was still there, but order had been replaced by a chaotic jumble. A Microlite sleeping bag and three extra blankets lay piled in a heap near the foot of an upturned camp bed, the lamp lay on its side, shards of broken glass from the shattered bulb scattered over the floor. On the other bed, a lumpy shape lay unmoving. The sharp tang that greeted his nose crystallised into the unmistakable stink of vomit and triggered a frown of sudden concern.

Chris stepped across and pulled back the blanket that covered the shape on the bed. Beckie lay there, pale and sweating, mouth open, saliva and vomit glistening on her chin.

'Beckie? Beckie, what's wrong?'

The girl moaned, leaned over and retched.

A barbed, unnameable fear lanced at Chris's gut. What the hell had they been doing? He put down the Thermos and looked around, eyes wide, registering the space where there should not have been one.

'*Shit.* Nia? Where's Nia? NIA?'

Ugly thoughts tumbled over in his head. Maybe the girls had eaten something. Perhaps they'd been stupid enough to try something. He pawed at the debris on the floor. Chocolate wrappers, Coke cans, phones. No sign of matches. No cigarette papers or syringes…

Syringes? What was he thinking?

No, he knew his daughter. Maybe she'd gone to the bathroom. He turned back to Beckie. She didn't look well.

'Beckie, love, what's wrong?'

She opened her eyes. Looked at him but didn't see him. Her eyes drifted up and over Chris's shoulder to the tack on the walls, the light beyond.

Something visceral and deep within him rippled and uncoiled.

Beckie giggled. He glared at her, but she still wasn't seeing him. She giggled again but he barely heard, because he was stepping back, his skin crawling, confused and unnerved. No syringes or cigarette papers maybe, but something was very wrong here.

Heart knocking hard against his chest, Chris moved forward again, stepped over Beckie, and leaned in to pick up the canvas camp bed. The expensive orange-and-grey sleeping bag lay like a collapsed cocoon on the floor. He picked it up to throw it back on the bed, but stopped as his eyes fell on a dark purple stain covering two handbreadths of the surface in an irregular smudge. Whatever fluid had been spilled, enough of it had leaked through to the inner lining to mimic the surface stain. Chris stared, the sudden trembling in his arms nothing to do with the freezing temperatures.

Behind him Beckie moaned again.

A dark liquid smudge. The colour of blackberry juice. Chris brought the material to his nose and breathed in a sickly mixture of iron and copper. *Blood.* The sleeping bag fell from his fingers. He turned, stumbling over Beckie, feeling his way along the walls to the outside, his mind buzzing with chaotic panic as he sprinted back to the house. He threw open the doors, calling out his daughter's name.

'Nia? Nia?'

She was not in her sister's room. Not in the bathroom, kitchen, living room. His frenzied search woke up the other children, and they watched with bleary, owl eyes as he yielded to blind panic. He ignored their frightened pleas for explanation, running from room to room, checking behind sofas and in cupboards.

Nia was not in the house.

Sara appeared on the stairs, but Chris was already heading for the door. He ran back out into the yard, heedless of his wife's calling, hurtling around the outbuildings, opening doors, stepping up on the four-bar fences that ringed the fields to call her name. All the while seeing Beckie's unfocused pupils and hearing that awful giggle in her voice.

'Nia? Nia?'

No answer but for the cawing of the rooks his yells disturbed.

He turned and ran back towards the house, the freezing air searing his chest.

Sara stood outside the front door, arms clutching her dressing gown about her. She grabbed at him. 'Chris! Speak to me!'

He could hardly breathe. There was no hope for words yet.

Her nails dug in to his arm. 'Chris, you're frightening me. What's wrong?'

He sucked in air and looked in to his wife's face, his legs trembling beneath him. 'Nia's not in the stables.'

Sara frowned, a half-smile began and then dissolved as his desperate fear ignited her own.

'And something's wrong… with Beckie.' He threw out the words in a broken whisper.

Sara moaned and ran towards the stables. He let her go and staggered to the front door until the noise of his other children crying reached him. He ushered them into the lounge, frightened and confused, plying them with false assurances. He hurried to the kitchen, picked up the phone and dialled 999, recalling the stark, pathetic images of desperate, sleepless parents in the glare of TV lights, begging for help in finding a lost child.

A voice answered the phone, efficient and practical, asking him which service he required. Chris's mind faltered, unable to respond to the simple question, wondering for a fleeting moment if he was overreacting. He stared at the kitchen door. Nia was going to walk back into the house at any moment, wasn't she? Hugging a dressing gown around herself, fragile on those long, coltish legs, wondering what all the fuss was about. Her eyes, so like her mother's, round and troubled from having caused her father the worry, spouting some improbable explanation so he could end this miserable call with an apology.

'Is it the police you require?'

The question burned away his hope. 'I…'

'Sir? How can I help you?'

He tried twice and failed, the words freezing in his larynx until, somehow, he managed to vomit them out. Hearing them was like having his heart squeezed in an iron vice. 'Ambulance and police. Something's happened. I don't know what. But my little girl, there's blood.' A sob choked off the sentence. He took a deep, tremulous breath and finished, 'It's my daughter… she's missing.'

CHAPTER ONE

Detective Sergeant Anna Gwynne stared out through the windscreen of her car at the massive grey wall of Whitmarsh Prison, with its odd cylindrical crown, smooth and bulbous and, accordingly, impossible to climb. She shifted in her seat and flexed and extended her neck, easing out the stiffness induced by the long journey from Bristol. Her eyes looked back at her in the rear-view mirror. Hazel eyes, the bunched-up muscles beneath them always making it look as though she was smiling when she wasn't; an attribute that men found engaging, but got her into trouble with stern teachers as a child. She lifted her chin in a quick inspection: minimal make-up; blonde hair stroked behind her ears in need of a touch-up on the roots; lips dry from the car journey. She reached into her bag for some balm.

The visitors' car park was half-full on this bleak Monday morning, but Anna's gaze settled on the heavy-set man hunched in a green raincoat and puffing on a cigarette some twenty yards away. He had his back to her, pretending to find the pay-and-display instructions meaningful, while he succumbed to his nicotine habit like the tobacco junkie he was. He turned, caught her looking at him, then took one final, defiant drag, stubbed the cigarette out under his comfortable shoe, and hurried towards the car. A bitter November wind picked up the thinning grey fringe of his hair and styled it instantly into a sparrow's wing. The passenger door opened and Detective Chief Inspector Ted Shipwright eased his ample frame into the seat.

'Right, Sergeant. Now that you've made me suffer for my sins, let's get on with this.'

'I'd never force you to have a cigarette, sir. Outside. In the bitter wind. And sub-zero temperatures.' Anna kept her face straight.

'We both know you bloody well did. Those recriminating glances are like porcupine quills. It's a look you and Mrs Shipwright uncannily share.'

This time Anna allowed herself a smile as she reached for the laptop in the space behind the passenger seat. The unspoken rule during their many car journeys together was that they'd take her car and she would drive. There were several reasons for this, the chief among them being the fact that she was a good driver and he could nap when he needed to, but also because his car smelled like the mobile ashtray it largely was. And, since one of his daughters from his first marriage was almost Anna's age, and flatly refused to get into the car because of the smell, Shipwright assumed – rightly but without even asking – that Anna would feel the same way.

On screen, Anna now brought up the video she wanted him to see.

'Hector Shaw, sir. From ten years ago.'

Shipwright grunted. He smoothed down his hair with a shovel-sized hand, his strong features set and suddenly serious.

The screen flickered into snow and then cleared as the clumsy edit settled. A room came into focus: low, scuffed cream chairs of tubular steel with padded arms of sweat-stained hessian, coffee-coloured walls and a brown needlecord carpet in need of cleaning. An officer was seated in one corner, arms folded, dressed in a prison-service uniform. The view focused on a man in prison-issue fatigues, seated at a table.

Hector Shaw had a pear-shaped face, heavy-lidded eyes behind myopic glasses and, at thirty-nine, when the video had been made, a prematurely receding hairline. He stared across the table at the interviewer who, out of shot, spoke first.

'Can we talk about your wife?'

Shaw tilted his head. 'How is she?' His accent was northern. The slow enunciation and the overemphasised vowels defining it as originating in Lancashire, more specifically, Mancunian.

There was a pause. 'She's dead. You killed her.'

'So, when you ask if we can talk about my wife, what you're really asking is how do I feel about killing my wife?' Shaw's gaze remained steady. When he blinked, he did so slowly. There was a suggestion of something crocodilian about it.

Off camera were the noises of shuffling papers and a throat being cleared. A pause and then, 'Do you think that your two years at Rampton prior to your transfer here have helped you?'

'Helped when it comes to talking about my wife, do you mean?'

'Have you been able to try and imagine what it might have been like for your wife when you killed her?'

Shaw sat back and folded his arms. Anna, watching the video for the umpteenth time, sensed that this, this single movement, was the giveaway. The moment Shaw decided that the interviewer was a complete imbecile.

'Are we talking about empathy or imagination? I have no conception of what it actually feels like to have a knife thrust into my liver, or to then have it slice my windpipe. I suspect very few people have.'

'You used the word empathy—'

'Because it's what you were trying to imply I don't have, isn't it?'

Some more clearing of the throat off screen. 'Erm, why don't you try now? Imagine you're a thirty-six-year-old woman at home alone. You hear a noise behind you. You stop and pivot. There's a man there. A man who grabs you and drags you into your kitchen, where he ties you to a chair and then uses your own kitchen knives to stab you and cut your throat. And what are you thinking, do you suppose, in that moment of supreme terror when you realise someone is trying to do you real harm?'

'If it was me, I'd want to get away. Definitely be somewhere else.'

'But you'd tied her up?'

'Yes.'

'Emotionally, what would she have felt?'

Still Shaw's expression was inscrutable. 'Terror. Sick maybe, but mainly terror. But we are talking about my ex-wife here, right?'

'Yes.'

'Then most of her feelings would have been blunted by the bottle of Smirnoff she'd been sucking on since ten o'clock that morning. The same as she did every day. Plus, she knew me, so I would not have been such a big surprise to her. Unwelcome, maybe, surprise, no. We hadn't surprised one another for years.'

'Afterwards, what about her parents? How would they have reacted?'

Shaw uncrossed his legs. 'I think they would have been quite happy to see me dead. They'd made that clear enough for some time.'

'Is that how you would feel if someone attacked your daughter?'

Another pause. This time Shaw moved forward, elbows on the table, eyes on the ball of his left thumb as he massaged it with the thumb of his right hand.

'I don't have a daughter.'

'But if you did?'

Shaw looked up. 'I'd want to see the bastard dead. But we don't have a death penalty, do we?'

'But you killed your wife because you felt she was responsible for your daughter's death?'

'Partly.'

More rustling of papers. 'Even though she, your daughter, umm, Amy—'

Another slow, crocodile blink from Shaw. 'Abbie. Her name was Abbie.'

'Sorry, Abbie, threw herself under a train?'

Shaw seemed to hesitate, his eyelids flickering momentarily as if he were calculating something. But he continued smoothly when he spoke. 'My ex-wife was drunk on the sofa when that happened.'

'Do you consider yourself to be judge and jury?'

'I consider her not to have been a capable parent.'

'Would you do it again?'

'Like a shot.'

A long beat of silence followed.

'You do understand that this interview forms a part of your continuing assessment for rehabilitation? You applied for certain privileges to be considered.'

Shaw's mouth split into an enormous grin. 'I wanted to test the waters. I guess it won't be happening this time.'

'No.'

Shaw smiled. 'Then we've both fucked up, haven't we? You need to be better prepared. Looking up notes during an interview is very rude. So is mentioning my daughter. Worse is getting her name wrong. And you need to ensure I don't put anyone else in the hospital wing, right?'

'You haven't.'

Shaw was still smiling. 'Not yet.'

The scene on the video erupted with the noise of scraping furniture and screaming as Shaw lunged across the desk out of shot before the watching guard could react. A blur of violent movement followed as Shaw pulled the interviewer across and buried his face into the exposed part of the back of the man's neck, before the screen froze and went blank.

'Who's interviewing?' Shipwright asked after several seconds of loaded silence.

'His name was Conrad. The consultant who normally attended was lecturing at a conference and thought it would be good practice for his junior colleague. Conrad needed twenty stitches and a skin graft. I think he retrained as a GP after this. I got a copy of the interview from a lecture I once attended.'

'What was the lecture called – "How to wind up a five-star psycho without really trying"?'

'Almost. The lecturer used it to illustrate how easy it is to get things very wrong. So, what do you think?'

'I think anyone who kills six people and puts another four in hospital during his prison term is a card-carrying nutter.' Anna nodded, but Shipwright saw that she was pensive. 'Come on, spit it out.'

'It's just that there was never an element of paraphilia in Shaw's crimes. No sexual motive at all. It started out as revenge for his daughter and spiralled up from there. He got a taste for it, literally.'

Shipwright shook his head. 'DNA doesn't lie, Anna.'

'I know.'

'When's Shaw due out?'

'His is a whole life sentence.'

DCI Shipwright smiled. It lifted the craggy jowls an inch and transformed the grizzly into a teddy bear. 'You meet the nicest people in this job. Shall we?'

They'd redecorated the interview room. This time there were drab grey walls, black plastic chairs and a metal-legged table with a Formica top. All in all an improvement on the brown, but despite liberal use of a sickly floral air freshener plugged into a socket at floor level, the room stank of old sweat and urine. Shaw looked thinner, harder, his face sunken, skin sallow from a prison tan. Blue bristles ran in a crown above his ears and around the back of his head from where he'd shaved off his remaining hair. He sat slumped and unsmiling, his arms folded, dressed in standard grey prison joggers and sweatshirt. His gaze flitted between Anna and

Shipwright. Yet, despite his posture, his eyes brightened as they sat down, calculating and sharp behind his thick glasses.

The room was equipped with recording facilities and the interview would be videoed. Shaw had declined the presence of a solicitor. Anna did the necessary for the recording.

'Interview at Whitmarsh Prison of Hector Shaw, under caution. Present are Detective Chief Inspector Edward Shipwright and Detective Sergeant Anna Gwynne. For the digital interview recording, the interviewee has declined the offer of legal representation.

'Mr Shaw,' Anna continued, 'thanks for agreeing to be interviewed. You understand that you do not have to answer my questions. If you choose not to answer my questions, but this matter is raised in court and you answer the same questions, then the court will ask you to explain why you did not answer here today. The tapes of this interview can be played in court, so that the court will be able to hear what has been said. Please indicate that you understand.'

'Yes, I understand,' Shaw said. 'What's this about? And who the fuck are you, anyway?'

Shipwright leaned forward on the desk, fingers steepled. 'We, Mr Shaw, are part of a major crimes review task force. What we do is take a fresh look at cases that have gone cold on our patch. The southwest, to be specific. I say, "our patch", though we end up all over the place interviewing witnesses. And suspects, like you. Amazing what things come to light when they're looked at from a new perspective. Especially in this high-tech world we now live in.'

'What's that got to do with me?'

'Good question. Remember the evening of 15th June 2002?'

Shaw snorted and shook his head. 'Yeah. Like it was yesterday.'

'Well, you should. Because that was the evening a fifteen-year-old girl by the name of Tanya Cromer was raped.'

Shaw continued to smile, but his jaw clenched, the muscles clearly working.

'Tanya fought,' Anna said. 'And there was blood. A few spattered smudges on her clothes and under her nails.'

Shipwright added, 'She'd fallen out with her boyfriend and everyone thought it was him. But he had an alibi tighter than a duck's arse and the case went cold.' He leaned a bit closer. 'It had rained. The DNA samples were mixed. Pretty hopeless then, but now…' Shipwright let his eyebrows crawl up towards his hairline.

'Riveting,' said Shaw. 'Where's this going?'

'What the chief inspector means,' said Anna, 'is that we've made significant advances in terms of lab technology, mathematical models and bio-statistical software since then. These days our forensic scientists can successfully separate contributors in mixed samples.'

'Couldn't have put it better, Sergeant,' Shipwright said. 'And guess what? One of those separated samples matches your DNA, Mr Shaw.'

Shaw looked like he wanted to say something, but his mouth stayed shut.

Anna watched for one of the slow blinks that had marked his aggression in the tape they had viewed. So far it hadn't happened. 'So where were you on the evening of 15th June 2002, Mr Shaw?' she asked.

Shaw still said nothing.

'For the DIR, the interviewee refuses to answer.'

Shipwright pressed on. 'Three months after Tanya reported the attack to the police she went missing.'

Three seconds of silence followed. So far it was a draw in the staring contest.

'If you want to say something, now is the time, sonny,' Shipwright said.

Anna pressed him further. 'If you know where she is, tell us. Give this poor girl's family a way out of purgatory.'

Still Shaw remained silent. His eyes looked back at them, his corneas reflecting the harsh ceiling lights, his irises the colour of oil spill on a grey sea. Anna waited and then said, 'For the record, the interviewee has refused to respond.' She looked at Shipwright. He shrugged in response.

'I have to inform you, Hector Shaw, that there is a positive match between your DNA and that found at the scene,' Shipwright said. 'Following a conversation with the senior prosecutor, I have the authority to charge you with the rape of Tanya Cromer contrary to the Sexual Offences Act, 1956. Do you understand this charge against you?'

Shaw glared.

'We need an answer.'

Another long beat of seething silence followed, until Shaw's eyes narrowed and his lips pursed like he'd thought of the world's best joke and he said, 'How about I volunteer for an identity parade?'

'Going to be difficult without the victim. But then you know that well enough. You're in for life, so I suspect there's no point us appealing to your sense of closure,' Shipwright said.

Shaw shifted in his chair. He sat up and unfolded his arms, hands on his lap, his gaze dropping to them for a moment before coming back up again. 'That's where you're wrong. I know all about closure.'

Shipwright sat back. 'Right, we'll be in touch. You might want to have a solicitor with you next time.'

'Time is now eleven twenty a.m. and we are terminating the interview.' Anna pressed the button to end the recording. Shaw blinked slowly. Anna caught it and felt her pulse canter.

'What about the rest of the sample?' Shaw asked.

'Sorry?'

'You said the DNA came from a mixed sample. Whose was the other sample?'

'We don't know,' Anna said.

'And it doesn't matter. We have yours,' Shipwright said, pushing away from the desk.

Shaw kept his gaze fixed on Anna. 'And what is your interpretation of that, Sergeant?'

Anna barely paused before replying. 'Who else was there?'

Shaw nodded and offered up a wintry smile. 'Do I look like someone who'd gang-rape a girl to you?'

He was challenging her, but all his question achieved was to trigger an instant unvoiced thought. *I don't know what monsters are meant to look like, Mr Shaw, but you'll do.*

When she didn't answer immediately, Shaw went on, 'I'll let you work that out, OK? You up for that, *Anna*?'

His words contained no menace but they hung in her ears like the ringing of a great bell.

The moment was broken by Shipwright, pragmatic as ever. 'Of course, it would save a great deal of time and effort if you told us, since you were clearly there.'

Shaw turned his face towards the chief inspector and nodded. 'Let me think about that, Mr Shipwright.'

Shipwright snorted and stood up. 'Let's go.'

They'd got halfway across the room when Shaw spoke again. 'Did they tell you I had a daughter once, *Anna*? I expect you came across it in your research, didn't you?'

It made her pause. Beside her, Shipwright shook his head. 'Don't,' he whispered, but she'd already hesitated. The minuscule delay gave Shaw the opening he'd been waiting for. 'She'd be about your age, *Anna*. Remember that.'

Shipwright took Anna's arm and ushered her out.

Shaw had seen something, or sensed something about her, Anna was convinced of it.

That was unusual, she thought.

Anna's sister, Kate, often commented on how she'd developed her professional 'death stare' to perfection, though there was nothing calculated about it. It was simply the way the muscles of her face arranged themselves when her mind was mining deeply for information. This happened most often in situations where the conversation was less than demanding. But sometimes, too, when she was concentrating hard. Most people interpreted it as inscrutability, or, less generously, arrogance, when it was nothing of the kind. Few, if any, saw it for what it truly was. Shaw seemed to be emotionally intelligent enough to pick up on it even in the brief time she'd been in his presence. He'd caught it and thrown it back at her with his question.

And what is your interpretation of that, Sergeant?

His words stayed with her all the way to the car. She'd seen photographs of his daughter. Small for her age, but pretty, with her mother's smile and her father's big, short-sighted eyes. The photograph showed Abbie with grey eyeshadow, and pink and black hair hanging low over her brow. The sweatshirt she'd worn had 'My Chemical Romance' in Gothic letters across the chest.

Yet, even worse than recalling Abbie and her untimely death, was remembering the way Shaw had spoken her own name. Slowly, emphatically.

You up for that, Anna?

The words echoed inside her head as she gunned the engine in the car park, and each time they did it made her scalp crawl.

CHAPTER TWO

They made a comfort stop at a McDonald's on the way to the motorway. Anna ordered coffee for both, explaining to a sceptical Shipwright that it wasn't at all bad since the fast-food chain got their coffee act together.

'Hmm.' Shipwright grunted and lifted one eyebrow. 'I'll soak mine up with a cheeseburger then, thanks, and none of that bloody pickle stuff.'

Anna ordered. Shipwright paid. He downed the burger in four bites and then took himself outside for a smoke. Anna finished her coffee before going back to the car and phoning Justin Holder, a detective constable and the third and youngest member of their unit.

'How did it go, Sarge?' Holder asked. Expectant, enthusiastic. Like a kid at a fair.

'Shaw did two cartwheels and offered me an interest-free loan after giving the boss a kiss.'

Holder chuckled. 'Yeah, I bet.' His accent was pure Acton. Like Anna, he was not an Avon & Somerset local.

'You?'

'All good. Chasing up the Ryder files from Northumbria. But you're on the way back, right?'

She caught the anxious tone in his responses. Holder was fresh but he wasn't usually needy. 'What's up, Justin?'

'Rain Man stuck his head around the door asking when you'd be back, that's all.'

'Was he carrying a bottle of champagne?'

'No. But he had that look on his face.'

'Look?'

'Yeah. A sort of desperate Labrador look.'

'You mean the "it's not important, honestly, but any time within the next five seconds will do" look?'

'Yeah. Trisha was in his office for twenty minutes and I haven't seen her since.'

Trisha Spedding was the squad's civilian support. A skilled criminal analyst with a cut-to-the-chase attitude and mind. Like the rest of them, she was on the squad at Shipwright's request. Rain Man – Holder's laddish nickname for their department head, Superintendent Rainsford – kept an arm's-length approach to operational tasks. His direct involvement usually meant something urgent.

'So, no victory celebration, then? Right, I'll warn the boss. Get the kettle on for about four. He wants to call in on the CPS.'

'Rainsford wants to know when we're back, eh? That does not bode well.' Shipwright was back in the car, still clutching his coffee, a miasma of stale tobacco surrounding him like an old coat. He sipped from the cup, grimaced, lowered his window and emptied the contents onto the road.

'I reckon it's a surprise party, sir,' Anna said as the damp November chill whistled in and ejected the car's heat.

'You will watch out for those flying pigs, won't you, Sergeant.' Shipwright powered up the window. 'One day, one of them will dump right on your head. Whatever it is Mr Rainsford wants, it'll have to wait until tomorrow. I'm on parental duty tonight at a concert. My youngest is a goat in *Old Macdonald Had A Farm*, the opera.'

'You're kidding,' Anna said.

Shipwright sighed. 'I'll thank you to leave the jokes to me, Sergeant.' He pressed a lever at the bottom of his seat and the backrest tilted rearwards. 'Now, let me meditate for ten minutes while that cheeseburger negotiates my digestive tract, especially that tricky bend near my liver.'

Anna winced.

'You mark my words, one day you will also find a post-lunch snooze essential.'

'Just ten minutes, sir?'

'Twenty max.'

Shipwright settled back and closed his eyes. Within two minutes he was in a deep and ugly sleep, mouth open, soft palate vibrating noisily.

Anna didn't mind. She relished the opportunity for reflection. They'd had a good result. Worth the trip to see that look on Shaw's rat-guilty face. And yet Anna felt a niggle. Shaw had denied any previous crimes and there was no record of violence prior to the killings that he'd been prosecuted for. Rape was a big departure from his modus operandi and nothing had been linked to him until the DNA hit flagged him on the database. She could still recall the words Professor Jane Markham had prefaced her lecture with when she'd used Shaw's interview as a teaching aid. Markham, a forensic psychiatrist, taught Anna as a visiting professor during her three years of a criminology degree, and her words had become Anna's mantra:

> *'Almost anything you hear in an interview with a patient suffering from a personality disorder should be taken with a healthy shovelful of salt. For most of these patients, lying is a way of life. Many are articulate, many are intelligent. Both of which make your job all the harder. It is you' – she'd pointed randomly towards her audience – 'who will be asked to make judgements upon which will often rest the freedom of the individual and the safety of the public. So, let's take a look at some examples…'*

An adrenalin squirt rippled through Anna. This job could be frustrating, boring, a real time-suck, and drive you to numb yourself with alcohol. But it could also be amazingly satisfying. There'd be justice for Tanya Cromer at long last, and some sort of closure for her relatives. It didn't matter how clichéd it sounded to anyone listening, bringing the perpetrators of harm to justice was what gave her the most satisfaction. It was why she put up with the crap hours and road-trip meals. Why she did the job.

Her thoughts drifted to the initial interview again. Now that Shaw was implicated, she'd drop Prof. Markham a line. She'd appreciate that. It would be a chance to tell her old mentor that at least one of her students was using what she taught to good effect. Even if some of Anna's own work colleagues thought it was not the best use of a stretched and salami-sliced budget.

The Southwest Regional Major Crimes Review Task Force began with twenty people culled from half a dozen different forces in a collaborative splurge, but as funds diminished over a two-year period, they were now limping along on what Rainsford could crumble out of a very thin slice of financial cake.

It didn't matter that over the last two years they'd closed twenty cases in five different force areas. Cold cases weren't fashionable, and they definitely weren't sexy. But Anna knew that working with an old warhorse like Shipwright was worth its weight in gold. The DCI defined 'old school'. So old that he still remembered writing on slate with chalk, or so he kept telling her. He could spot a bullshitter from two hundred yards, possessed an elephant's memory, and, come to think of it, quite a bit of its gait. There'd been barriers to clamber over, but Anna felt she was at least over the barbed wire and heading for the trenches. So long as she kept looking, she knew she'd keep finding little nuggets of buried gold, which weren't in any training manual, invariably delivered in Shipwright's laconic style.

Contrary to what many thought, his secondment to unsolved crimes was not a pre-retirement doss, but Rainsford's attempt to add teeth to what might so easily have become a paper tiger. Shipwright and his squad had proved this in the first six months by solving two murders, and an abduction that had languished for over fifteen years. Mostly, Anna had been amazed and impressed by his doggedness. Once Ted Shipwright's teeth were sunk into something he never let go, no matter how bad it tasted. He'd taught Anna never to back down if you thought you were right. And even more so if you didn't, so long as you thought you would be right eventually. And she was an apt pupil, he'd admitted that.

'You're like me, Anna. Mrs Shipwright insists I was a mule in a previous life,' he'd said. 'Notice I didn't say ass' – he'd paused before adding –'that's what I am now, apparently.'

He was right there. Stubborn as they come and with connections across almost every region in the country, Shipwright was an invaluable tool in investigating historical crime because, in most cases, witnesses and suspects had spread their wings and flown a long way from where the crime had been committed. It meant long days and literally thousands of miles.

Yet Anna harboured no regrets. Police banter naturally referenced the cold cases, and Shipwright had variously been nicknamed Captain Birdseye or, more commonly, the lollipop man – though never to his face, of course. Anna liked it. The idea that Shipwright was cool and calculating, just as she was, only made her feel they were a better team. Plus, in a gently derogatory tilt at his age, she, like the other officers, grasped the irony and tried to imagine him in a yellow, hi-vis full-length coat, waving a Stop sign outside a school – though they'd probably have to change the school hours to accommodate his fag habit. It made her smile. His team had naturally become 'lollipop boys' and, in her case, 'lollipop lady'. She wore it like a badge, mainly because of its association with Shipwright, even though it was only a short hop and a skip from that to 'Anna the Ice Queen', which she'd also heard as a locker-room whisper.

Now, heading south on the M5, with the cruise control set at seventy-five, she pondered why the thought of being labelled a frosty bitch didn't bother her one little bit. Perhaps it was because in all the books she'd read, ice queens were powerful and usually got their way. She could drink to that.

Forty minutes after the coffee stop, she nudged Shipwright awake. 'On the M32, sir. We'll be at the CPS in fifteen minutes.'

Shipwright rubbed his eyes and then let the backrest up, put his glasses on and peered at his watch. 'Christ, Anna, twenty minutes from Worcester to Bristol? Can this thing fly?'

'I may have lost track of time, sir. You know, meditating.'

'Sarcasm can be a very unattractive trait, Sergeant.'

'Sir.'

Their caseworker at the Crown Prosecution Service kept them waiting for half an hour. Someone made them more coffee. Anna found it undrinkable, Shipwright smacked his lips as he sipped from a steaming mug.

'This is what I call coffee, Sergeant. Undissolved granules floating on the top and no bloody froth with a leaf drawn in it.'

She was prepared to forgive him. He was a lifelong smoker, after all, and probably had few functioning taste buds left. But she kept her thoughts to herself, fetched a plastic cup of cold water from a cooler, and read an uninspiring gardening magazine while Shipwright went over Shaw's charge with a prosecutor.

They got back to HQ at Portishead a little after five. The MCRTF was housed on the second floor of the sprawling site. White walls, ash-effect desks, open plan for most. As they entered, DC Holder looked up from his desk in the room they all shared.

'Good day?' he asked, grinning. Mid-twenties, no tie, he wore his dark hair close cropped, and even with glasses still managed to look no older than fifteen.

Shipwright sat down on the edge of a desk that creaked in protest. 'A good day indeed, Justin. About to be ruined, I understand, by an urgent meeting with Superintendent Rainsford?'

'He had to go to a different meeting, sir. And Trisha's gone home, too, but the super got her to prepare these for us. Called it homework.' Holder made an apologetic face and handed round three large sealed envelopes. 'And he wants us in by eight tomorrow morning.'

Inside each envelope was a cardboard file holder containing a sheaf of papers held together by a paper clip. Trisha had written the word 'Emily Risman' on the cardboard cover. Inside were case notes and clippings from newspapers, along with copied typed-up sheets.

Shipwright let out a low whistle and muttered, 'Neville Cooper.'

'Who?' Holder asked.

Shipwright looked up. 'Come on, Justin. Last year's shit storm? I'll give you a clue. One more Central Counties Regional Crime cock-up and press feeding frenzy.'

When Holder continued to look blank, Shipwright added, 'The Woodsman?'

Holder's eyes lit up behind his glasses. 'He's the bloke who was wrongfully imprisoned.'

'The cigar is yours.' Shipwright nodded.

Anna peered at the papers, her memory of the case flooding back. Of all the miscarriages of justice perpetrated by the notorious CCRC squad, the wrongful imprisonment of Neville Cooper for the murder of Emily Risman was one of the most despicable. Cooper's walk to freedom on the steps of the Royal Courts of Justice had taken place in a blaze of public and press indignation some eight months before, his guilty verdict deemed unsafe on the basis of a catalogue of prosecution gaffs and undisclosed evidence.

'Why the Woodsman?' Holder asked.

Shipwright answered, 'Body was found on the edge of the Forest of Dean. The killer had half hidden it under an arrangement of leaves, branches and sticks over a shallow depression. The team suspected the killer had been meaning to set a bonfire, but may have been disturbed. The press, ever ready for a catchy headline, nicknamed the killer the Woodsman.'

Holder nodded, his mouth forming the ghost of a sanguine smile.

Anna continued to read the file. At the time of Cooper's release, he'd served seventeen years.

'They made up his confession, withheld evidence, locked him up and threw away the key,' Shipwright muttered, scanning the papers.

'What's that got to do with us, sir?' Holder asked. 'We're not anti-corruption.'

'We're not,' Anna said. 'But this is also a cold case.'

Holder frowned behind his glasses.

'Cooper's conviction was deemed unsafe,' Anna explained. 'By definition that opens up the possibility that someone else must have carried out the crime he was wrongfully prosecuted for.'

'Right.' Holder nodded.

'I thought West Mercia were making a big fuss about reopening the case?' Anna said, still scanning the papers.

'Indeed.' Shipwright got to his feet. He hadn't bothered taking off his coat and now he put the papers back into the file before tucking it under his arm. 'Up until three weeks ago when the CPS, bless 'em, decided that they had enough evidence for a retrial. According to the *Guardian* article I read, Cooper is going back into the dock some time in the New Year. God knows why Rainsford is giving us this. I daresay we'll find out in the morning. Go home, children. Come back ten minutes early in the morning, bright-eyed and full of background information. You can fill me in over coffee and a croissant. My treat. Now, I have a concert to attend.' He moved off and started humming 'Old Macdonald', but turned back at the door. 'How do you spell unmitigated enjoyment, Justin?'

'Umm, u, n—'

'Wrong. It's E-I-E-I-O. Tomorrow.' He waved a hand.

Bemused, Holder turned to Anna.

She shrugged. 'Married-life humour.'

Holder blinked.

'Definitely an acquired taste.'

Anna made the 6.30 p.m. kettlebell class at a gym off the Gloucester Road. One of the half-dozen franchises that had opened in Bristol. She trained or ran whenever the chance arose. In a job that held no warnings for what lurked around each corner, it paid to be as hard and trim as possible. After an appropriate hour of sweating, she called in at a Sainsbury's Local for some essentials before returning to her flat. Whenever she passed by, it was her custom to glance in at the estate agent's window beside Sainsbury's, as a depressing reminder of how unlikely it was that she would ever be able to afford her own place. Horfield had not escaped the property-price madness. Two-bedroomed terraced houses on the Hughenden Road were going for £250k plus.

Well, good luck with that, she always thought. A deposit and a mortgage would wipe her out. As things stood, her bloody student loan was still eating into her pay packet. *Student loan. Christ, at almost thirty*, Anna reminded herself.

She arrived at her flat and unlocked the door. The one-bedroom, ground-floor apartment with kitchen and living room in an Edwardian terrace had been a find. Especially as it bordered a park as well. Though close to the city, in the summer she could be running out of her front door and over Horfield Common within a minute. Now, on the downward slope to winter, and with the hour turned back, she missed the light at six in the morning and only ever saw the park trees in daylight at the weekends.

By 8 p.m., she was showered and fed. She hung up her dark suit and threw her white blouse into the laundry basket, poured herself a glass of wine from a bottle in the fridge and took it to her desk in the living room. As she waited for the computer to boot up, she sipped the bargain Riesling from Aldi. One glass only. She'd convinced herself that the wine helped her sleep, though Sunday magazines espoused as many views on that as there were bottles in an off-licence.

The Woodsman file lay open on her desk. Background stuff that she needed to research. Carole King's 'A Natural Woman' came to an end, and Anna went over to adjust the volume. The equipment was modern – an Akai direct drive with Bluetooth links to speakers on a shelf – but the vinyls were old and had once belonged to her father. Anna and her sister had ended up splitting the collection, because her mother had shown no interest in it. She had even threatened to throw the records out during one of her 'clear-outs'. Anna's sister, Kate, younger by a year and a bit, kept her half in the box room of her nice little house twenty miles north of Cardiff, but Anna liked listening, imagining her father doing the exact same thing in his teens. Somehow it helped keep his memory alive, and it felt like much more than simply a homage to the man who had died before he'd seen her graduate and make her career choice. Sharing his music made a connection she cherished.

'I Feel the Earth Move' kicked in and she returned to her desk and the computer. She scanned Facebook and looked up some of her old college mates. She considered adding a line or two of comments but then dismissed the thought, shut it down and punched in 'Ellison Institute'. Professor Jane Markham was still listed under 'faculty' and, conveniently, possessed an email address. Anna spent ten minutes drafting a paragraph, not wanting to come across as sycophantic, but genuinely believing that Markham would be interested in anything Shaw-related. At draft five she told herself she was being stupid and pressed 'send'.

When she typed in 'Neville Cooper' the search engine came up with 110,000 hits, most with the Woodsman sobriquet added to the line, the first twenty from newspapers. She opened a few, simply to get a feeling for what had taken place.

The Court of Appeal had ruled that a vital piece of evidence corroborating Cooper's alibi, which placed him at an amusement arcade on the afternoon of the murder, had been suppressed deliberately in order to secure a conviction. The reports recounted the systemic victimisation of Cooper and made her blood run cold. The wine was gradually losing its chill in the glass as she turned away from the screen to the file Trisha had prepared.

Emily Risman was eighteen years old when she was murdered. A posed black and white photograph of her at sixteen, in a school uniform, showed a pretty girl with the remnants of puppy fat filling her cheeks and lessening the definition of what were unspectacular but well-defined bones. Her smile looked perky and knowingly defiant; the grin of a teenager with no academic pretensions. Emily left school shortly after the photograph was taken and went to work as a hairdresser, escaping the environment that shackled her and earning, for the first time, money to spend on herself. Emily knotted her tie a good eight inches below her chin, over a deliberately unbuttoned blouse. Her teachers were kind in their guarded obituaries, not wishing to speak ill of the dead. Emily had not been a troublemaker, but though she'd been a girl whose interests lay outside the curriculum, they were as shocked as everyone to learn that their ex-pupil was three months pregnant when she was killed.

In the middle of February 1998, Emily went missing on her half-day, a Thursday afternoon. Her parents reported her absence on the Friday morning on discovering her empty bed, having not stayed up for her return on Thursday night. The attraction of a neighbouring town's football club dance meant that they had not expected her home much before midnight—

Anna's personal mobile rang. The display showed the caller as her sister Kate. She let the answerphone kick in. Now was not the time for chit-chat.

—They found Emily on the Saturday in a densely wooded area less than two miles from her home in Millend, Gloucestershire. A woman out walking her dog spotted an arm sticking up out of the sodden leaves and dirt, the wigwam of sticks covering her having collapsed. Disturbed, in all probability, by a fox attracted by the smell of the body.

In stark contrast to Emily's pretty school snap, the scene-of-crime photos made unpleasant and ugly viewing. The body had been dumped in a shallow depression and left with only a hurried and half-hearted attempt at concealment by the killer. Her lower half remained covered by decaying leaves, but the February winds had blown much of her torso clean. The impression it gave in two of the photographs was an oddly disturbing one. From twenty feet, it looked as if Emily was struggling upwards out of the ground, as if the earth was attempting to swallow her. She lay on her stomach, face turned to one side, mouth open, eyes staring beseechingly, with lustreless corneas, at the surrounding trees. Her left arm was raised and resting on a log, as if she were signalling or calling for help. Blood had stained her clothes black. Her jeans lay rucked around her ankles, sweater yanked up to expose her back. Many of the thirty or so fatal stab wounds looked like flecks of dirt. Some had trails of blood caking the skin like cracked lacquer. Anna knew that the stab wounds without bloodied snail tracks had been inflicted after death.

The pathologist's report gave the cause of death as multiple stab wounds to the neck, chest and abdomen. Marks on her neck implied attempted strangulation. The post-mortem examination had also been the first indication to anyone that Emily had been pregnant. The estimation came in at eleven plus weeks. She had been dead for at least thirty-six hours.

The forensic work-up, though extensive, yielded little in the way of hard evidence. No fingerprints on the victim's skin, but also no ligature marks. The suggestion was that the killer had worn gloves. The weapon used had a four-inch blade, but a careful and painstaking search of the surrounding area had not brought anything to light. There was clear evidence of sexual activity, but no semen; vaginal bruising suggested that the sexual activity had been forced. Traces of lubricant indicated condom use. Fingernail swabs yielded nothing useful. Emily's blood contained enough alcohol for the police to surmise that she had been drinking on Thursday afternoon or evening. Since no one came forward to advise them otherwise, they assumed that she'd been drinking with the killer. The most significant forensic findings came in the analysis of Emily's sweater, which threw up several foreign fibres. But, paradoxically, it was the absence of an item of clothing that led, finally, to an arrest. And it was Emily's mother who had complained to the police on receiving her daughter's clothes, following extensive analysis, that her pants were missing.

Investigating officers' reports made up the bulk of the photocopies that filled the file. Initially, things ran relatively smoothly. Emily's pregnancy had been a key feature and provided a motive for her murder. But it also provided the loose thread, which, on pulling began to unravel the fabric of Emily Risman's far-from-innocent life. An only child and kept on a tight rein for years by a hard-working and respectable father, Emily rebelled at school. As a teenager, she'd become a good-time girl in the truest sense.

The hair and fibres found on her sweater matched that of two local youths, both of whom had been spotted with her at the football club on the Wednesday evening prior to her murder. Both were from the same village of Millend as Emily, and both were taken in for questioning. One, Roger Willis, had DNA typing consistent with being the father of Emily's child. Willis broke down and admitted that Emily and he were lovers, but he vehemently denied murdering her and the police were hamstrung. Willis had a solid alibi for the whole of Thursday and Friday morning, with twenty or more witnesses at a hospital appointment and, later, at a local pub attesting to his presence. More importantly, at eighteen, Willis showed symptoms of the early stages of an inherited disease called retinitis pigmentosa. Theirs was the rarest type in terms of genetic transmission being X-linked. Willis's mother bore the defective gene and also suffered from the disease in a mild form. Medical evidence showed that he displayed a classic symptom of the disease, namely severe night blindness. In the dim and dark environment of the Forest of Dean on a February afternoon, his vision would have been severely impaired.

Emily's boyfriend at the time, a nineteen-year-old carpenter named Richard Osbourne, admitted sexual involvement with her over the previous couple of years, but could account for his whereabouts on the day of her murder. Other witness statements claimed Emily was willing to take boys into the woods for a 'seeing to'.

From the reports, Anna could sense that the mood of the investigation had changed as time went on. No longer considered completely innocent, Emily started to be viewed as a rather unruly, precocious girl. The net widened, and as the sordid details of her death began to emerge, the press began hounding the police for results. By the end of a month, that hounding became shrill provocation. The police's decision to protect the family by withholding some of the more unpalatable aspects only served to fuel press speculation. Emily and the Woodsman became a national obsession.

Neville Cooper had already been questioned by CCRC officers – the regional team put in charge of the investigation once the local CID's efforts had not borne fruit. The same age as Emily, Neville lived one street away and neighbours had reported that from his back garden he would sit on a wall and consider the Risman property, and watch Emily sunbathe. Despite the similarity in their age, Emily and Neville were not schoolmates. Cooper had attended a special needs unit in Hereford since the age of eleven. By the age of two, it had become obvious that he had behavioural problems and, at six, he had thrown his first epileptic fit. An IQ test at the age of nine measured eighty-four. His parents adopted a typically overprotective attitude, and for years Neville was not allowed to play with other children for fear of this triggering 'one of his turns'.

A lack of boundaries meant that he was seldom disciplined for his unruly behaviour and, as his mother put it to social workers, he 'ran rings around her'. This entailed absconding from home, staying out late, and playing truant. When the opportunity arose for the eleven-year-old Cooper to attend the special unit, the disciplined, structured regimen did wonders for his behaviour. But, once at home during the holidays, it became all too easy for Cooper to revert to his old ways. Ways that were compounded by the continued absence of a father, whose job as a long-distance driver took him away from home for days if not weeks on end. A friendly and charitable neighbour felt obliged to relieve Mrs Cooper of her responsibilities at least one night a week, and insisted on taking Neville to the local youth club. There, the neighbour supervised as best he could.

Five weeks after Emily's death, they found her pants in the Coopers' garden shed, together with an assorted collection of women's underclothes culled from Millend's clothes lines. Neville Cooper was arrested and held. The arresting officer was DI John Wyngate and the confession extracted by DS Maddox from Cooper became the foundation stone of the prosecution's case, despite its retraction during and after the trial. But the true extent of the police's role in suppressing evidence and coercing key witnesses came to light only after Cooper's appeal had at long last been upheld.

In his defence, Cooper stated that on the Thursday afternoon in question, he'd caught a bus to Coleford, 'hung about' at the Klondike amusement arcade, watching kids playing the slot machines and space invaders and then gone to the cinema. His friend and alibi, William Bradley, was a petty thief and truant from a neighbouring village, whose previous record of appearances in court, and reputation as a compulsive and hopeless liar, were all brought unremittingly to the jury's attention at the trial. Mehul Patel, the owner of the Klondike, was never called as a witness, but his affidavit of having warned Cooper for pestering smaller children for change was a vital element in the Appeal Court's decision to release Cooper seventeen years later. When asked why he had not come forward before, the Klondike owner merely responded that he'd made his statement to DS Maddox seventeen years before and had been told that he would not need to give evidence. Subsequently, in the light of several appeals, Maddox visited Patel and warned him about getting involved with tricky lawyers who might twist his words. Unwise, Maddox had said, for someone from abroad, who wanted to stay in this country, to get caught up in a murder investigation. Patel, despite flourishing as a successful businessman, had only felt safe in speaking out once Maddox's hold over him ended with the officer's death. Such was the fear that the policeman had instilled in him.

By the time she'd finished, Anna already knew how their investigation would pan out. They'd have a head start because of the work done for the appeal, but it would still mean tracing investigation files, officers' pocket notebooks, witnesses and relatives. By this time, the individuals could well be anywhere in the country, or even abroad. More important still would be the hunting down of forensic exhibits. The original investigating force would have used laboratories long since defunct, or which might have moved premises. The exhibits themselves would likely have been divided and split.

And, of course, there would be the police personnel. Given the nature of the Woodsman fiasco and the criticisms that were levelled, she deemed it unlikely that anyone involved was going to welcome a dirt-digging lollipop man or lady with open arms. The Ice Queen was in for a frosty reception.

She sipped at the wine and grimaced. The glass was still half full, the contents now warm and unpalatable. She threw it in the sink and then listened to her sister's message.

> *'Hiya, babes. Just checking in. I guess you're too busy to chat with your little sister. No biggie. Just a reminder about Sunday lunch. Mum is coming and the good news is that Rob's mum and dad can't make it. Oh God, I don't mean that. Another emergency babysit for my sister-in-law, because her boyfriend's been picked for Cardiff against Sale in some rugby cup. Anyway, give me a ring if you're not too busy. Byeee.'*

Anna toyed with phoning back but exhaustion prevailed. Kate knew her far too well to expect an effusive response. Or any response. Anna would, no doubt, end up getting flak for it, but Kate could wait until tomorrow and a carefully worded text. Yawning, she went to the kitchen, drank a glass of cold water and went to bed.

CHAPTER THREE

At the same time as Anna struggled to find solace in sleep, twenty-five miles away, near a spill of red ochre under a canopy of oaks, a figure paused. Unmistakably male he stood in contemplation, having finally found what he'd been searching for under the frozen November moon. He seemed immune to the biting cold. Instead of shivering, he bathed in it with his face upturned and his arms open wide in supplication. The moon energised him just as the rain quenched his thirst, and the sun warmed his bones, and the night enveloped him in her concealing gloom.

The moon was not yet full, but this evening it was gloriously gibbous and bright enough to light up the scene perfectly. A hollow in the landscape; a setting. This would be the place where he would be born again. They'd witness his re-emergence as with a moth from its cocoon, though the truth of it was very different. He had not been sleeping for all these years. Rather he'd existed in a different form. A patient predator who'd never strayed over the red line. But now he would express himself again and they would say his name and tremble.

Reading that name in the newspapers had transformed his life all those years ago. Given him purpose. He took it as their gift to him. An acknowledgement that allowed him to relinquish all constraints and become something so much more than merely a man. The woods had called to him, sheltered and hidden him. Provided his hunting ground.

He had fresh prey, captured and alive in his lair. And now that he had found a suitable place, there would, finally, be a deliverance.

The creature known as the Woodsman sucked the freezing air into his lungs and smiled.

CHAPTER FOUR

She was running. Familiar paths and sights danced in and out of her imaginings. She was invisible, feet pounding the pavements under a burnt sky until, as so often in reality, the streets gave way to greenery. Her usual 'long' run, her endorphin fix, took in Horfield Common, a mile or so of streets, and then the ten-hectare oasis of Badock's Wood. She followed the path, revealing the odd recognisable image, and some that had no place there.

Shipwright appeared as she ran, incongruous on a bicycle on the wooded path, face straining from the effort, looking as if he might topple at any moment. Across a field, a man in a grey tracksuit grinned at her, his hands shackled to the earth beneath him. He opened his mouth. It kept opening like a basking shark's, hopelessly, abnormally wide, until it took up half the space of his head. Yet though his grotesque jaw moved, no words reached her. But his presence disturbed her enough to turn away.

Now she was in a different place. A strange, unfamiliar woodland, the trees ancient and gnarled high above her, looking down on where she tried to run. The long straight path was gone. Now she followed a winding track, fending off denuded branches that hung like elongated fingers and brushed at her face and clothes. Black peaty water oozed up from around her feet where she stepped, her breath like dragon smoke in front of her. The way became more difficult and she slowed, dark branches crossing, brambles snagging her legs. But something drove her on.

She glanced behind. Still the grey man in the field was shouting. She pushed on, breaking through into a treeless depression, looking down into a gouged-out leaf-strewn bowl in the landscape.

She stood, surveying this place that had drawn her to it. A noise, high up near the sentinel trees drew her gaze. The thud of steel against wood echoing in the air. An axe.

At the edge of her vision, down in the hollow bowl, something moved beneath the leaves. The movement grew into a shape.

She wanted to turn and run, capture the freedom she'd had moments before, but her feet had sunk into the peat. They would not, could not move.

The axe again, louder this time. She jerked her gaze up but there was no one there. When she turned back, Emily Risman stood just feet away, hand outstretched, looking at her with white, dead, coagulated corneas.

Anna jerked awake, the memory of the dream pounding the pulse in her throat as she gasped. Was there something in Emily's hand? But it shimmered and shifted like a pixelated face as she tried to recall it. Unsettled, she got up and drank some water, letting the image fade, but knowing it would not be the last time she would see it. Her curse, whenever crime-scene photographs were pored over, was to dream of the case. Dreams that were vivid and startling, taunting her with meaning.

During her time as a student at Goldsmiths she'd volunteered for some tests in the psychology department. One of them involved measuring memory. Anna had always been good at exams, but to be told that she was off the psychometric scale for a certain type of visual recall came as a complete shock. Like a colour-blind child, who knew no better, she'd assumed that everyone could remember the way she did.

But it had motivated her to reflect on the personality traits she'd struggled with over the years. She had always disappointed her mother by wanting to dress only in jeans, never been big on hugs and kisses. She'd never fitted in, striving for achievement as a teenager and being labelled an arrogant princess for it. At school, she'd learned early on to deliberately flunk the less important tests, or the odd question even in the important ones, so as to avoid the worst of the name-calling. 'Geek Anna' hurt at ten years of age. Her gifts, she very quickly realised, came with consequences, and her initial survival response in the sprawling state school she'd attended had been to deliberately underachieve. And as for boys… they had to be at least as good as her at *everything* to even stand a chance.

She ran and reran tests on herself in the college library, introspective self-report questionnaires, which put her in the category of an INTJ on the Myers-Briggs Type Indicator. So appropriate that she should find out in a library annexe; the kind of calm, silent place she'd always gravitated to.

INTJ: an Intuitive Introvert who prioritised Thinking and Judgement. Big words that didn't mean a great deal to anyone outside a psychology department. But it was a big deal to the doctorate student she'd discussed it with.

'Way to go, Anna. You and Mark Zuckerberg. Bill Gates, too. Oh, and there was Lewis Carroll. Seen any white rabbits lately?'

'That doesn't exactly make me feel better.'

'OK, well, only four in every five hundred women end up with this. How about Jane Austen and Jodie Foster?'

She'd liked that. She wasn't big on literature, but Jodie Foster she could certainly live with. Still she remained sceptical, but the doctorate student was adamant.

'I've seen you sitting alone in the refectory, reading a novel. So, you're happy to be alone, right?'

'Yes, but—'

'When you go shopping, you'll make a list and try and combine everything into one trip?'

'That's just efficiency.'

'Not big on surprises? Parties need planning and an exit strategy? Oh, and not a big hugger, am I right?'

That made her sit up and take notice.

'Better wear a badge to work though,' the doctorate student had grinned. 'Hate the mundane, independent, despise authority. Hate the water cooler even more, and people will confuse your confidence with arrogance. Ever thought of medicine?'

She hadn't. She'd thought about the police instead.

The doctorate student had asked her out, but he'd only lasted one date, falling at the first hurdle by not knowing that Ray Bradbury had written the screenplay for *Moby Dick*. An obscure fact of little importance, but something he'd argued with her about. Given his analysis of her, he should have known better.

She'd never told Shipwright. In fact, she'd only ever told Kate and one significant other about any of this, but the chief inspector read it in her anyway and had couched it in his own, inimitable terms.

What I like about you, Anna, is that you see patterns where others see mess, you ask questions no one else does, and you don't let emotion cloud your judgement. That's rare in this job.

In fact, knowing what she was at last helped only to an extent and four letters could hardly do justice to a whole personality. But it had provided insight into how others saw her. What people had the most difficulty with was reconciling her natural reserve with her physical appearance. Blondes were meant to have all the fun, weren't they? And hazel-eyed, physically fit, imperious-looking ones especially. But that was simply the wrapping. This blonde genuinely enjoyed being alone. Happy to be in her own mind, even energised by the thought of it. She needed reason and logic and liked to plan. *Meet Anna Gwynne, freak.*

She blew out a dismissive snort and went back to bed pondering these thoughts and knowing that they needed to be put away, back in the cupboard where they belonged. Perhaps it was the hour, or that she was alone, or that she'd spent the day dealing with the very worst that humanity could offer in a poky interview room at Whitmarsh. Whatever the reason, as she lay in bed waiting for sleep to come again, Anna couldn't shake the irrational conviction that seeing Emily Risman rise from her grave had connotations besides the simple explanation of her brain not letting her forget.

Beyond the transient horror of the dream lay reason. Emily Risman *was* calling to her. Asking her unspoken questions that echoed inside her own head. Where would the key be? What hidden thing needed to reveal itself to her? What smell, or sight, or sound? What buried thing that the original team had missed?

'Seeing the patterns,' Shipwright had said. The N, the misnomer in INTJ, stood for *in*tuition. Drawing from the deep well of experience, other people, books, art and personal interactions, which were filed away and stored in her capacious memory. That was what she needed to do now. Then she could do the 'T', the thinking bit, the analysis. And the outcome would be closure. Judgement was something she craved more than anything.

She was made to be good at this job.

Come on then, Anna. Prove it.

CHAPTER FIVE

She was at her desk at 7.45 the following morning. Holder arrived shortly after, shrugging off his backpack and unscrewing a bottle of water, which he upended and drained.

'Rough night?' Anna asked.

'Been to an early spinning class,' Holder replied.

They both looked up as their civilian support walked in on her trademark three-inch heels.

Trisha Spedding called out a cheery 'Morning', and unbuttoned a woollen coat which she hung on a coat hanger. The heels came off and were replaced by a pair of black Nikes kept hidden under her desk. Style tempered by pragmatism was one of the things Anna loved in Trisha.

'So, what do you think?' Holder asked, pointing to his copy of the files. 'The Woodsman,' he added with a theatrical wave of both hands.

'Not exactly Bridget Jones,' Anna said.

Trisha looked concerned. 'I hope it was enough. Superintendent Rainsford didn't give me much time…'

'More than enough, Trish,' Anna said. 'Did he say why there's such a rush?'

Trisha shook her head and pursed her made-up lips. 'Just said anything and everything I could lay my hands on.'

Anna nodded. Trisha was the glue holding the thinned-out squad together and was as motivated as the rest of them. Divorced and a single mum to two teenage boys, Trisha looked after herself and everyone else. Anna had huge respect for her professionalism and the way she'd worked her way up from filing clerk to being a highly organised criminal analyst. She knew the job and knew how to get it done, and with a better attitude than a lot of warranted officers.

'Bloody unbelievable, though. I mean, in prison for seventeen years—' Holder shut off the flow as the door opened and Superintendent Rainsford entered.

Anna couldn't resist glancing at her watch. Seven fifty-five on the dot. Rainsford did things by the book. He'd been in the job for only five years, significantly less time than Anna. One of the new breed; a direct entry superintendent levered in without the usual slog up from constable. Eighteen months of training and a further eighteen of probation saw him go from uniform to operational and into plain clothes with meteoric speed. He kept tabs on many operational and task-force teams, but he seemed to have a soft spot for them. No one was entirely sure of his background, but everyone assumed it was the forces, because of his military bearing, the old-fashioned cut of his wiry hair, and his clipped delivery. Early fifties and rake thin in a blue suit, plain tie and crisp white shirt, he looked at them in turn. A couple of seconds each, making the connection. 'Rain Man', ironically, made a big deal of eye contact.

He closed the door and addressed the team. 'Thanks for coming in early. I know you're wondering what this is all about. Best we get on with it.' Anna caught Holder glancing in the direction of Shipwright's empty office. It spurred her on.

'Begging your pardon, sir, but shouldn't we wait for DCI Shipwright? I'm sure he won't be—'

Rainsford let his eyes drop momentarily before pinning Anna in his gaze. 'I'm afraid DCI Shipwright will not be in today, nor for the foreseeable future. He woke up with chest pains in the middle of the night and got rushed to the infirmary. He's awaiting tests.

I spoke to him this morning. Angina. He'll need stents, if not a bypass.'

Anna's tongue turned to wood.

'Oh, dear.' Trisha put her hand over her mouth.

The tension in the room hummed like an over-tight guitar string. Seconds of silence ticked by while people found their voices.

'Is he OK, sir?' Holder asked.

'Stable, so his wife says. Which in my book is a great deal better than deteriorating.' Rainsford offered up just the right amount of comfort in a reassuring smile.

It got Anna wondering if he'd used words like this before to relatives of injured troops in some far-flung corner of the Middle East. It sounded like it. But it was one of a thousand thoughts bouncing around inside her skull as her brain writhed like an eel with its head cut off. A fractured image of her dream – Shipwright puffing on an unstable bicycle – flickered behind her eyes. A bit of her realised what was happening; her brain was distracting her to stop her properly processing the enormity of the news and all its implications. The alternative was to give in to emotion. Let the tightness in her throat close completely. But she wouldn't let tears come. Not now. She zeroed in on Rainsford's words.

'I have to ask you not to go to the hospital. He's on strict bed rest while they carry out further tests. Is that clear?'

Holder and Trisha muttered acknowledgements. Anna said nothing.

'Sergeant Gwynne?'

Hearing her name brought her back. She swallowed hard. 'Yes, sir.'

'You three are all that's left of Ted's squad and I know he'd want you to get on with the job in hand.'

Anna sat up, willing her mind to compartmentalise the shock. There was a job to do. 'DCI Shipwright did manage to speak to the CPS about Shaw yesterday, sir,' she said, bringing herself back to business. 'Shaw's admitting nothing. We'll let him stew.'

'Good, then that's in hand. Let's see if it triggers a response. But I want you to drop everything else and concentrate on the Risman case.'

Anna frowned. 'Sir, this wasn't really on our radar. We thought West Mercia—'

'It is now,' Rainsford cut in. 'You've had a chance to look at it, I take it?'

Anna and Holder nodded.

'Good.' Rainsford paused, choosing his words. 'Unless you've been on Mars for the last week, you'll all be aware that the Serious Crimes team in Gloucestershire have a major search operation under way for a missing schoolgirl by the name of Nia Hopkins. You'll have seen the bulletins. Most of you, no doubt, will have seen the press conferences.'

Everyone had.

'The facts are that Nia was abducted from a stable up near St Briavels on the edge of the Forest of Dean, roughly the same area where Emily Risman's body was found. Today is Day Four. They are considering another TV appeal. What makes this so' – Rainsford paused, searching for the right word – 'sensitive, is that Neville Cooper works for Nia's father, and I've heard he's already being considered a suspect. So far, they've managed to keep all of this out of the press, but it is only a matter of time until someone sniffs it out.'

Anna frowned. She'd got a taste of the press circus that ensued during the Risman case from Trisha's notes. If they heard that Cooper was implicated, the Woodsman would fill the paper's pages once again, and their window of opportunity for investigating other suspects in Emily Risman's murder would shrink severely. 'Sir, I read the file, but I wasn't clear on how this was left. DCI Shipwright told us Cooper is still being charged?'

Rainsford's smile contained no trace of humour. 'The Court of Appeal overturned Cooper's conviction last year, but the CPS has not been happy. A month ago, they threw their toys out of the pram good and proper. They are convinced that they still have enough evidence and so made an application for a retrial, which the Lord Justice of Appeal granted.'

Anna tried to read Rainsford, but he was a blank page.

'So how is this a cold case, sir?' Holder asked.

The superintendent ran a finger between his shirt and his neck, where his tie was knotted. The gesture made Anna give a little mental cheer. *The bloke is human after all*, she thought.

'At the request of the police and crime commissioner, the chief constable has agreed that we should re-examine the case *de novo*. Cooper's mistreatment has raised a lot of questions with… critics of the police. Let's say that the commissioner feels that every "i" needs to be dotted and every "t" crossed before another complete balls-up takes place.'

Anna exchanged a glance with Holder, but said nothing.

Rainsford continued, 'I want you both to liaise with Sergeant Slack at Gloucester immediately. He will brief you. Get up there and just get a taste of what's happening with Nia Hopkins' disappearance. See how well Cooper fits the frame and how keen they are to implicate him. But I want you to concentrate on the original crime. The powers that be don't think it would a good idea for West Mercia to involve themselves in any way. They, like Gloucestershire, have too many links to the old Central Counties Regional Crime squad. When it was disbanded, some key personnel ended up in those two regions.'

'Why were they disbanded, sir?' Holder asked.

'The CCRC had members from Gloucestershire, West Mercia and West Mids forces. Let's just say they didn't cover themselves in glory. At least thirty convictions quashed. After a series of scandals, the squad was disbanded in 2002 and the fallout is still haunting them.' Rainsford sighed. 'Cold crimes like Emily Risman's murder are a minefield of half-forgotten details with fragments spread over several jurisdictions. Not all of them will be throwing a party at the thought of you asking questions. I'm sure there'll be some conflict but, well, you can wear a stab vest if you need to. Your brief is to look at everything without preconception. If it involves Cooper, it's fair game for obvious reasons, but don't get stuck between the rails. Shipwright says you have a nose for this kind of work so stay focused. Everyone clear?' Rainsford's laser eyes drilled the message home into the watching faces in turn. 'I also realise that the loss of a DCI leaves you severely depleted. I am in the process of trying to source some help. In the meantime, Sergeant Gwynne will be acting up as a temporary inspector.' He pinned her with a glance. 'Use Shipwright's office. Report directly to me. Any questions?'

Anna had a thousand, but none seemed relevant in the light of Rainsford's grenade statement.

Satisfied, Rainsford pushed up from the desk he'd perched on. 'I suggest you two head for the Forest of Dean sharpish. Slack is the designated liaison. I'll get someone to forward directions.'

Anna exchanged a glance with Holder. They both wanted Rainsford to leave so they could discuss all of this with Trisha. Instead, the superintendent waited while they put their coats on, effectively ushering them out of the squad room.

'You drive,' said Anna, in the corridor.

'Yes, Sarge.' Holder did a double take. 'Sorry. Yes, ma'am.'

Anna thought about telling him not to be bloody facetious, but there was no sign of mockery in his expression. She let it go and followed him to the car.

The Ford smelled of silicone polish and vanilla. A pine-tree-shaped air freshener hung from the rear-view mirror, and a large kitbag sat on the back seat. They were quiet for a while, just sitting there, both stunned by the news of Shipwright's hospitalisation, and Anna, at least, equally stunned by her temporary promotion. The average age of a detective sergeant was around twenty-nine or thirty. Inspectors at least five years older. OK, it wasn't a substantive post but…

'I need a coffee,' she said. 'With lots of sugar.'

They found a Costa Express bar in a BP petrol station, and, back in the car, Anna clutched her coffee in both hands as she watched the traffic roar by on the M5.

'I'm gutted about the boss,' Holder said. 'I know he smoked and that, but…'

'I suppose it was on the cards if you add in the amount he ate as well. But what do you do? Everyone knows the risks.'

'But do you, though? I mean do you really? I reckon they should ban fags, full stop.'

'They never will. Too much tax revenue in turning people into smelly tobacco addicts.'

'I hope he'll be OK.'

Anna tried to unravel the knot of anxiety that tightened in her gut at hearing the concern in Holder's voice. 'He will. He's tough.'

Conversation lapsed as they both wrestled with their thoughts. Music droned from the radio, too low for it to be meaningful in any sense, failing miserably in its attempt to lift the mood. At eight thirty, Holder's phone rang.

'DC Holder.'

'Morning. This is DS Slack, Serious Crimes, Gloucester. I've been asked by our super to give you a call.' Slack's accent was local to his patch. Holder put the phone on speaker.

Anna answered. 'Sergeant Slack, you have DS— sorry, acting DI Gwynne and DC Holder on the line from Avon and Somerset. We've picked up the Risman cold case and we've been asked to look at any likelihood that the Nia Hopkins abduction ties in. What can you tell us?'

Slack stayed concise. 'Nia Hopkins' father is a well-respected businessman. Animal feeds. Owns horses and stables. The girl is horse mad. Rides whenever she can. It was her birthday on Thursday night. As a treat, they allowed her to sleep outside in the stable block with a friend. An adventure. On Friday morning, her father found her bed empty, a trail of blood, and her friend drugged with a big dose of ketamine. There's been no sign of Nia since.'

'And we heard that there's a link to Neville Cooper?'

'Hopkins' and Cooper's mothers are childhood friends. So, when Cooper was exonerated of the Emily Risman murder, Hopkins offered the bloke a job. Magnanimous gesture. Cooper is "challenged". In old money, a bit simple. If the retrial acquits him too, he's in line for a useful settlement for wrongful imprisonment, when the lawyers sort it out, but that hasn't happened yet. So, for the last six months, Cooper has been a stores man at Hopkins' Ledbury feed depot.'

'Do the press know about the Cooper connection yet?' Anna asked.

'Not yet.'

'They'll eat Cooper for breakfast.'

'Like sharks,' agreed Slack.

'Does Cooper have an alibi?'

'Says he was at home with his mother all night. Paper-thin as alibis go, especially as his mother lied through her teeth for him at the trial,' Slack said.

'With good reason, it now seems.'

'But lies nonetheless, ma'am.'

'But Cooper was exonerated,' Holder said.

'The boss isn't a great believer in coincidences.'

'And who's the senior investigating officer?' Anna asked.

'DCI Harris. Long in the tooth, but a good copper. He knew quite a few of the boys in the Central Counties squad who were involved in the original Woodsman investigation, so he knows everything there is to know about Cooper.'

Great. He's laying this on with a trowel good and thick.

Anna let Slack's words sink in, knowing that a great deal more lay hidden in what he'd left unsaid. Referring to Cooper as the Woodsman showed that Slack still attached Cooper to Emily Risman's murder, still demonised him in the same way the media had. And if DCI Harris knew people at the discredited CCRC, this wasn't necessarily the positive spin that Slack was trying to make it out to be. Coppers weren't very good at thinking clearly when it came to other coppers. 'Us and them' ruled the day. They said love was blind, but camaraderie and loyalty among officers was sometimes as bad. It often meant that it seemed like they were wearing rose-tinted glasses when it came to finding fault. She mentally filed the subtext away in capitals under 'NB. THIN ICE'.

'We ought to introduce ourselves to DCI Harris,' she said. 'Hopefully our paths won't cross too much, but if there is anything that links to Cooper we'd like to know.'

Slack gave them a postcode and Anna punched it in to the satnav.

When she'd rung off, Holder seemed worried. 'Sounds like we're in for a nice warm welcome, ma'am.'

'Open arms, Justin. Open arms.'

Anna and Holder headed for the parish of St Briavels on the English side of Offa's Dyke. Though it was a village, it contained the remnants of a medieval castle. Once part of the frontier with Wales, and a judicial centre in the twelfth century, these days it hosted walkers as a youth hostel.

They drove through the village, west towards the border. The sign announcing 'Cotty Hill' was painted on a slate board on a large post to one side of an open five-bar gate. The entrance broached a tall bank topped with hawthorn. In the shadow of the bank, frost still clung to the grass in ghostly clumps. A white ITV news van sat parked awkwardly on the verge in front of a couple of cars. Its satellite dish and assorted telecom paraphernalia stretched up from its roof at odd angles, like the broken legs of some damaged insect. Anna hoped that its occupants had the good sense to be somewhere warm having breakfast. She didn't fancy being part of a bulletin clip. The really good news was that the gate, as the property boundary, stopped them getting any further in. It meant they weren't able to stick intrusive microphones under the Hopkinses' noses, or waylay anyone entering the front door, as was so often the case.

The house itself stood bathed in sunlight as they crested the small rise above the drive leading down to it. Smoke spiralled up from the chimney over the property to stall in the freezing stillness. A few sheep and horses raised their heads as they drove by, watching them intrude. Anna stared at the horses. Inquisitive faces above powerful bodies. What violent secrets were trapped behind those dark eyes?

They parked in a stone courtyard to the side of the main yard and were met by two officers. The taller of the two had a long face matching a lanky body clad in a flapping raincoat. Restless eyes devoid of humour acknowledged her presence. He exuded hostility like heat from a stove. She couldn't work out if the anger she sensed was directed at her personally or was just his reaction to having someone else on his patch. Plus, it was never easy to retain a sunny disposition towards the world when you spent your nine to five dealing with murders, rapes and assaults, she knew that well enough. The man next to him was shorter, squatter, and, as they pulled up, Anna put money on him being Slack. Late forties, paunchy with silvery wisps of hair above heavy-framed glasses and a standard black anorak over grey Trutex trousers and comfortable shoes. The shoes were the giveaway. Cheap, thick-soled. Comfort over style. Anna and Holder got out and the shorter man stepped forward, hand extended.

'DS Slack, ma'am. You made good time.' They shook. She introduced Holder before Slack turned to the taller man behind him. 'And this is DCI Harris.'

Anna exchanged a cursory handshake with Harris. She put him in his late fifties, within sight of early retirement, which she knew he would be unlikely to take. Coppers like him never did. They either hardened to a point and became a sharpened tool, like Shipwright, or wallowed in the mire, scared of becoming as fallible as the great unwashed they served to protect. Above the eyes and a swarthy skin sat a busby of unfashionably parted hair, which looked unnaturally dark. She knew it was unwise to judge Harris based on a first impression, but her instincts were generally quite good, and already she didn't like him.

Greetings over, Harris began proceedings. 'So, do you want the tour?'

'I'm not sure it's—'

'I insist,' Harris said. 'Professional courtesy, let's say.'

Anna read challenge in his eyes, but she didn't feel like sparring this early in their relationship. They followed Harris around the property to the stable, where a huge horse turned its head and gazed at them suspiciously. Harris pointed out the small stall where Nia Hopkins and her friend had slept. It stood empty now, everything removed for analysis or logged as evidence. Slack told them that the blood on the sleeping bag had been identified as Nia's.

'What about the friend… Rebecca? Has she remembered anything?' Holder asked.

'She's still in hospital under observation,' Slack explained. 'Whoever did this gave her a hefty dose of ketamine. She's lucky to have survived. As it was, she aspirated some vomit and has been treated for suspected pneumonia. All she remembers is a pillow over her face in the dark and a pain in her leg where she was injected.'

'So, there's no chance this was a drug experiment gone wrong?'

'Always a chance, Constable,' Harris said, speaking for the first time since they'd entered the stable. 'If it was and Nia has run off in a drug-crazed high, she managed to do it after clearing up all traces of ketamine or drug paraphernalia. Of course, we could ask the horse.'

Holder reddened. Anna tagged it mentally. So Harris didn't suffer fools gladly, but there were ways of letting the inexperienced down that did not involve the verbal equivalent of GBH. She knew then that she was never going to like him.

'Obviously, early observation suggests that Nia Hopkins has little in common with Emily Risman,' Anna said. 'Different colouring, build, age.'

'And she wasn't a little tart,' added Harris.

'Even little tarts don't deserve to be strangled and stabbed,' Anna said.

Harris didn't respond. Anna and Holder walked out of the stable block. The paddocks surrounding the property ended in fences bordered on two sides by woodlands. The abductor could have found his way in from almost any direction. Holder turned and looked back at the house.

'Don't even think about it, sonny,' Harris said, joining them.

'We have no intention of crowding you, sir,' Anna said.

'Good. I'm glad to hear it. Now, I think a little discussion about ground rules is in order, but not here. I need to speak briefly to the family.'

They made arrangements to meet at the Robin Hood pub in Quedgeley before Anna and Holder made their way back to the car. They watched as Slack and Harris went towards the house, where the family stood.

Sara and Chris Hopkins wore the haunted, sleep-deprived faces of people in a waking nightmare. Anna knew the look. She'd seen it many times on the faces of relatives outside mortuaries and intensive-care units. Faces with irreparable damage written all over them. Anna wondered if she should nod, at least, but decided against it. Best they remain simply anonymous officers, ancillary to Nia and her family.

Even so, as they followed the serious crime officers' vehicle, Anna caught Sara Hopkins' eye. In that one split second, she read desperation and terror. Like a primate caught in the coils of a python. The family liaison officer would stay with them. They would have talked about the need for calm and the possibility, however remote, that there might be a ransom call. They were stuck, prisoners in their own home, victims of their own imaginations. Abductions were a form of mental torture for those involved. Emotions were laid bare and see-sawed between wild hope and soul-wrenching fear. It tore families and relationships apart. It remained the thing she found most difficult to forgive of abductors, and of suspects, who continue to plead innocence, denying a victim's family closure, answers… a body to bury.

Her mind did an easy cartwheel to Hector Shaw and his enigmatic reply to Shipwright's request that he let Tanya Cromer's family grieve. She had no doubt that he knew exactly where her body was buried. But getting Shaw to acknowledge and confess would not be easy, not without Shipwright's help. Might there be a way in to his troubled psyche? She parked the thought and let it brew.

Beams on the ceiling, specials chalked on a board on the wall, abstract carpet on the floor… Anna didn't like pubs with carpets. Might as well rename them all the Petri Dish Arms. In the Robin Hood, they sat at a table with an L-shaped banquette upholstered in red velour. Through the windows, the hum of traffic on the ring road was almost hypnotic. Four other members of Harris's team sat at another table. Harris didn't bother to introduce them. Fraternisation was not on the menu.

Anna sipped a lime and soda, while Slack and Harris nestled against the wall, nursed beers, and shed a small avalanche of crumbs each time they bit into huge, crusty ham rolls. Holder sipped his second diet Coke.

'So,' Harris said, after pouring half a pint of bitter down his throat, 'this is nice, isn't it? Lunch with colleagues.'

Holder kept his eyes on his drink.

'Have you any leads at all?' Anna asked.

Slack grunted. 'There's a fourteen-year-old neighbour with a photograph of her on his phone.'

Holder looked up. 'If he's fourteen, where would he get ketamine from?'

Slack had a mouthful of roll. It didn't stop him from answering. 'Same place everyone else gets it from. Nicked from vets or stables. Special K from your local drug dealer.'

'Is he a drug taker?' Anna asked.

'Not as far as we know,' Harris answered. 'But we have fifty people knocking on doors, getting people to check their outhouses and sheds in case she's dosed up and incapable. We've searched the properties of everyone who knows the family and found sod all, so we'll take anything we can get at the moment. He's on our radar because of the fact that he knew her.'

'Does he have access to a vet?'

'No. But the family does have horses,' Slack said.

Harris put down his drink and stared pointedly at Anna. 'Look, OK, the kid didn't take her. But there's a chance he knows someone who was sweet on her. Or maybe he's seen someone hanging around, some bloody maniac with an agenda he keeps in his own private box of frogs.'

Anna wasn't prepared to let it go. Harris was angry. Every squad member in the pub was angry, and that was understandable. Most of them had daughters or sisters. None of them needed more incentive than they already had. But she couldn't help but believe that it would do no harm to bring a little cold, analytical thinking to the situation. 'Maniacs, as you put it, very rarely abduct anyone. Something less than one in two hundred of all referrals to regional secure units are involved in abductions. Those that do get referred are male and have personality disorders but very rarely psychoses.'

Harris rolled his eyes up and applauded with three slow claps. 'Great. So, you went to the bloody lectures.' He downed the rest of his pint and burped.

This was old-school button-pushing and Anna wasn't going to play. 'We're not here to interfere.'

'Well you are. Inter-bloody-fering.' Harris spat the word out through clenched teeth. 'How long have you been an inspector?'

'Since this morning.'

His eyebrows went up. 'Since this morning. And they think they can send a…' He checked himself.

Anna smiled. *Go on, say it. I dare you to say it. Woman? Girl? Bint?*

'… you up to oversee my investigation?'

'Not oversee. We were told to get a handle on things, that's all.'

Harris nodded. 'I know Ted Shipwright. If I rang him in his hospital bed, would he give you his backing?'

'Yes, sir. He would.'

'Then you know as well as I do that if he was here we wouldn't be doing this stupid little dance.' Harris's eyes bulged. He cupped his ear and turned to Holder. His turn to be poked. 'Can you hear it, Constable? The trumpeting?'

Holder frowned. 'Trumpeting? No, sir.' He glanced at Anna in panic.

Anna put him out of his misery. 'He means the elephant in the room, Justin.'

'The big, grey, shit everywhere, elephant in the room. Neville Cooper.' Harris nodded, a joker smile on his face. 'Ted Shipwright would have brought a big gun in case we needed to shoot the bastard.'

No, he wouldn't. Not the Ted Shipwright I know, Anna replied silently. But what she actually said, was, 'Sergeant Slack says he has an alibi.'

'His dear old mother. But Cooper had seen Nia with her father at the feed depot where he works. He knew who she was, where she lived.'

'That's hardly—'

Harris didn't let Anna finish. 'And something else I know, and that I didn't need to go to a bloody lecture to learn, is that sexual predators reoffend.'

'Cooper has not been convicted as a sexual predator yet,' Anna said.

Harris dropped his head. 'No, he hasn't. Despite spending seventeen years in prison. But he's out of prison now, and if he is the bastard who killed Emily Risman, the Appeal Court, in their great and liberal wisdom, gave him the opportunity to do it all over again.'

Only if he's guilty, Anna wanted to shout. Calmly, she said, 'If you arrest him, there'll be a press feeding-frenzy.'

'He's a person of interest,' Harris said, his eyes cold. Anna realised then why Rainsford had been so careful with his words that morning. Harris, unlike the politicians and her managers, couldn't care less about fighting fires. He was more inclined to set them.

'But there is a chance Nia is still alive, isn't there?' Holder said.

The question dropped into the group like a grenade. Conversation fell away and the whole of Harris's team turned to Holder, looking at him as if he'd spoken the punchline of some terrible, inappropriate joke. Anna read hope and fear in equal measure in their faces.

Harris said, 'Believing that is what keeps us all going, Detective Constable.'

'Are you extending the search?' Anna asked.

'Divers in the rivers and a flooded quarry next,' Slack said. 'Then the press conference.'

Anna's stomach swooped. Everyone in that pub was desperately hoping against hope that there was a chance, however slim, that Nia would be found alive. But the reality was that the search teams were now looking for her body. Anna didn't say anything. There didn't seem to be much point. But she could see in the faces around her the grim reflection of her own misgivings. Young girls sometimes went missing of their own volition, in pursuit of misguided adolescent dreams. But they were hardly ever abducted for purposes other than the most dire, and Slack and Harris knew it. As for any links with Risman, they were tenuous, flimsy threads, but they clung annoyingly to Anna and she couldn't shake them off. Cooper's shadow loomed, but it remained insubstantial, a disquieting and unsettling presence that had no business being there.

Anna finished her drink and she and Holder left. Someone started whistling the Lollipop song by The Chordettes. If they were hoping to offend Holder, they were way off. He didn't even know what it was.

Anna chewed some gum in the car, but the minty freshness did nothing to relieve the bad taste that the visit to Cotty Hill had left in her mouth. She was glad when Holder asked her a question.

'What you said, ma'am, about abductions. Is that true?'

She knew the stats. She remembered them with ease. 'I used a bit of artistic licence. The stats are almost split in half. Maybe fifty per cent of child abductions are by perpetrators known to the victim. The other half are by strangers, and only a quarter are successful.'

'But this looks planned. I mean, why didn't he take both girls? And surely he didn't just stumble across them in that stable?'

'I don't know why he didn't take Beckie, Justin. Maybe he didn't want to risk it. But I'm with you on the planning. It feels thought-out to me. Most abductions involve the use of a car, are opportunistic and sexually motivated. The usual predatory preoccupations are the triggers: indecent exposure, touching or feeling. Rape is rare. Murder is rare. Our man is not your usual.'

Holder sat quietly for a while, driving, processing. After a minute, he asked, 'How common is it, ma'am? Child abduction, I mean.'

'More than fifty, less than a hundred per year. And this is not your usual type of grab and go. Not in the slightest.'

'So, how could they think that Cooper...' Holder let the statement hang.

Anna knew what he was alluding to. Slack had said it himself in his own politically incorrect and inimitable way: Cooper was 'In old money, a bit simple'. Could he have planned all of this, sourced a drug, used it on Beckie so she'd be rendered incapable while he took Nia?

Holder echoed her thoughts. 'I mean, is Cooper honestly capable of that kind of sophistication? DCI Harris seems a bit... fixated.'

Anna glanced at Holder. He still looked about fifteen. 'Now you know why Rainsford wants us on this. We're the buffer between Harris and Cooper. We need to pick up the other threads in the Risman Case, and soon.'

Holder blinked. His mental cogs were now in overdrive. 'This has a really bad smell about it, ma'am.'

'Don't worry, Justin. That was just the stale beer and testosterone in the pub. Gets stuck in the sinuses,' Anna said.

Holder blinked and she knew that he was trying to work out if she was being serious or making a joke. And he was clearly struggling with it as people around her so often did. It was amusing to watch the mental battle.

After a few more seconds of studying the panic flickering in Holder's eyes, she said, 'You're allowed to laugh, Justin.'

Holder let out an unconvincing titter before turning his gaze back to the road.

Anna told herself she needed to try harder at this social interaction caper.

CHAPTER SIX

They got back to Portishead to find Trisha had already set up the incident room. In truth, it was more an incident wall, consisting of a large whiteboard studded with photographs and a map. Setting up a lines-of-inquiry flow chart was a hugely underestimated skill and Trisha excelled at it. Patient, thorough and clear in her approach, she'd set out the timeline of Emily Risman's murder with precision.

Anna peered at the whiteboard, trying to absorb the information and get a feel for what happened all those years ago, but her eyes kept coming back to that one image from the crime scene: Emily's body pushing up out of the leaves, as if reaching for one last desperate grab at life. Or, said her imagination, waiting for Anna to see her, like a beseeching child in a classroom.

Here I am, Anna. Find out.

On the other end of the board, a series of individual photographs were pinned under the heading 'CCRC'. Half a dozen old images from personnel files. She zeroed in on three: Detective Superintendent Briggs, DS Maddox and DI Wyngate. Next to the single images hung a photograph of the three of them together, arms around each other's shoulders in celebratory post-trial euphoria. Craggy-featured men, Briggs the oldest. Smiling. Jubilant. Briggs and Wyngate would need to be found and interviewed. Slack's comments over Harris's connection with this squad echoed in her head. Did he mean the inevitable professional acquaintances one made over a lifetime's work, or something else? Friendships, perhaps, that could lead to closed ranks and resentment. In either case, it was an unwelcome wrinkle.

The necessary fraternity that existed between police officers helped them to cope with the dirty job they did, but sometimes it got in the way. Despite the new evidence that, had it been presented at the time of the trial, would have undoubtedly caused the jury to doubt the dubious links between Cooper and the murder, Anna knew that there were those out there who would still like to have Cooper neatly tucked away behind bars. The CPS certainly believed he should be.

The fact was that more than one officer involved in the original investigation had colluded in an unsafe conviction. It was difficult to credit now that the CCRC officers extensively interviewed suspects without solicitors being present, and that selective disclosure of evidence had been rife. Shallow remarks from the prosecutors involved in the trial, in response to allegations, seemed hopelessly inadequate. That such actions were said to be 'routine at the time' earned little in the way of merit for a justice system on the rack.

A face appeared at the door. Female, Asian, clean hair and dark eyes, the body that followed smart in a grey skirt and black blouse.

Holder looked up. 'Can we help?'

'DC Ryia Khosa. Superintendent Rainsford said you needed a hand.'

'Great,' said Anna, smiling. She introduced herself and the others. She asked Holder to bring Khosa up to speed, while she went back to her desk and began making notes, pulling out 'names', trying to piece together twenty-year-old relationships from the dry and dusty police files. It was mainly background material, though sketchy to say the least. But amid the big wad of papers stacked by Trisha on her desk was a paperback; one with a black spine and menacing artwork and the title in bold red type that read: *Tracking the Devil.* The author, Eric Lentz, was an unfamiliar name.

Curiosity piqued, Anna walked across to Trisha's desk.

'Where did you get this?'

Trisha's cheeks flushed pink. 'The second-hand bookshop on St Nicholas Street. You know, Crime Time? I had a brainwave and rang them up. I've walked past the window often enough. Anyway, I knew that they had a True Crime section in the window, so I just asked. The bloke there's a real nerd. Knew all about it. I nipped in at lunchtime and bought a copy. There's a whole chapter on the Woodsman. I thought it might help. With background, you know.'

'Trisha, you are an absolute star.'

Pleased, Trisha grinned. 'But there is some bad news, ma'am. I've been chasing up addresses and I found out that one of the other main suspects, Roger Willis, is no longer around.'

'Why?'

'He died in a car accident, ma'am. I spoke to his brother' – Trisha's fingers danced over her keyboard – 'umm, yes, here it is. Charles Willis.'

'OK, then we'd better speak to him instead.'

Anna went back to join Holder and Khosa. 'What's your background, Ryia?'

'I've been with the robbery squad in Plymouth for two years, ma'am. Before that I was in Stafford, organised crime.'

Anna nodded. Just what they needed. Someone with a bit of experience under her belt. 'As you can see, we're a much smaller team. I'll want you to sort through the CCRC personnel. See who's still around or still in the job. Justin, you concentrate on Emily Risman. I'm going to get us all some tea. Sugar and milk, Ryia?'

'Just milk, thanks.'

There was a machine that dispensed warm brown fluid in plastic cups, but Anna preferred the communal kitchen with its old-fashioned kettle and teabags. She sourced four mugs, washed them out and put a teabag in each. When the kettle boiled, she poured boiling water over the teabags and let them brew for four minutes. She distributed the tea and went back to work.

There were other cases pending at various stages of investigation, and though Rainsford's instructions were that they concentrate on the Woodsman, there were reports to file, queries to answer, feelers to put out, emails to read…

Anna wondered if Prof. Markham had replied.

Trisha left at 5 p.m. Anna suggested Holder and Khosa should go too, but they both declined the offer and stayed, glued to their screens. Feeling mightily guilty, but knowing she could read Lentz's book and the crime-scene reports just as easily at home, Anna excused herself.

In the flat, she showered, made herself a stir-fry and put on Free's 'Fire and Water' before checking her emails.

> *DI Gwynne. Intrigued by your email. Be happy to talk. I enclose my mobile number.*
> *Best wishes,*
> *Professor Jane Markham*

Pleased, if a little daunted, Anna finished her supper and called the number Prof. Markham had enclosed. The voice, when it answered, was instantly recognisable from a dozen lectures.

'Professor Markham, this is Anna Gwynne. Thanks for getting back to me.'

'Pleasure. And it's Jane.'

'Right… I don't for one minute expect you to remember me—'

'Of course I remember you, Anna. I remember the ones that stand out from the herd. It's no surprise to me to hear you're hunting monsters.'

Anna took a moment to absorb that. She hoped it was a compliment.

Jane continued, 'How is our friend Shaw?'

'Friend is not a word I'd use when it comes to Shaw.'

'Indeed, and my apologies. Though it's no accident that I use the word. People like him see the world in a very simple way. Either friends or enemies.'

'I revisited your teaching materials. The Connor interview.'

Jane sighed. 'Connor was naive and poorly prepared. I felt for him and his boss. Were you teaching?'

Anna got straight to it. 'Not exactly. We have a historical DNA match for Shaw in an unsolved rape case going back almost a year before he was imprisoned.'

The line stayed silent.

Anna continued, 'Three months after reporting the attack, the girl, Tanya Cromer, disappeared. We think Shaw is responsible.'

Static crackled on the line. Anna could hear Jane breathing. Eventually she spoke. 'Shaw… he's capable of just about anything. But I am a little surprised. Sexual predation was never his motivation. How much do you know of his background?'

'I know he's killed more than once.'

'He has and never denied any of that. But his case, as despicable as it is, remains interesting.'

Anna tried to find something appropriate to say, but, before she could, Jane spoke again.

'Shaw worked at Government Communications Headquarters in Manchester. He was a network operations specialist, though I can't remember what his role was exactly. I seem to remember it being glossed over at trial as "sensitive". These days it would be cyber intelligence, or something like that, but they didn't call it that back then. What I'm saying is that he was more than tech savvy. He and his wife had been separated for some time. His daughter lived with her mother. Abbie was bright and followed her father in that. He saw her regularly alternate weekends. The separation came partly as a result of his wife's alcohol problems, but she still held down a job of sorts, though sickness absence was on the up.

Their relationship was troubled, but neither Shaw nor his wife were prepared for what happened to Abbie.'

'You mean when she threw herself under a train?'

'It sounds horrifyingly simple when said like that. The fact is she'd shown no sign of depression. Good in school, not sexually active, but later it transpired that she'd fallen in with a group, an emo crowd. It was they who led her to the online games. Have you ever heard of the Black Squid?'

Anna hadn't and said so.

'People dismissed it as an urban myth. An online game that goads people into killing themselves sounds far-fetched. But Abbie's death proved that it wasn't.'

'I don't understand.'

'The game works by finding vulnerable teens through suicide groups. For the victim, there's the thrill of discovery and, once an administrator accepts your request, you're set thirty daily challenges. It originated in Eastern Europe. Sites get shut down constantly, but they simply go underground. They're still there if you know where to look.'

'Abbie Shaw joined one of these groups?'

'She did. The tasks condition the victim. At first, they're easy, like not talking for a whole day. But they soon escalate to antisocial or dangerous behaviour. Things like sitting on a high roof with legs dangling over the sides, or carving a number into your arm with a razor. In both cases the instruction is to send an image of the completed task to the administrator. The players are warned that if they pull out of the game they will be found and killed. The last task is to draw an image of a black squid on your face, send a photograph, and then, complete the final task. In Abbie Shaw's case, throw herself under a train.'

'It sounds…' Anna struggled for the right word.

'Incredible, I know. But those who have fallen victim are all emotionally labile teenagers. It's an ideal pool in which to fish.'

'It must have been hard for Shaw to take.'

'He reacted badly. Blamed his wife for not knowing who Abbie was spending time with. He had a point there, but he blamed himself as much. What we now know is that he spent the next eighteen months devising ways of getting to the administrators. He trawled the dark web, visited chat rooms, posed as a teenager himself, made his own variant of the Black Squid game to see if he could trigger a reaction. Eventually, he did. He then used his network-tracking skills to trace an administrator from the game. He found him and killed him. But not before torturing the man into telling him about the other devisers of the game. He found them too.'

'What about his wife?'

There was a pause and the noise of swallowing, and then the gentle knock of a glass being replaced on a table. 'Shaw, when he was caught, had abnormally low levels of serotonin. There is a subgroup of borderline personality disorder patients with very low levels of this hormone.'

'Serotonin? Doesn't that modify aggression and impulsivity?'

'It does. Shaw controlled his aggression prior to Abbie's death. Some people have theorised that his work, and more importantly his daughter, allowed him to keep a lid on it. With her gone, he was a bomb waiting to explode. When he did, his wife got caught in the shrapnel.'

'But it doesn't preclude him from sexual aggression as in Tanya Cromer's rape?' Anna wanted reassurance. When it came, it was far less effusive than she'd hoped.

'No, it doesn't. But it's an anomaly.'

The line crackled feebly as silence ballooned.

Jane broke it. 'I didn't ring to rain on your parade, Anna. If there's anything I can do, just pick up the phone.'

'That's good to know. Thanks, Jane.'

'Don't thank me yet. My main reason for ringing was to warn you… I presume you'd like him to confess to the rape and abduction?'

'It would be so much kinder on Tanya's family if he did. That would mean no trial. Just evidential presentation and sentencing.'

'Then I wish you the best of luck. Genuinely. But you need to try to understand Shaw's mindset.' She let out a little laugh. 'Truth is, no one's really achieved that. Of course, we as professionals have been desperate to label him. Is he BPD? Is he a sociopath? Or, is he truly psychopathic? As so often is the case, it's blurred. He had some classic signs of a borderline personality before it all happened. Chaotic interpersonal relationships, anger issues, poor intimacy skills. My own interpretation of the killings is that he was a coping BPD who, under severe psychological stress, descended into full-blown sociopathy, perhaps even psychopathy. I don't want to lecture you, but BPD patients struggle with nuance. The world is black or white for Shaw. If he's stable and has taken to you, then he may well appear to let you in to his world. But he can't help being manipulative and exploitative. That's the default setting. He lies. He does things only for his own benefit. Be prepared.'

Jane rang off, leaving Anna anxious and unsettled. She'd devoured the stir-fry through hunger, but now it wallowed like a lead weight in her stomach. She wished, not for the first time that day, that Shipwright was at her elbow. He'd been her shield for the last two years, and after talking to Jane Markham she felt his absence keenly.

On impulse, she rang Mrs Shipwright.

'Fran, it's Anna Gwynne. How is he?'

'Desperate for a fag. Even more desperate knowing he now has to give them up for good.'

'Any news?'

'He's in the queue, they keep telling me. Can you believe that? You queue for a bus, not to have your heart fixed.' Concern made Fran's voice waver.

'I'm sure he'll be fine. You know him, he's made of different stuff from the rest of us.'

'I know he likes everyone to think that, Anna. But he's scared. I can see it. This has put the willies up him. And I know what you're going to say. It does serve him right.'

'I wasn't—'

'No, I know you weren't. But we've all thought it. The way he eats and smokes and… oh shit, shit. If anything happens to him, I'll blame myself. I should have—'

'Don't do this, Fran. We both know that he's at least fifty per cent mule.'

Fran let out a helpless little laugh. 'I tell him that all the time and then he'll say that mules have other attributes below the waist and that's why I married him. Oh God, he's such a bastard.'

Anna didn't think she'd ever heard 'bastard' delivered with such tenderness. 'Say hello for me, will you? Superintendent Rainsford has told us no visitors yet.'

'No work, he means. But he'll see you, Anna. Any time. You know that.'

Anna went to the fridge and poured herself some wine before settling in an armchair in the living room to read the chapter in Lentz's book. Paul Rodgers wooed her with some white blues vocals, but even he couldn't lessen the horror of what she read.

On 15 February 1998, Deliah Lambton was walking her dog near her home in Millend in the Forest of Dean. The previous few days had been exceptionally warm for winter, with nearby Bristol airport recording an unheard of eighteen degrees. Rain was forecast over the weekend, but Sinbad, Deliah's Labrador, made the most of the fine weather, searching for rabbits and squirrels. However, when Sinbad refused to come back from where his nose was buried near a collapsed pile of branches, his odd behaviour made Deliah curious. Sinbad's tail was between his legs and he kept darting forward and retreating. When Deliah got close enough to see, the sight of a body under the makeshift covering of branches would be one she would never forget.

What Sinbad had found was the slain victim of the killer known as the Woodsman.

Emily Risman had been missing for two days. Strangled, raped and then stabbed almost thirty times, her death and the death of her unborn child led police to believe that they were dealing with a deranged killer. A fun-loving girl who travelled every day to work in Coleford, Emily was popular with the boys. The police investigation, led by the Central Counties Regional Crime squad, centred around three main suspects.

Richard Osbourne had been dating Emily for two years. Older, working, with money and a car, their relationship blew hot and cold for months, as Emily experimented with other boys. But it was Osbourne she went back to when her flings with the other men blew apart. Osbourne swore that their relationship was open, and yet could jealousy have unleashed the beast inside him?

And then there was the father of her child. Roger Willis cut a tragic figure. A good-looking boy and an athlete, Willis's life was falling apart as he began developing symptoms of a blinding hereditary condition. Willis had inherited a condi-tion known as retinitis pigmentosa, which caused nyctalopia, rendering him virtually blind in dark conditions. Emily had already broken up with him by the time of the murder and the police feared this rejection might well have triggered a violent reaction.

Thirdly, lurking in the background was Emily's neighbour, Neville Cooper. An epileptic, educationally challenged, ado-lescent youth, with a mild behavioural disorder characterised by aggression directed mainly towards immediate family. His epilepsy was reasonably controlled by drugs and he did well at the residential training unit he attended, but his social worker admitted that the designated regimen, which was meant to encourage accepting greater responsibility for his behaviour, was not working out at home. Cooper, in the words of his contemporaries, was wild. Perhaps, with teenage hormones raging inside, his wildness could have spilled over into something much, much worse.

It would take police three months before the vital clues that led to the Woodsman's conviction came to light. Three months in which the community cowered at the prospect of the Woodsman stalking the countryside, searching for yet another victim.

Lentz liked adjectives. Emily was a 'fun-loving' girl, her killer was 'deranged'. Osbourne was a potential 'beast', Willis cut a 'tragic figure', Cooper was 'wild' and 'raging'. This was history as written by the victors. By the time of publication, Cooper was in prison. All too easy to accept and believe that the aggressive, challenged youth, frustrated by the pretty girl, turned on her in a frenzy. It was like *Beauty and the Beast* without the talking teapots. Cooper had been an easy target from the outset. Best to hive him off from society as the devil that he was, and everyone could sleep a little more soundly in their beds. Sensationalism sold, everyone knew that.

But there were a few little nuggets here that were worth exploring.

Had Emily really been that popular with the boys?

And Osbourne, the older man, the bad boy that Emily was attracted to, were they really in an open relationship?

Lentz had taken the path of least resistance. Sound bites that echoed, she suspected, press fixation on the lurid aspects of the case. A fixation that might have fed into the police's approach to the investigation. And if that was true, what else might they have missed or glossed over?

And then there was Willis.

She put down the book and went to her laptop, typed in 'retinitis pigmentosa' and clicked on a medical information website called Medoracle.

In terms of symptoms, RP patients first notice loss of peripheral vision, and nyctalopia, another common symptom (night blindness), is due to the poor adaptation of the eye to dim illumination as the decline of rod sensitivity progresses. As the degeneration spreads to the central area of the retina, the initial 'tunnel vision' leads to eventual blindness.

Other than a slightly better understanding of who the main players were, Lentz's account contained little of any real use to her.

She needed to let her mind disconnect from the present, allow it the freedom to travel the roads where a young, pregnant girl would find herself in an isolated spot with a killer. Did she go there of her own accord, or had she been taken against her will? Did she know the man who'd done this to her or was she the victim of that most difficult of crimes to solve, a random attack? What significance should they attach to the pregnancy? Or was it a more important element, something with a deep, and as yet hidden, emotional significance?

Anna let her mind generate these questions and noted them down. In her experience, not all of them would be answered, but, if some of them were, it would inevitably lead to a better understanding of the circumstances surrounding the crime. She sensed that this was what she needed to do. Understand. And that applied to both victim and perpetrator.

Suddenly, the enormity of the task threatened to overwhelm her. Rainsford, at Shipwright's behest, was taking a big punt on her to deliver. And here she was, staring at a blank wall, trying to look through it and see the threads of the case reaching out into the street and the city and the past. There were many, but she knew she'd have to pick the one that would lead on to answers, if she were to have any chance at all of solving this case. This was a huge responsibility and a great opportunity. Yet it was also obvious to her that there were some people in her own profession, and her life, who would love to see her fall flat on her face.

The music reminded her, as it always did, so much of her father. A man who had loved her and protected her and emboldened her to be true to herself. Whereas Shipwright's advice was that of a mentor, delivering his criticisms of her flaws with blunt honesty, her father had couched his encouragement with a tender smile. But looking back, Anna realised that sometimes what she'd read as tenderness was in reality a kind of sadness. Because even then he'd known full well that Anna's gifts came at a cost.

The music rolled over her and she let it engulf her, pulling her knees up to her chest like she had done as a child.

It helped. Like it always did, to wash away the doubts.

CHAPTER SEVEN

The televised public appeal for help in Nia's disappearance was the third Breakfast News piece the following morning, after an allegation against a government minister and another terrorist bombing in Israel. Gloucestershire's assistant chief constable led the press conference, with Harris next to her. The ACC read out a statement, her delivery suitably deadpan:

'We are continuing in our efforts to find Nia Hopkins, now missing for seven days. We would like to appeal to the public for any information regarding her whereabouts. In particular, we would urge the community to spread the word through social networks. We are grateful to everyone who has already given their time in the search. We appreciate the difficulties searchers are experiencing in covering the terrain, and the relative remoteness of the environment. Mr and Mrs Hopkins are with me today and, though understandably distraught, have asked to speak.'

Someone had convinced Sara and Chris Hopkins that an emotional appeal to the public was worthwhile; that it might trigger feelings of guilt in someone who knew the killer. Anna watched as first Nia's father and then her mother broke down and sobbed and begged Nia to get in touch, and for anyone who knew something to come forward. The form of words they'd recommended the Hopkinses use came straight out of the training manual. At this stage, the couple were incapable of any rational thoughts of their own. They would have been guided, if not cajoled, by someone in authority into appearing like this. Anna sat with her arms folded, unsure as to what difference this sort of harrowing display ever achieved, but also knowing that the team needed to keep the momentum going. Increasingly infuriated as the cameras hid nothing of the Hopkinses' pain from the viewing millions, all she wanted to do was ring Slack. Was it worth it, seeing all that pain on display? Was it worthwhile?

At HQ, Rainsford met Anna as she made her the way to the squad room a little before eight.

'Quick word, Anna.'

Rainsford's office was a minimalist's dream. One photograph of the family – a wife and two children – an open laptop, a filing cabinet and a whiteboard with pinned-up sheets of monthly statistics.

He offered her a seat and she sat.

'First, I have to apologise for the way I railroaded you into the inspector's role. We haven't talked about it much.'

'You don't need to apologise, sir. I appreciate it.'

'Ted wouldn't have it any other way. He's a big fan.'

Anna nodded, secretly pleased. Even when not physically present, Shipwright had her back.

'Your impression of the situation re the missing girl?'

Anna sighed. 'Difficult to say, sir. Obviously, Cooper is on the investigating team's radar. Why wouldn't he be?'

'But no hard evidence?'

Anna shook her head.

Rainsford nodded. 'Bring me up to speed with Emily Risman.'

'We're about to start interviewing suspects who were in the frame at the time, beginning with Richard Osbourne.'

'Good.' Rainsford nodded encouragement.

'Sir, Chief Inspector Harris—'

'Is resentful and cantankerous. I know. And there's bound to be more of that. But you have your brief, Anna. All I need to know is that you can handle it.'

Can you, Anna?

'Yes, sir. I only wanted to let you know that Harris sees it as interference. His words, sir.'

'They messed up badly the first time with this. I want to make sure that we, and they, don't mess up again.'

The biography that Trisha provided told Anna that Richard Osbourne had left the village of Millend, where Emily Risman too had lived, when he was twenty-four. He'd drifted around the southwest as a jobbing carpenter on a succession of building sites, until he'd settled near Banbury to set up a business venture. There was no arrest record.

She took her car and Khosa as company.

They drove towards Banbury, eventually leaving the A361 at Bloxham and heading up a lane to an open gateway and a rutted and stony single-track road that meandered for a quarter of a mile before opening out into a sawdust-strewn yard. On a post at the entrance hung a sign reading 'Osbourne Oak'.

The drone of a saw cut through the air. It came from a dilapidated wooden barn on the far side of the yard. Next to it, a light burned in a Portakabin. At right angles to the barn hunkered a stone cottage, which appeared to be in the middle of major refurbishment. Plastic sheeting covered two windows, and a quarter of the roof was bereft of tiles.

Anna parked the car in the yard and then she and Khosa got out and headed for the Portakabin. By the look of the yard, either the business needed to expand or was in a severe decline. The bio had said that Richard Osbourne built cruck barns. Anna was ashamed to admit that she had no idea what that meant.

Inside the barn were three people, two of whom wore goggles and worked at feeding huge pieces of wood, supported by chains, into a massive beam saw. The third man stood apart from the rest, marking the sawn beams with yellow chalk. He looked up at their entry, wiped his sawdust-coated arms on a rag, and walked towards them. His expression, under a dusty tangle of brown hair, was one of muted surprise at the sight of visitors.

Anna began the introductions, but the buzz of the saw drowned out her voice and the man gestured towards a small office at the rear. Inside it, an oil stove hissed out heat from the corner, and filled the room with a musty, stifling, atmosphere. The air was redolent with the smell of wood and engine oil that was carried on the sawdust pervading every surface. Khosa did the introductions again and Osbourne's face gave way to nervous suspicion.

'What's all this about?' he asked in a voice like gravel over zinc.

'Some routine questions, sir,' Khosa said.

'We won't take up much of your time, Mr Osbourne,' Anna added. 'You're obviously very busy.'

'We've been lucky enough to get some orders recently.'

Osbourne got up and pointed out through a rear window to an area of gravelled yard not visible from where they'd parked. He was thin under his clothes. Hard work and cigarettes keeping his bones lean. Anna moved forward and stared out at two huge wooden frames with curved beams from floor to apex.

'These are cruck as opposed to box frames. Originally, they used the halves of crooked trees as blades to support roofs. There are a variety of styles – we build the frames in oak then take them down again before delivering to buyers to assemble, either by us or as self-build.'

'These are houses, are they?' asked Khosa, who had joined Anna.

'Houses, barns, summer retreats.' They turned back into the room and Osbourne added, 'But you're not here to talk to me about barns.'

'Emily Risman,' Anna said.

Osbourne's face clouded in annoyance before a sour smile appeared. 'I knew it would only be a matter of time…'

'You are aware of Neville Cooper's release then, sir?' Khosa asked.

Osbourne snorted. 'You here to try and get a confession out of me, is that it?'

'Just a few routine questions, sir.'

'I've answered them a hundred times already.'

'We have the facts of the case, Mr Osbourne, of course,' Anna said. 'And we're not here to try to catch you out. We're coming at this investigation afresh and I don't have to remind you that, as of this moment, the murderer remains at large.'

Osbourne glared at her before dropping his eyes and nodding, grudgingly.

'Tell me about your relationship with Emily Risman.'

Osbourne stared out of the window into the yard for a long moment before answering. 'We were kids. She was up for it.'

'You had a sexual relationship, yes?'

'Yeah, we did.'

'And would you describe Emily Risman as promiscuous?'

Osbourne swung his gaze back towards Anna. 'You know she was. That was the main attraction. Most of the girls of her age were scared stiff of sex. Emily was into it. But always made me use a condom.'

'You began your relationship when she was what, fifteen?'

'Yeah.' Realising what he'd said he added, 'But no sex until she was sixteen.'

'But she did go out with other boys?'

'After the first year, yes. I mean neither of us wanted to get married and have kids, for God's sake. We both wanted other things, other experiences.'

'But you never severed the relationship entirely?'

'No. We still met up occasionally.'

'For sex?'

'Sometimes. Sometimes just for a drink and a laugh.'

'How did you feel about her seeing other men?'

Osbourne shrugged. 'It wasn't an issue.'

Khosa took out her notebook. 'Sir, there was some talk at the time that Emily Risman took money for sex, is that true?'

'She never asked me for any.' Osbourne's mouth set in a thin, defiant line. Khosa tilted her head, allowing him space in which to finish. Finally, he sighed and said, 'Look, she was from a rough background, but she looked after herself. She was young, sure, but she knew what she was doing. At least I thought she did.'

'You were surprised when you heard she was pregnant?'

'Yeah.' Osbourne nodded. 'She took precautions. Always.'

'With you?'

Osbourne nodded.

'But not with Roger Willis?'

'Maybe that was a slip-up.'

'So, she wasn't trying to get him to commit where you wouldn't?'

'There was never a question of commitment. Not for me and Emily. She liked blokes too much.'

'You never encouraged her to ask for money at any time?' Khosa persisted.

'What are you trying to say?'

'It's a simple question, sir.'

'Like I was her pimp you mean?' Osbourne rolled his eyes up to the ceiling. 'It wasn't like that. She was easy-going, that's all. Maybe some blokes gave her presents, I don't know. Maybe they were grateful.'

Khosa scribbled something down in her notebook. Anna held back a smile. Khosa knew the drill. Nothing like seeing your words written down to instil a little edge.

'What about Neville Cooper. Did you know him?' Anna asked.

'Knew him to say hello to and to avoid. He was younger than me by a good couple of years. Bit of a nutter, always had been.'

'When they arrested and charged him, did you think that he was capable?'

'I didn't know what to think. I mean, he confessed, didn't he? The whole village was simmering, crazy like. Everyone had a theory. Then they arrested Neville Cooper and suddenly that was the answer that had been staring everyone in the face for weeks. People were ready to accept it.'

'Roger Willis, was he a friend of yours?'

'Not a friend, as such. We'd been to the same school, but he stayed on and I left early.'

'Did you know he'd been seeing Emily?'

'Only afterwards.'

'It didn't bother you?'

'I've already told you it didn't.'

'They had already broken up, hadn't they?'

'That's what I was told.'

Anna nodded and glanced down at her own notes. The heat in the room pressed down on her and she took a deep inhalation of musty, warm, resin-laden air.

Osbourne said, 'Look, I didn't keep tabs on Emily. We weren't an item when all this happened.'

Anna nodded and glanced over at Khosa. 'Just a few more questions, sir.'

Anna left them to it and walked out into the yard that held the huge cruck frames and gulped in clean fresh air. A cool wind fanned the moist sweat that prickled her neck and she arched her back to straighten out the kinks. Her thoughts were full of guilt. Not her own. Someone else's.

It was possible that someone had enjoyed seventeen years of freedom at the expense of an innocent man. She tried to imagine how anyone could live with that. She chided herself. No, that was far too easy a trap to fall into. Someone capable of the brutal murder of a young girl was not going to worry about a miscarriage of justice. And yet it was something that couldn't be dismissed altogether.

She let her fingers run over the rough-cut surface of a massive nine-inch wooden beam. There was something about the wood that made her want to touch it. Under her hand it felt solid and strong. More than could be said about the case against Neville Cooper.

She turned back to the office. Inside, Osbourne was sitting and the truculent expression on his face was back in place.

When Anna entered the room, Khosa stood and snapped closed her pocket book. 'You have children, Mr Osbourne?'

'No, we're trying, but…'

Khosa moved towards the door but Anna hesitated. 'There is just one more thing I'm not clear on, sir. On the day Emily Risman was killed, you were working in Gloucester?'

'That's right. They were putting up a new estate in Hucclecote. I was hanging doors all day.'

'Did you work on your own?'

'What do you mean?'

'Hanging doors is a one-man job, is it?'

'Yeah.'

'So, were there other people working in the house at the same time?'

'Sometimes. It depended how far along the plasterers and electricians were.'

'Statements from the foreman on the estate say that you were given a free hand. He would come along in the afternoons to check how many doors you'd hung, is that right?'

'Look, people saw me that day. The police took statements.'

'You drove to work, sir?'

'Yes. I drove.'

'Thank you, Mr Osbourne. We'll be in touch.'

Osbourne looked confused, his face flushed. 'I know what happened to Neville was awful and I'm sorry he's been inside, but I've really tried to put all of this behind me. I didn't like being a suspect then and I don't like it now.'

'Is that what you consider yourself to be, Mr Osbourne? A suspect?'

'Christ, no. It's just that you lot coming here after all this time… I've got a partner.'

'And the Rismans still have a dead daughter, sir.'

Anna drove back. She liked the way that driving freed her mind, letting it meander along diverse trails of thought until something stopped it in its tracks. This time the obstacle was all about arrogance.

'Why didn't he do this again?'

Khosa looked across, alarmed. 'Who? Osbourne?'

'Perhaps Osbourne, who knows. But I'm referring to the killer. He got away with it. Emily was attacked and killed in a frenzy. Or what turned into a frenzy. Either way, he believed he'd got away with it. It feeds a need and empowers arrogance. Even if he hadn't planned to kill, he'd always be wondering if he could do it again.'

'Maybe he didn't do it because he was locked away in prison, ma'am?'

Anna looked at her. That was the most obvious conclusion, she agreed. The one Harris and Slack would no doubt have championed.

The one that put Cooper right back on top of the list. The one she found most difficult to accept.

'Maybe,' Anna said, surprising herself, but troubled, too, at how unconvincing the word sounded in her ears.

CHAPTER EIGHT

He'd been patient. Watched them with their hi-vis tabards and long probing poles, crossing the landscape in a single line, searching for something they would never find, because he had not been ready to let them. Now the searchers had moved on and the woods were once more his.

In between the scudding clouds, the moon hung silver and bright enough to navigate by as he exited a narrow path onto a wider track. There he halted, aware that he was not alone. Twenty yards away, something large lifted its snout and grunted; a lead sow and her sounder of wild boar. She watched him, assessing the danger. He turned his face up to reflect the light of the moon in response. The sow, huge at fifteen stone and six feet in length, observed in silence before turning away to disappear into the undergrowth.

He read it as an acknowledgement. His right to be in the forest.

His passenger moaned from where he'd slung her over his shoulders, her body warm against his neck. She was his prey and he was the predator, stalking the woods. His woods. He'd carried her off the ground so that the tracker dogs couldn't trace her passage. The drugs were wearing off, but it didn't matter now. If he wanted to, he could leave her by the pigs to be discovered. They would not have objected. But that was not his purpose. What he was about to do would trigger an upsurge of anger and hate and outrage after days of letting the anticipation build. He craved these monstrous approbations because they suited his purpose. Fed and validated his existence.

He would make it to the designated spot in twenty minutes.

He would be away and safe within forty. If there was any jot of feeling, it flickered like a guttering candle before sputtering to die completely. She was blameless. As blameless as calves before they became veal. Yet everyone had to eat. Such was the nature of the food chain.

Purpose, as twisted and gnarled as the roots he stepped over, drove the Woodsman through the depths of the forest, the apex predator going about his business with silent efficiency.

CHAPTER NINE

Friday dawned bright and cold. There'd been no developments in the Hopkins Case overnight and no news from Shaw. Anna needed to get the Risman case interviews ticked off, so she took Holder and they headed west in his car.

Beacon Cottage, Alburton, nestled on a knap hidden amidst the rolling Monmouthshire hills on the western reaches of the Forest of Dean. The roads had been excellent until the last two winding miles between the Severn Valley floor and the Wye. The cottage was whitewashed in the vernacular style and stood a good thirty yards off the narrow lane that led past it. They parked on a gravelled area adjacent to the wooden gate and got out, stretching their legs and taking in the freshly painted windows and doors, and the neat heather garden. The view looked out onto a green expanse that fell away and ended in the silver ribbon of the Severn with Gloucestershire beyond. The old bridge was just visible, and, in the foreground, a five-acre field was being turned over by a farmer driving a red tractor.

Crunching their way to the front door, Anna again became acutely conscious of the unorthodoxy of this approach. She needed a point of focus. Her own mind remained muddled and unclear. The snippets she was getting were not gelling and if there was a pattern emerging, it was not immediately obvious to her.

It was a still, grey day with little or no breeze. Adjacent to the cottage stood a garage full of everything but the two cars that were parked outside. She noted the new Isuzu jeep behind a beaten-up Astra, which looked very much on its last legs.

A small porch framed by ivy led to the front door and, as they approached it, the air was suddenly pungent with the smell of fields freshly sprayed with slurry. It caught in Anna's throat as Holder knocked. The woman who opened the door wore jeans, a fisherman's smock and a warm smile. Her black hair was shorn close to her head with little wisps around her ears and down onto her neck. The face was devoid of make-up and belonged to someone in her late thirties. The only concession to any form of frivolity consisted of a pair of large parrot earrings and an incongruous smudge of yellow paint on one cheek. Glancing down, Anna registered the yellow smudge repeated on one forearm, where it joined an abstract collection of muted greens and blues.

'You must be DC Holder,' the woman said holding her hand out. 'I'm Gail Willis. How was your journey?'

'Easy, thanks to your map,' Holder said.

Gail laughed. 'The map's been perfected over the years since we moved here. Coffee? Tea?'

'Coffee for me,' Holder said.

'Tea would be good,' said Anna.

'Could I tempt you with something herbal?'

'Well…'

'I make them myself. Try some camomile. I guarantee you'll like it. Charlie's popped out for a walk. He usually does after lunch. Come into the kitchen and we can chat.'

They followed Gail into the kitchen. Holder ducked, conscious of the low ceilings. The surfaces and shelves were laden with brightly coloured pottery of unusual design. Anna picked up a pale green mug, hand-painted in a flowing floral pattern.

'These are interesting.'

'Thank you,' Gail said, with a smile.

Anna caught the genuine pleasure in her voice. 'Did you make them?'

'Make them and try to sell them.' Gail pointed out of the window at a large wooden outbuilding, which might once have been a summer house, but which now had pink dust coating the inside of the windows and unglazed pots all over the small veranda. 'That's my workshop. One of the reasons we moved here was for the extra space. I can work anywhere if I've got clay and an oven, and Charlie does all of his stuff from home.'

'The home office concept?'

'Especially in Charlie's case. He can't really function without his CCTV now.'

'CCTV?' Anna stared blankly and saw Holder's puzzlement register too.

'You don't know?' Gail asked.

'I'm afraid I know very little. We're here to speak to him about his brother,' Anna said apologetically.

Holder glanced at his notebook and chipped in, 'We have Mr Willis down as an electrician.'

Gail's smile was full of pain. 'That's what his trade was, but he had to retrain. The CCTV is a tool he uses. You can't tell from reading his work, but Charlie is sight impaired. He has retinitis pigmentosa.'

The penny dropped with a thud. Anna recalled Lentz's chapter and the Medoracle website's explanation about how the condition was inherited. Charles, like his brother, had lost the gamble.

'I knew his brother Roger was affected,' Anna said.

'It's progressed slowly. We're hoping that it won't get much worse. Charlie copes amazingly well. Gets his bad days, obviously, but he's determined not to let it hinder him.' Gail shrugged. 'You can't tell by looking at him. I thought it best that you knew though.'

Holder said, 'You mentioned just now that you couldn't tell from reading his work. What work is that?'

Gail's chin tilted upwards a degree. A gesture full of defiant pride. 'He does a little freelance work as a journalist. Mainly technical writing. Assessing new equipment and tools for the trade journals. Writes for the local paper too, though; lighter stuff, news snippets, articles. It's a huge struggle, but it's his passion.' She poured boiling water into a pot in which she'd already placed some dried green leaves. 'Sugar?'

Anna shook her head.

'Their mother was a carrier. As you can imagine, she was mortified – in those days there was no such thing as genetic counselling.'

Gail Willis was insightful enough to sense the discomfort her statement caused in her audience. 'Don't worry. We're fully aware of the genetics. Charlie is adamant about that. And children were never on my agenda. We've only known each other for six years and I'm sad that I never met Charlie's mum. She shouldered all the blame for both her boys.'

She poured steaming liquid into a mug and handed it to Anna.

'Smells lovely. Sort of grassy and warm.'

'Good?' asked Gail as she watched Holder sip his coffee.

'Lovely.'

Anna felt unable to hide her surprise and pleasure. 'It's smooth with a hint of mint.'

'Refreshing isn't it?' Gail giggled enthusiastically.

Anna found herself liking this woman. She exuded a warmth and genuineness that was almost palpable.

'Can I get you anything else?' Gail asked, clutching her own mug in both hands and leaning against the sink.

'I'd like to have a closer look at your pottery.'

'Really?'

Anna nodded. 'Really.'

She spent a pleasant fifteen minutes wandering around Gail Willis's workshop and studio, amazed and surprised at the craftsmanship and natural earthy beauty in the designs that Gail had imprinted onto the plates and jugs she made. The patterns were floral and natural, but there was nothing twee about the bold colours. Anna was drawn especially to a corner cabinet laden with Gail's most recent design; an oceanic motif full of swirling blues and greens.

'Do you have an outlet?' Anna asked, admiring a large milk jug splashed with yellow, green and blue sealife.

'I have a shop in Cheltenham with a flat above it. I stay there three nights a week from Tuesday through Thursday. I come home lunchtime on Fridays. It's a bind, but a sacrifice I readily made for the chance of living here. A friend of mine does Fridays through Mondays.'

Anna saw Holder watching her from the kitchen, clutching his coffee, bemused by her interest in pottery, no doubt. She hoped he was learning. Shipwright had taught her always to find common ground, where one could, with the major players of any investigation. She'd found it counterintuitive at first, preferred to root out the hard facts, the unimpeachable truths for her analytical brain to play with. But so often said truths were hidden inside the layers of lies everyone lived by. A concept that the original investigative team had spectacularly failed to grasp. And if she felt any guilt at this tactic, she buried it.

Besides, she really did like Gail Willis's stuff.

'These are fantastic,' Anna said with feeling, moving from one piece to another. For a brief moment, she lost herself in the art, almost forgetting her reasons for being there, until a voice hailed them from outside.

'We're in the studio,' shouted Gail in response.

Charles Willis was not as tall as Holder, but just as lean beneath the padded jacket that he unbuttoned and removed as he walked into the workshop. Gail went over and kissed him gently on the cheek. She took his arm and brought him over to where Anna waited. Holder followed behind them.

'Inspector Gwynne, this is Charlie, my husband.'

Anna noticed how Willis looked directly at her, staring unremittingly. It was almost disconcerting.

'I saw the car,' he said, grinning. 'I guessed it was you.'

'And this is DC Holder.'

They shook hands as Gail explained, 'In daylight, Charlie has very poor peripheral vision. What he has is a central tunnel. He sees best directly in front of him.' It was all delivered as matter of fact and without a trace of embarrassment to either of them.

Anna studied the man in front of her. He had been almost fifteen when Emily Risman was murdered and echoes of his youth persisted in a long face dotted with freckles. He had a full head of wiry hair that curled naturally on his head in dark spirals above a lined forehead. As Gail explained, his damaged eyes showed no external sign of defect and were of a dense brown colour that made his pupils all but invisible.

'I see Gail has already done refreshments. Would you like something else?'

'Another camomile tea would be lovely.'

Gail took her mug and Charles said, 'Let's go into the office.'

Anna watched as Gail took her husband's coat and adjusted a wayward collar of his checked shirt. Her face filled with pride and Anna's admiration for her grew in that moment. Charles's illness was a burden that this couple shared and Gail struck Anna as a woman who entered into the relationship with the dice loaded but with her own eyes wide open.

Charles's office was a high-tech workstation, all order and neatness. On a large desk against one wall stood a Mac, next to an odd-looking grey box perched on two struts twelve inches above a tray. The box, which had two large knobs like eyes on the front panel, was connected to the tray by the legs that stood at the rear of the unit.

'We'll get straight to the point,' Anna said, when they were all seated. 'We realise that it was a long time ago, but we have to go over statements and facts pertinent to the Risman case.'

Charles shook his head. 'It's difficult to believe Nev Cooper's been inside for seventeen years for no reason, isn't it?'

'We're really here to talk to you about your brother, but before we do can I ask, what were your impressions of what went on?'

'You'll have to remember that I was only fourteen at the time. The cops scared the crap out of me. They seemed big, hard men. They weren't too bad, I suppose, but I can imagine what it must have been like for Nev.'

'You knew him well?'

'Everyone knew Nev. He was wild. He'd do anything you'd ask him to do as a dare. I suppose it was nothing more than a need to be accepted, but he'd eat worms, steal fags, anything, if he was in the mood. He didn't know where to draw the line. That's why people were ready to believe it could have been him.'

'Was he violent when you knew him?'

'Not really. Throwing stones at the windows of empty buildings was about his limit. But he was wild. Ever since I read about what the police did, the confession and suppressing evidence' – Charles Willis shook his head – 'it's made me boil inside.'

Holder had a notepad in his hand but sat back, letting Anna take the lead.

'That's understandable,' she said. 'A lot of people feel like that.'

'Seventeen years.' Charles shook his head.

'And you moved here sometime after your brother's death. Is that correct?'

'We've only been here six years. Roger died twelve years ago.'

'A car accident, wasn't it?'

'Yeah. We were abroad. In France. I still had a licence then. We still had some money left over from when Mum died and we decided to spend some of it on a proper holiday before Roger's vision got too bad. Just the two of us. I suppose I should have given up driving, but I could see well in daylight. It was getting late, not dark but heading towards dusk. I shouldn't have been on the road.

Someone tried to overtake us. I panicked, swerved… I was thrown clear, broke my arm in two places, but Roger didn't make it.'

'I'm sorry,' Anna said. 'It must be painful for you.'

'It's OK. I only get the nightmares a couple of times a month now.'

'If we can go back to Emily Risman. Roger was the father of the child she was carrying, wasn't he?'

Willis nodded. 'He admitted it freely and the tests were all positive. He'd always fancied her, even though she was a bit easy. Funny really. I never understood that. I mean she wasn't a bad-looking girl; she didn't need to put it about like that. I suppose she just liked it. Rog had been with her a couple of times. Bought her a few beers and got his leg over. He thought he'd been careful but…'

'He hadn't used a condom?'

Wills threw his hands up.

'It wasn't what we might call a steady relationship then?'

'No way. Emily Risman was the original "wham, bam, thank you, ma'am" girl.'

'And you brother was eighteen when all this happened?'

'Yes.'

'Do you remember Richard Osbourne?'

Willis smiled. 'Yeah. Flash bugger with a car.'

'Did he object to the fact that Roger was seeing Emily?'

'I don't think he liked it much.'

'What do you mean?' Holder asked.

'Tried to warn him off. After a couple of drinks, Osbourne could be a bit mouthy.'

'So, there was bad blood?'

'A bit. But Roger was never serious about Emily. At least, I don't think he was.'

'You mentioned that you drove until twelve years ago. That would have made you what, nineteen or twenty? Does that mean that your condition came on later than your brother's?'

'By a couple of years, yes. By the time Rog was twenty, he was struggling. He hated the winters, hated the dark nights. Like I do now.'

'He didn't have a driving licence?'

'Yeah, he did. He passed his test as soon as he was seventeen in our dad's old Granada.'

Anna shuffled through some papers on her lap. 'On the day of the murder, your brother attended the hospital, is that correct?'

'Yeah. Check-ups every three months by that stage. RP affects the retinas of your eyes, but you can also get cataracts at an early age. They were monitoring him.'

'And you went with him?'

'Yeah. It was half term. Rog had an afternoon appointment. That meant he would have to come home in the dark. He needed someone with him. Mum was too busy at the factory and my dad worked in lumber. He'd be in the middle of nowhere, mostly.'

'And you travelled by bus?'

'To Gloucester Royal, there and back. Nearly an hour each way.' Willis shook his head, as if remembering slow, trundling journeys.

'And what time did you get home?'

'I think it was around half-five, maybe six.'

'Your brother's statement says five forty.'

'Then that's what it was. I think he went to the pub after that.'

Holder came in with a question. 'Can you remember the last time your brother saw Emily Risman?'

'Must have been the football club the night before she went missing. He danced with her. Everyone danced with her. Most of the guys were hoping for a quick feel outside in the car park. Emily was a very friendly girl. A fact that was common knowledge amongst the local boys. Just how friendly depended on how much cider she'd drunk.'

Anna steered things away, asking general questions about Charles's work. He showed them the grey box next to the screen and used a newspaper to demonstrate. Placing a sheet of the paper on the tray, he took the mouse and the icons on the PC screen flashed across until he found the one he wanted. He double-clicked the mouse and part of the page on the tray appeared on the screen. The grey box on legs was a camera. The words blurred and sped across as Willis adjusted it until he found something to show them. An advert appeared, huge and surprisingly clear.

'Big help this,' said Charles, looking from Anna to Holder. 'Couldn't survive without it.'

Neither of them commented.

'So, are you interviewing everyone involved? Eighteen years is a long time to remember stuff,' he said.

Anna nodded. 'We can but try.'

She made to leave and Holder took his cue. 'Uh… you don't mind if we contact you again? We might need to check some detail.'

Willis shrugged a yes.

Anna took the signal and couldn't help but wonder what he was going to think if and when Cooper was dragged back into the limelight again.

She left shortly afterwards, with one of Gail Willis's wonderful milk jugs wrapped in newspaper in one hand. Kate's birthday was looming. Problem solved. They said their goodbyes on the doorstep of the idyllic cottage, Anna leaving with a promise that next time her visit would be less rushed. Gail walked with them to their car and they stood for a moment admiring the Willises' shiny Isuzu jeep.

Gail said. 'It gets very wet around here and there's a lane at the bottom of the hill that floods regularly. Once the sun goes down he's effectively blind. He tries to make the most of daylight and depends on me to do all the driving, of course. I've kept the old Astra for running around in, but the Isuzu should keep us mobile in all conditions. It was Charlie's idea really.'

'He is remarkable,' said Anna.

'Yes, he is,' said Gail.

'They were close as brothers, were they?'

'I think so. I never met Roger but I think Charlie took his death hard. He was devoted. His dad never really recovered from an accident at work and Charlie more or less became Roger's carer after their mother died.'

Anna again caught tender admiration in the glance that Gail Willis threw across to her husband as he stood in the doorway, before she walked over to join him.

Holder drove. Anna still had the list of questions she'd asked herself at the beginning of all of this in her notes. She glanced at them again now.

> *Emily.*
> *Goes to woods of her own accord to meet, or taken against her will?*
> *Does she know the man who'd done this to her or victim of a random attack?*
> *The pregnancy?*
> *Other?*

'Charles Willis's recollection of his brother's relationship with Emily Risman suggests that her pregnancy was an unfortunate accident,' Anna commented.

'What do you mean, ma'am?' Holder frowned.

'Well, why didn't Emily insist that Roger used a condom? And then there's Richard Osbourne's statement that he didn't keep tabs on Emily. Yet, according to Charles, he did and he even threatened Roger.'

'And Osbourne had a car, ma'am.'

'What's the significance of that?'

Holder shrugged. 'It means he'd be mobile.' He nodded out of the window. 'I mean, you'd need to be mobile out here.'

Anna flicked her notebook shut. He was right. The villages and hamlets were not far from each other in the forest, but getting to them was a logistical nightmare. 'Why do you think Osbourne lied about not caring?'

'Because it shows he wasn't really Mr Cool and that he did give a stuff, ma'am.'

Anna turned back to look out of the window. *Right again, Justin.* None of that was enough to suggest Richard Osbourne was a murderer, but it did mean that their presence was making people nervous. And nervous people made mistakes.

Anna tried not to think of what Charles Willis must have endured knowing he'd been responsible for his brother's death. Guilt like that never truly left you. She had no real answers to her questions, no pattern yet, but there was some comfort in knowing they were definitely the right questions to be asking.

CHAPTER TEN

On Saturday morning, Anna's work phone rang at a little after ten. She was surprised to see Shipwright's name come up.

'Sir? How are you?'

'Sitting here bored to tears waiting my turn for an angiogram. Never mind about me, how are you, Anna?'

'Good question, sir.'

'Fancy a chat?'

'Not sure that we should over the phone.'

'Who said anything about a phone? Come to the infirmary.'

'OK. What are the visiting hours?'

'*Inspector* Gwynne, you are leading a murder investigation. They are not going to ask you to wait outside. Flash your bloody warrant card, woman.'

She left the flat and went to her favourite coffee shop. Bean and Gun was run by a couple of thin Italian guys who flirted outrageously with virtually every customer. She loved their coffee, but went there as much to prove to herself that she was not a nun. She knew the two boys were a couple but somehow that made it even more fun.

She took a flat white, which oozed a gorgeous liquorice aroma, to a corner table and spent half an hour reading the remainder of Lentz's chapter on the Woodsman. His portrayal of the detectives involved was full of hyperbole, but it served its purpose as a reminder to Anna, and provided a glimpse into public opinion of the time.

Detective Superintendent Ewan Briggs was a thirty-year veteran with vast experience of every facet of criminality when he and his team were brought in to investigate the murder of Emily Risman.

Briggs had served in the Royal Navy before becoming a police officer. He brought to the job a discipline and ethos that he'd learned in the service of his country and applied it in the service of the people who suffered at the hands of criminals. By the time he commanded the Central Counties Regional Crime squad he had hunted rapists, blackmailers, drug dealers and murderers.

> *'With the newspapers baying for blood and criticising our every move, it became almost impossible to carry out normal police work. The kind of routine interviewing and checking of facts that get you there in the end. They wanted a big splash, a chase, a showdown or a confession. Of course, what would have really pleased them would have been another murder. I fell out with the press over this Woodsman nonsense. They were like wild dogs.' – Detective Superintendent Ewan Briggs*

Working with him on the team was another experienced officer, Detective Inspector John Wyngate, who had a reputation as a policeman who cared deeply about his job, but more importantly about people and the victims of crime. He also cared about right and wrong and justice, along with philosophical aspects of the law; things so often at odds with one another in today's politically correct society. It was Wyngate's promise to the parents of Emily Risman that drove him to ensure that the Woodsman would be brought to book.

Lastly, and crucial to the eventual capture of Neville Cooper, was Detective Sergeant David Maddox. A charis-

matic and dogged investigator who never baulked at putting in the long and extra hours needed to pull together the many strands of information that the murder investigation threw up. It was Maddox's work in exploring Cooper's dubious alibi that finally clinched his capture.

Three musketeers if ever there were any, Anna thought, as she closed the book.

By midday she was walking through coronary care into a male four-bedder with every bed occupied. Shipwright was sitting up in a chair, leads from his chest attached to a monitor. There were newspapers strewn over the blue blanket covering the bed, and a radio with a long snake of earphone dangling on the bedside table.

'I brought Lucozade. Didn't know if coffee was allowed and this has,' she held up the bottle and read off the label, 'the unmistakably awesome taste, now without the calories.'

'Oh, joy,' Shipwright said, grinning.

He looked somehow diminished. She was used to seeing him in larger-than-life control. Here, he was but another one of life's victims and it bothered her. 'You look...' She made a play of searching for the adjective.

'Well? Like crap? Don't leave me hanging!'

A couple of patients looked up. She finished the sentence. 'You look OK, is what I was going to say.'

'Good. All that clean living has to pay off some time. Now, let's get the unpleasant details out of the way. I am not dying. I'm going to have an angiogram and maybe a stent or more if needed. Miraculously, in the time since I phoned, they've scheduled that for today. So, this is your last chance before I'm whisked off to a catheterisation lab, and I quote, so they can do whatever voodoo it is they do.'

'So, what should we talk about?'

'I want to know what's going on.'

'Shouldn't you be, I don't know, resting?'

Shipwright waved a hand towards the bed. 'I am, as you can see. But I'd rather have something to distract me up here' – he tapped the side of his head – 'so that I don't have to think about someone pushing bloody wires through my veins.'

'It's not exactly private here, sir.'

'Draw the curtains. Best we can do.'

Anna did as asked, going over everything that had happened and what the team had done. And then she told him in hushed tones about Harris's attitude.

Shipwright snorted. 'Always a hard-nosed bugger. Don't let him push you around. Rainsford has your back.'

'Harris is going after Cooper.'

'Of course he bloody well is. No smoke without a bloody great bonfire in Harris's narrow little mind. That's the way he thinks. The way a lot of people up there still think. So, you're either going to have to prove him right, or prove him wrong by solving the original case once and for all. Stick to your guns.'

'I've been trying to get my head around the CCRC squad.'

'Unbelievable, isn't it?'

'Did you know them?'

'Briggs, slightly. The Woodsman case made him. He went from zero to hero in the press. Maddox, I didn't know. Poor bugger took the brunt of the criticism later, though at the time everyone thought he'd just done a bloody good job. He was the CCRC's Rottweiler, there was no doubt about that. But he ended up being crucified and it got to him in the end.'

'Do you know when he died?'

'Must be a few years ago now.'

'What about Wyngate?'

'I did a spell with Wyngate in Thames Valley. Bit of a dark horse. Never quite worked him out.'

Anna remained puzzled. 'From what I've read, the media had the squad under the cosh. What do Briggs and Wyngate think now, do you reckon?'

'Are you asking me if they feel foolish or resentful? Praying that a retrial will exonerate them? I wouldn't put it past Briggs. As for Wyngate, who knows? Look, I know this is bloody hard. There's what's going on now and what went on then. But don't get sidetracked by any of it. Open mind, Anna. It's what you're good at.'

Shipwright was right.

He watched her nod and then asked, 'Talking of sidetracks, where are we regarding our friend Hector Shaw?'

There it was again, that word 'friend'. Surprising just how often people used it as an aphorism. Even Shipwright. And she wasn't sure just why it rankled so much in this context. But it did. Still…

Anna trod on her musings and suppressed the wince that wanted to show itself. 'Nothing more yet, but Professor Markham got in touch. I'm not sure how, but I think she may be useful to us.'

Shipwright tilted his head and his eyes became slits. She recognised it as a signal of wariness.

'Is there something I should know?' he asked.

'Only that she was surprised to hear that we'd tagged him in a sexual assault case.'

'Like you, then.'

'There is nothing in his history to suggest that kind of paraphilia.'

'We didn't plant that DNA, Anna.'

'I know that, sir. But why did Shaw go on about the other part of the mixed sample like he did?'

'Perhaps he wanted to put a stone in your shoe. From the sound of it he succeeded. You have lots of balls in the air, Anna. But I know you'll cope. Let the CPS handle Tanya Cromer's link to Shaw. As for Nia Hopkins, you're there as an observer, so observe. And treat Emily Risman's case as if it's happening now. You know the drill. You've started interviews?'

Anna nodded. She briefed him on Osbourne and Willis.

'Visited the crime scene yet?'

She shook her head this time.

'Then get down there. Soak it up. Let that Anna Gwynne brain kick into gear. But no flying solo, Inspector.'

Anna scrunched one corner of her mouth involuntarily. Something she'd done since she was a child whenever she was caught out.

'I mean it. I know you like to, but this is too big to crack alone. Use the team. *Our* team.'

Anna brought both hands up, palms forward at shoulder level, surrendering to Shipwright's shot across the bows. 'OK.'

The curtain twitched open and Mrs Shipwright's face peered in. 'Oh, good, it's just you. For a minute, I wondered what was going on.'

'Fran, I'm sorry.' Anna stood.

'Don't be sorry. He's been going slowly mad.' She looked at her husband. 'So, this afternoon then?'

'I'll miss the bloody rugby.'

Fran threw Anna a glance. 'See what I have to put up with?' But her lips trembled as she said the words and her eyes brimmed. Shipwright saw it. He stood up and they embraced. Anna read the signals and took her leave, but not before he left her with a welcome approbation.

'Show them what you can do, Anna.'

At six, a relieved Fran called to say that Shipwright was out of theatre. They'd stented two of his arteries and he'd gone straight to ITU and would be out of commission for a few days. 'Thanks for calling to see him today, Anna. It meant a lot to him. He's felt so useless.'

'It's me that should be thanking him.'

'He thinks the world of you, you know that.'

'The feeling, Mrs Shipwright, is totally mutual.'

'Anyway, go out and celebrate. It's Saturday night. Anything planned?'

Another hour making notes about the Woodsman à *la Eric Lentz; Dine in for a Tenner, which I'll split in two and refrigerate one half for Monday night; two glasses of wine; some chocolate; a Scandi noir on television at nineish; then bed. Adrenalin junky that I am, I have it all laid out, thanks…* 'Oh, you know, see how it goes.'

Not a lie as such, but enough to feed the conventional expectation. She'd learned to do that a long time ago.

Fran sighed. 'Oh, to be young again.'

Sunday arrived foggy and cool, but behind the mist the sun lurked tantalisingly. When it finally broke through, Anna was halfway through a five-mile run. The first and last miles were urban; Bristol pavements heading north from her flat. But the middle loop was well worth it. Badock's Wood was a local nature reserve in a limestone valley. An oasis of broad-leafed trees and grassland in the heart of urban sprawl. She tried to get there at least a couple of times a week. Quite apart from the aerobic benefits, what it did for her mind and soul was equally important. It provided space for her eyes and ears and, if she was lucky, little moments of solitude. She'd grown up in Pendare, half an hour north of Cardiff, a town that had suffered greatly from the loss of heavy industry. Even so, within a twenty-minute walk of her house she'd be in the open country of hills and moorland. It came as a surprise to her to learn how much she missed that when she moved to the city: first London for college and now Bristol. She needed her runs to the woods as much as she needed water or air.

Her circuit began and ended in Horfield Common, just a few yards from her door. The sharpness of the air made her chest burn from the final sprint. She drank thirstily from the bottle she carried in a tiny backpack and stretched her limbs on a low wall. Endorphins suitably boosted, she re-entered the flat, opened the curtains and tried not to see the mess in her living room. It was more like a second incident room now. She needed to get on, to interview Briggs and Wyngate. Resisting the urge to engage with the stacked files and papers, she showered, made herself a coffee, and by eleven was in the car and on the way to Kate's.

Her little sister by a year and a bit, Kate had married the local boy she'd met in the summer before university. The relationship had survived against the odds. He worked in his family's haulage business and, according to their mother, Kate had 'married well'. She lived in a new-build detached property on the edge of a small estate, within three miles of where the Gwynne girls had grown up, which meant that the journey Anna was making that morning was a very familiar one. Mist hung over the Severn as she crossed the bridge, but the roads were clear, with the M4 as quiet as it ever was and the valley road she took north after passing Cardiff almost deserted. It meant that she drove through her sister's wrought-iron gates and onto the yellow gravel drive ahead of time, for once.

The door opened when she was half a dozen yards from it. Rob Riordan stood in the doorway, grinning. He was big, broad-chested and, of necessity, something of a gym fiend, because he still turned out on Saturdays for the local rugby team. He shifted his hips to one side as something wriggled to get out. Harry Riordan, a smaller version of his father by some three feet, burst through the door, yelling, 'Aunty Annaaaaaah!'

Three seconds later, she was being hugged and thrown instantly into a conversation about a cat who'd sat on the fence and licked its paw, the most important news in the world in Harry's three-and-half-year-old opinion. Rob hugged her around Harry, apologising for his son's jabbering. One of the good guys, Anna loved Rob because she knew he took good care of her little sister. He, like his son, was on Anna's very limited hugger list.

The kitchen had her salivating in seconds, the smell of roast pork and duck-fat roasties as seductive as any drug. Kate, in an apron and wielding a slotted spoon, beamed at her.

'Hello, stranger.' The usual teasing remark laced with a tinge of vitriol. Kate was her mother's daughter, but with a wicked sense of humour attached.

'You look... organised. As usual,' Anna said. 'Can I help?'

She put Harry down, and he began pulling her towards the living room, demanding that she see his shark book.

'You already are,' grinned Kate. 'Mum's in the living room with Elin.'

In the living room, Sian Gwynne had the eighteen-month-old Elin on her knee, reading about Peppa Pig going to the shops for the hundredth time.

'Hi, Mum,' Anna said and leaned in to kiss, only to be pushed away by an irate Elin, who said, 'No, Ammma read Peppa Big.'

They ate at one. Pork with crackling, potatoes, cauliflower, swede and red cabbage. Elin didn't want it. Harry finished his in three minutes. They put up with Elin's tiredness until Rob finished his meal, at which point he volunteered to take both children in the car with the promise of duck feeding for Harry and a nap for Elin. That left the women alone to linger over the home-made dessert: bread and butter pudding with extra sultanas, topped with Joe's Ice Cream.

Food of the gods.

They talked mostly about the children; Harry's propensity for serious statements and how Elin was turning into a toddler with a mind of her own, which brought forth a nod of sanguine understanding from their grandmother and several anecdotes about Kate's notorious toddler temper. It was good, it was family, and as they cleared away the dishes, Anna began to believe that their mother would behave.

Until they were at coffee.

While Kate fussed over the Nespresso machine, Anna sat in the dining room with her mum who turned to her brightly. 'You'll never guess who I bumped into outside the post office last week.'

Anna bit back the caustic remark. She left those to Kate these days. She didn't trust her emotional brakes enough.

'Tim's mother,' said Anna's mum, after a dramatic pause.

'Tim who?'

'Tim, you know. Your Tim. Timothy Lambert, the boy you almost got engaged to!'

Anna suppressed a grimace. 'How was she?'

'Very well. She was asking after you.'

Anna stayed silent. There'd be more to come.

'Don't look so surprised. You went out for almost three years, remember? Such a nice boy. Lovely manners.' She shook her head. 'I still don't understand what went wrong there.'

'Isn't it enough just to know that it did?' Anna said. This was old and well-trodden ground. Well-trodden, rutted and now riddled with mines. But her attempt at dismissing the conversation fell on selectively deaf ears.

'Oh, we had a lovely chat. He's doing well for himself. Travelling salesman for a drug company. Lovely car. A BMW, I think.'

Anna sighed and dropped her head.

'What? Aren't you pleased for him?'

'If it was true, I might be. But it isn't, Mum.'

Kate came in with the coffees.

'I was just telling Kate about my meeting Tim's mother. Tim's doing so well for himself.'

Kate nodded. 'Really?'

Clever Kate. Just the right word, with eyebrows raised, placating her mother with implied interest, and then adding an off-stage one-eyed squint at Anna to let her know that her mother was batshit for even suggesting it.

Her mum turned her gaze back to Anna. 'Perhaps you ought to look him up.'

Somewhere in a dark and locked cupboard of her brain, Anna could hear herself scream. Her mother was a gossip, very much of her generation, but had been a godsend for Kate with the kids. And the kids were a godsend in return, giving her a purpose and a distraction from Anna when her father had died. But when they were together, just the three of them, it did not take long to draw up the old and well-established battle lines. And Anna's single status was one of the bloodiest, opening old wounds with every skirmish.

Kate must have read something in her sister's expression. 'Well, I've heard that he is in a steady relationship now.'

Anna's mum's face fell, the pillars of her imaginary matchmaking crumbling. 'Oh, don't say that. And anyway, how would you know?'

'Facebook,' Kate said, without missing a beat and causing her mother to frown. Social media proof brooked no argument.

'Well, it wouldn't do any harm if you poked him, would it?'

Kate suppressed a guffaw. Anna shook her head and muttered, 'I wouldn't poke him with a fifty thousand volt taser.'

'There's no need to be sarcastic,' their mother said. 'It's not as if your social life is crammed, is it?'

'Mum,' Kate said, with a stony glare.

Anna's work phone vibrated on the dining-room table, where she'd left it. Maybe she did have a guardian angel. But not even in her wildest dreams did she imagine it would be Sergeant Slack.

'Inconvenient?' he asked, by way of greeting.

'No. Fire away,' Anna replied, moving away from the table into the empty living room.

'Sorry to spoil your Sunday, ma'am, but we thought you'd better know. We've found Nia Hopkins' body.'

Slack didn't sugar-coat it. No point. Anna squeezed her eyes shut. 'Fuck!' The expletive emerged as an expulsive whisper. Even though she knew that seven days after an abduction the chances had been slim, a tiny part of her nestling in the core of her humanity hoped that for once someone might hold two fingers up at the stats. But it was not to be.

'What does it look like?' she asked.

'Something you ought to see, ma'am.'

She went back into the dining room.

Kate must have read her expression. 'Bad news?'

'Yes. I have to go.'

'Oh?' her mum said. 'Anything interesting? Must be more *important* than visiting your sister and your family.'

'If you call murder interesting, then yes.'

'My God.' Her mother's hand went to her throat.

'Not that poor little girl in the Forest of Dean, is it?' Kate asked.

'I really can't talk about it,' Anna said.

'Why on earth are you involved in something like that?' Horror raised the pitch of Mrs Gwynne's voice.

Anna snapped. 'What do you think the police do, Mum?'

'I know what the police do. But you could have done anything. Your father would be—'

'Proud. He'd be proud. I'm doing what I bloody well want to do. When are you going to accept that?' It came out sharp and bitter. 'Sorry, I can't do this. Not now. Bye, Mum.' She turned and walked away. Kate's chair scraped back and she caught Anna's elbow at the door.

'She doesn't mean any harm by it, Anna,' she whispered.

'Yes, she does. You know she bloody well does.'

'She's losing the filters. She just says what comes into her head.'

'Yeah, and she might as well stand on the table, wave her hands around and say, "This! This is what you should have. Not a rented flat and a can of mace as your perfume of choice."' She raised her voice a notch, knowing her mother would hear. 'Well, guess what? I like my rented flat. I like making a sodding difference.'

Kate winced and put a calming hand on Anna's arm. 'I know you do, babes. And you do have all this, too. Rob thinks you're a rock star. The kids love you to bits. This is here for you, whenever.'

'Tim fucking Lambert?'

'She doesn't know the dirty truth though, does she?'

Anna sighed. 'No, she doesn't. And I've just been reminded of why I didn't tell her.' She hugged Kate. 'Say goodbye to the monsters for me.'

'I'll come up one Saturday. Leave the kids with Mum and Rob. Just us two, OK?'

'That would be good. Really good.'

'Take care, Anna. I'm just on the other side of that bridge, remember. And on the other end of the phone. You know, black oblong? Touch screen?'

It broke the tension. Anna smiled and they hugged again.

Holder rang Anna five minutes later. They agreed to meet at the Severn View services and travel up to Gloucester together. It was Sunday. He didn't have to, but she was grateful for him offering nonetheless.

Driving fast along the M4, Anna couldn't shake the thought of Tim Lambert. Even after all these years it made her feel sick. What was her mother thinking of? Guilt followed. Her mother had probably thought of nothing at all. And yet...

She'd analysed the why and the wherefore of just when her relationship with her mother started to go south and concluded that her father's death, though not the actual trigger, was the catalyst that allowed a suppressed stream of constant negativity to pour forth. There was probably a PhD psychoanalysis thesis here, if she dug deep enough or even scratched the surface. But knowing that didn't help.

Anna had been close to her father, much closer than Kate. He'd engaged in and encouraged her interests, and possessed enough emotional intelligence to screen her from the carping criticism that her mother seemed unable to stop. Kate, on the other hand, could do no wrong in her mother's eyes. Her three years at the university in Cardiff meant that she'd been close enough to nip home most weekends to be with Rob and provide emotional support for their mother, whereas Anna's end-of-term visits were kept to the minimum, and, after a couple of days, she'd be itching for London again. No, that was wrong. She'd be itching to be away from the chintzy curtains and antimacassars, and the silent drone of disapproval. More than once Anna asked herself, and occasionally Kate, if their mother had suffered some sort of localised stroke. A targeted embolism, which demolished that part of her brain capable of empathy, or, as said in typically blunt Anna fashion, 'recognising when she was being a hypercritical cow'.

She had her phone in a holder on the dash and pressed a key to bring up Siri. 'Phone Kate.'

Her sister answered. The noise of children giggling in the background abated as she changed rooms. 'Anna? Everything OK?'

'I made inspector. Temporary, but still inspector.'

Kate squealed. 'Why didn't you say anything?'

'You know why.'

'We would have opened champagne.'

'Now's not the time for celebration.'

'Was the news really bad?'

'The worst. Keep that bottle on ice for the next time and I'll stay over. I miss having a three-year-old crawl all over me at six in the morning.'

'Hah! When was the last time anyone crawled all over you at six in the morning?'

'*Thanks*, Kate.'

'Any time, babes. Right. I'll sort out that Saturday and we will drink Prosecco because you're a cheapskate and I will definitely sleep over.' The rest of the sentence was sung in a dramatic soprano. 'Oh my God. My sister the detective inspector!'

CHAPTER ELEVEN

He'd made sure they'd find her and it had been easy. There'd been no resistance. The drugs ensured that. He'd used ketamine alone the first time and far too much of it. He'd almost killed her in the barn. But they'd worked a treat once he'd reduced the amount and mixed it in with the other stuff. It had kept her quiet and subdued while he waited.

She'd bled a little when he'd taken her. He'd stuck her in the thigh with the dart as she slept in the barn – *who let two kids sleep in a fucking barn?* – and she'd jerked from the pain, tearing a gash in her thigh. But he'd got enough in to subdue her. Later, she'd lain, quiet, pale, unmoving. Exactly the way he liked. Ever since that first time with Emily had awakened the excitement within him.

The drugs were a new departure. Previously he'd had to use his hands to suppress and choke, but the drugs… he wondered why he'd never thought if it before.

They'd ensured she hadn't fought at the end. He'd hardly needed to use his hands on her throat even, except that he liked to feel, to squeeze the apple. She'd only reacted when he'd stabbed her. Then she'd bucked and flopped like a fish. He'd made sure to stab her exactly the same number of times that he'd stabbed Emily. With exactly the same knife. It had to be the exact same number of times. Yet even he was surprised by how much it fulfilled him. How much he'd missed this. His hand had been forced by circumstances and yet… and yet he knew that there would be no going back now. No more being careful not to cross the red line.

He had a good supply of the drugs left. He knew how to hunt. A new chapter was dawning. This one had been a necessary target. He'd watched her ride. Knew her movements. But she was different. Chosen because of who she was, not what she was. Much more risk than he would normally take. But he'd taken care. Extra care.

Even the wild boar he'd encountered on the track had stayed away. Boars knew real danger when they came across it.

Now that they'd found her, they'd used his name again. He liked that. Couldn't wait to read the words in the newspapers, hear them emerge from the mouths of those perfect English newsreader's lips. Him. His name. He felt elated at the thought as it burned through him, from within.

But first, he needed for his carefully planned and constructed scenario to play out. It shouldn't take long. Confirmation. Affirmation. That's what people needed.

And afterwards? Afterwards he would be free to continue. A new chapter in his story. Spread his wings. Find another forest in which to hunt, even.

Watching, from a distance, the men and women in their stupid white suits swarm around the place *he'd* chosen for them to dance to his tune, he trembled. *So much power. So much fucking power.*

The cold was unremitting. The sun, sinking, stained the sky magenta as the day ended. It presaged another clear day to come and, with it, the promise of a new awakening for the Woodsman.

CHAPTER TWELVE

Anna parked in Quay Street and she and Holder walked up under the overhang of the Gloucester county offices. The police station, a seven-storey concrete-and-glass monstrosity, cast a cold, architectural shadow over the simple domed beauty of the Crown court entrance opposite. Slack met them and took them upstairs. Within minutes he'd furnished them with strong tea and put them into a tiny room with a glass wall looking out onto the busy squad room. Sunday was forgotten and at least ten people were at work. It came as no surprise to Anna. The Hopkins Case was now a murder investigation for Harris and his team. With a killer at large, the danger for the local community had increased incrementally, and the public hadn't even seen the body yet, or made the connections to Cooper, to Emily Risman… to the Woodsman.

With the door of their room closed, Anna and Holder could see the bustling activity and conversations taking place through the glass wall, but the soundproofing was excellent. Occasionally, someone in the squad room would glance in, wondering what it was that kept them so engrossed on the TV monitor.

Thankfully, no one in that workaday room could see what they could.

No one in his or her right minds would ever want to.

A dog team had found her in desolate woodland just four miles from the Hopkinses' property. In a place that had been searched some days before. One handler had noticed activity from a couple of magpies as he'd made his way through a copse, his dog quickly repaying his sharp-eyed observation. The SOC video showed the layout. A narrow path led up to a crest, which rapidly descended into a bowl surrounded by naked ash and beech. From the approach, there was no way of knowing that such a depression existed in the landscape beyond. But the killer obviously knew.

The camera led the way down to the body and Anna was struck instantly by the similarity to Emily Risman's SOC photos. The arrangement of branches and sticks forming a wooden tent over the body stood out. This time, a circlet of twigs entwined the crown. Someone had edited the video and the scene shifted to some time later, when the forensic team had done their preliminaries, to a point where the sticks had been removed. The cameraman was by necessity a true pornographer, visually probing all exposed parts of the victim's body. This was his thankless role in the CSI team; finding and zooming in on every stab wound and bruise.

The similarities between Nia and Emily stood out as vivid and stark. Nia was also on her stomach, her lower half also covered with leaves, her face turned to one side, left arm half raised, pyjama bottoms pulled roughly down around her ankles. Anna knew that if she counted the stab marks, they'd number the same as were found on Emily's body.

'It's the same. Exactly the same,' she said finally.

'You all right, ma'am?' Holder asked.

'As well as anybody after seeing that,' said Anna. 'The branches over her body. Has anyone given them a thought?'

Slack shrugged. 'Half-hearted concealment maybe.'

'I'd say he wanted her to be found,' Anna shook her head. 'Evidence of sexual molestation?'

Slack nodded. 'There is bruising on the thighs but no semen. He used a condom.'

'Knife?'

'Four-inch blade. Same as with Emily Risman. Same number of times.'

Holder, sitting next to Anna, winced. He looked grey under his normally glowing brown skin.

'Bathroom's on this level, through the swing doors and take a left.'

Holder got up, mumbled some thanks and hurried through the door.

Anna watched him leave with a sympathetic grimace. 'They didn't tell him about this stuff at the academy. Preliminary forensics?' she asked.

Slack consulted a file. 'Remnants of adhesive on the wrists and mouth. Probably from tape. Strangulation was not fatal but prolonged. The ground was badly trampled. It looked as if he played cat and mouse with her, or she tried to get away. The blood spatter is all over the place.'

'Time of death?'

'Late yesterday evening.'

Anna squeezed her eyes shut. Nia'd been alive all this time. Hidden away. She swallowed down the frustration and hot anger. It wouldn't help.

Slack continued, 'No adhesive on the ankles but evidence of chafing on the left as if she'd been tied. He didn't want her to get away, but didn't want to restrict her movements either.'

'Carried her to the killing ground. Easier to do if they're not completely trussed up,' she said, before exhaling loudly and reaching for the A4 pad she'd been scribbling notes on.

'And, like Beckie, she was dosed up on ketamine and something called thiafentanil. A narcotic analgesic used by vets.' Slack shook his head. 'Do you need a copy of the video?'

'No. Just send me through a few stills.'

'Harris asked if you'd give him a ring once you'd finished here.'

She tried to read Slack but failed. She outranked him through nothing more than luck. If he was resentful, he was keeping it under wraps. She liked to think that catching Nia Hopkins' killer was more important to him. Unlike his senior investigating officer.

'Where is he?'

'At the scene. He has a mobile.'

Slack reeled off the numbers as Anna dialled.

Harris answered with a barked hello. He sounded tired and brusque and blunt. 'So, what do you think?'

'My opinion is that we're looking at an organised killing.'

'You think whoever did this planned to kill this girl from the outset?'

'Of course he did. Drugging Beckie. Abducting Nia to a place he clearly chose. He knew what he wanted to do, presuming this is not a copycat?'

'No way. This is the sodding Woodsman. It's Cooper,' Harris said. 'And don't try telling me anything different.' He killed the line and Anna pocketed the phone. His vehemence was understandable and all the more unwelcome for it. He wasn't thinking clearly at this point. Though the similarities were obvious between Nia's and Emily's murders, there were differences, too.

Emily had not been hidden away and then killed. Her death had occurred on the day she'd gone missing. The abduction was a new departure. Why had the killer kept Nia? There were obvious reasons, despicable and harrowing ones that she didn't need to dwell on, which the autopsy might reveal. But there may have been more practical and devious reasons, which she had yet to think through.

Anna saw no point in quizzing Harris further at this point. He'd hardly been receptive up to now, and, judging from his reactions on the phone, the drawbridge was most definitely up.

'Is he happy?' Slack asked.

'Couldn't you hear the hysterical laughter?' she replied.

They both swung round at the noise of the door opening. Holder, looking a lot less grey, walked in.

'Sorry, ma'am.'

'Don't be. I'd think a lot less of you if you hadn't thrown up. I was a whisker away from it myself.' Anna turned to Slack. 'We'll want all the evidence and files duplicated, obviously.'

'No problem,' Slack said. 'I'll make sure of that. You know the way out?'

Back in the car, Holder looked confused. 'So, are we investigating this case, too, ma'am?'

'No. But we need shared access now that there are so many similarities. Slack and Harris know how this works.'

Holder nodded, a deep frown creasing his brow.

Anna snorted. 'Don't ever play poker, Justin. Come on, out with it.'

'Something Sergeant Slack said, ma'am. When he phoned through with the news, he said that DCI Harris wanted to pick Neville Cooper up for questioning.'

'And so it begins,' she said, and the smile that graced her lips bore no trace of amusement.

They drove back to Bristol in the darkening afternoon, Anna unable to shake off the despondent mood that had settled over her. There was no denying it might be the Woodsman, but that didn't immediately incriminate Cooper, and she desperately needed to investigate her other leads. What if the killer killed again?

As she drove, Anna found herself hoping that Slack and Harris wouldn't have shown Nia's body to the parents in that state, although experience told her that someone must have made the identification since Nia's Rupert the Bear pyjamas did not constitute enough in the way of confirmatory evidence. She assumed it would have been Chris Hopkins. How would he cope? How did anyone survive such a thing? You didn't. But if you were lucky, if you had others you could care about, you endured.

CHAPTER THIRTEEN

Anna called the team together for a briefing on Monday morning.
Rainsford joined them. It was a sombre affair. Since Nia's body
had been found, the Risman Case had taken on a new and
sinister complexity; they had a potential serial killer on the loose
and everyone looked pensive. But Anna could hear Shipwright's
words in her ear.

Stick to your guns.

She briefed the team on the similarities the crime scenes shared,
asked Trisha to liaise with Gloucester and asked Khosa to chase up
the whereabouts of Briggs and Wyngate. Her conversation with
Shipwright was ringing in her ears as she waved a hand to the
rogues' gallery pinned on the whiteboard.

When she'd finished, Rainsford led her into his office. 'Tough
weekend,' he said. A statement not a question.

'Not the best I've ever had, sir.'

'There's even more good news. Shaw wants to talk.'

'*What?*'

'I know. Never rains but it pours. We can't ignore it. You need
to get up there tomorrow morning and hear what he has to say. I
know you're busy with Risman—'

'No. I'm on it, sir. We're heading up to Millend today. I'll be
free tomorrow.'

'Millend?'

'Where Emily Risman lived, sir.'

'In the Forest of Dean?'

Anna nodded.

'Then we both know that's on the way to nowhere at all, but I'm grateful for your enthusiasm, Anna.'

'Yes, sir.'

'I don't know what Shaw's up to and I'm sure you could do without the distraction. If you think he's going to be too much for you to handle, just say the word. I'll get someone up there to see him and let you concentrate on Risman.'

'No, sir. I'd like to see this thing with Shaw through.'

'I thought you'd say that and I'm glad you did. Shaw says he wants to speak to you and you only. I was prepared to try with someone else, make your excuses if need be, but I think we'd lose his cooperation if we did that.'

Anna nodded. Listening to Rainsford she could see how he'd got to where he was. He had his faults, didn't everyone? But the ability to lead was not one of them. And neither was the ability to read ambition in other people.

Anna and Holder headed for Chepstow on a dull afternoon that seemed to leech the colour out of the landscape. By the time they reached Blakeney it had begun to rain in heavy downbursts, which had the wipers on overdrive and made the going slow on a winding road. The satnav made them take a left at Buckshaft and drive directly into the heart of the Forest of Dean. Within a couple of miles, traffic had all but disappeared and Anna stared out at unending acres of Forestry Commission land to both sides. Holder surprised her by supplying a stream of bland commentary, telling her that there were more deciduous broad-leafed trees, such as oak, ash and beech, in this forest than in any other in the UK. Though it seemed like another world, the map showed them to

be only about ten miles from where Nia's body had been found
the day before.

'These roads go on forever,' Holder muttered. He was right.
The only hope you had around here was with a car, and even then
it seemed to take an age to get anywhere.

They got to Millend just before one. It was a small village with
a fenced in cricket green and two unpretentious pubs. The road
climbed away from the village, and after a quarter of a mile, they
were out into forest again. Holder was reading a map from the file
he'd brought and asked Anna to slow down as they approached a
sign that read 'Miller's Pike Lake picnic area'.

'It's around here somewhere,' he said, peering through the
blurry glass.

Anna drove on slowly until he found the right spot, and then
pulled over on to a gravelled lay-by, opposite a turning into a rutted
lane guarded by a closed gate.

'We'll have to walk from here,' Holder said, reaching into the
seat behind for his coat.

They both got out of the car and crossed the road, the rain
mercifully slowing to a spattering drizzle.

'What is this road?' Anna asked.

'This whole area is riddled with abandoned mills and old forges,
apparently. They were mining here as far back as Roman times. Iron
ore, coal, even quarrying for stone. There're miles of abandoned
railway. This lane could have led to anything, but historians think
that the scowle a mile or so in points to surface mining.'

'You've done your homework, Justin. Or did you pick up a
tourist leaflet? What's a scowle?'

'Local term, ma'am. Shallow hollows. Evidence of cave systems
or excavations.' Holder gave her a lopsided grin, put his file in one
hand so that he could hold on with the other, and climbed over
the gate.

Anna followed.

The track wound around and upwards until they were out of sight and sound of the road. Holder's map led them up a muddy path to a point where they could look down into a clearing in a natural dip in the ground. A bowl surrounded by tall oaks and chestnuts, interspersed with Scots pine and larch.

'The Forest of Dean,' said Holder.

Anna didn't say anything. There were no birds singing, only the solid plops of rain dripping from the leaves and branches onto the forest floor.

'The village kids used to come here. There should be a picnic area just behind us.' Holder pivoted towards the remains of some tables. 'Yep, there it is.'

'And no trace of tyre- or footmarks at the time?'

Holder spread the file open under a plastic sheet on one of the tables. 'It had been cold and dry for days,' he said. 'There were footprints but they were numerous and not particularly fresh.'

'Where exactly did they find Emily Risman?'

Holder handed her some black and white prints, rotating them this way and that in the thin drizzle before pointing to the east edge of the hollow under a large oak. 'Looks like it was about there.'

He walked across and Anna joined him. Eighteen years ago, someone committed murder on a gloomy February afternoon at this ancient spot, and the only witnesses were these towering trees. To the north, the land fell away. On a ridge above stood the forest; dark and silent and menacing, as if the trees were waiting to march back and reclaim what was rightly theirs.

Some of them looked incalculably old; huge gnarled trunks suggesting centuries of growth. It was not difficult to imagine that this natural amphitheatre might have attracted people from the very beginning. Anna frowned, wondering from where such a thought might have sprung. The place had a definite pagan feel to it. Her mind filled with imagined horrors. Sacrificial groves, wicker men for burning, robed druids spouting arcane rites. She shook her head to clear it, but her thoughts had left her unsettled. She looked down, blinking away the dampness, and when she looked up again, she thought she saw something move on the horizon. A shape, fleeting and blurred, flitting between the trees.

'There!' She pointed.

Holder followed her finger. 'What is it?'

'I thought I saw something move.'

Holder peered. 'How big?'

'Difficult to say.' She paused, analysing why his question sounded odd. 'Why?'

'There are wild boar here, ma'am. Sometimes there's a cull if their numbers swell. They've been known to attack dogs and horses.'

'Wow, there was a lot of information on that tourist leaflet.' She tried using humour to deflect the disquiet that gripped her, but despite scanning it several times, nothing moved at the tree line now. The place smelled of earth and leaf mould, and Anna guessed it would even in summer. Hundreds of years' worth of rot under her feet, the ground spongy and damp underfoot. For a moment, she feared she might sink into it and be swallowed up by the forest and its secrets.

'Creepy spot here, isn't it?' Holder spoke for them both.

'It all started here,' she said. '"The evil that men do lives after them."'

'That sounds like something I should know,' said Holder, with a nervous little laugh. 'Is it Shakespeare?'

'It is.' Anna turned away as the rain escalated from drizzle to shower. She'd planned on asking Holder to go back to the car to wait for her, wanting time alone to let her mind roam over the landscape of Emily's last minutes. Imagine the possible scenarios that could have led her to this lonely spot, alone with her killer. But now, even if Holder had gone and left her, she knew she wouldn't feel alone in this place. The flash of movement in her peripheral vision had unnerved her, leaving her with the unpleasant and unshakable sensation of being watched.

'Come on,' she said after another moment's contemplation, 'let's go and see Emily's family.'

Holder drove back to Millend. A smattering of scattered dwellings were the heart of the village. The biggest building was another Forestry Commission property; a field centre for outdoor studies. They doubled back and Holder stopped opposite the cricket pitch and pointed across the road at a concrete post tilting at an angle just short of forty-five degrees, with a bus stop sign at the top.

'That would be where Emily caught the bus to Coleford or Gloucester.'

Anna looked up and down the road. No cars or houses to the north and south for fifty yards.

'It's not overlooked by anything,' she stated.

'No,' Holder agreed.

The Rismans lived in a bungalow a quarter of a mile outside the village, on the edge of an estate of 1930s-built semis. The bungalow was a low, dirty, cream building flanked by two rows of quick-growing leylandii hedges that had been someone's bad idea some fifteen years before. A weed-strewn lawn and some bedraggled shrubs led the way to a paint-flecked front door. Holder knocked and introduced himself and Anna to a bespectacled, portly man in a tight-fitting knitted polo shirt that had once been canary yellow, but which now bore several stains that were a timeline of past meals. Bill Risman was balding and he pulled back his lips to reveal nothing but pink gums.

'You must be the police. Been expecting you,' he said cheerfully.

Anna followed Bill and Holder down a narrow hallway to a clean but cluttered living room. A mock coal fire hissed quietly in one corner in the middle of a brass surround. A herd of china shire horses marched across the mantelpiece, and polished brasses and horseshoes hung at eye level on every vertical surface. Two faded, brown velour armchairs were pulled up around a big TV that glowed colourfully in one corner. Above it stood a glass-fronted cupboard full of framed photographs of Emily at different ages.

The TV droned out a mid-afternoon chat show full of the sound of a sycophantic audience overeager to applaud everything mentioned by hawker guests and bland hosts.

'Joan,' Bill sang out. 'The police are here.'

The corpulent occupant of one of the armchairs turned an incongruously small round face towards them before levering herself up. She bobbed, favouring her right hip, and waved at them to enter.

'Come in and sit down. Bill, go put the kettle on.'

Bill scooped the open pages of a tabloid off the sofa and brushed away some crumbs with his hand.

'Tea? I remember the police always liked a drop of tea.'

'That'll be fine, sir,' Holder said, and waited while Anna seated herself. 'We're sorry to disturb you like this, Mr Risman,' he continued.

'S'all right, we're used to it. We gets half a dozen or so people a year from newspapers and TV and such. More so now, o'course,' Bill replied on his way to the kitchen. The accent wasn't heavy, but the absence of teeth made Anna listen hard to understand.

'They've always wanted to know about my Emily,' Joan explained. 'I can't count the number of times we've had copies of her photos made. Newspapers are the worst, mind. Say they'll send back pictures but they never do. So, I just charge them now. A tenner to cover our costs, innit, Bill?'

'A tenner, yeah.' Bill's voice floated in from the kitchen.

'Trouble is, pictures don't give you the whole story, do they? Lovely nature when she was little, she had. A proper madam, mind, always wanting to sing or dance, the centre of attention. Did wonderful in school concerts and the like. Wasn't too good at reading to begin with, but she'd caught up by the time she'd got to the comprehensive. I wasn't surprised. I mean, no one in our family liked books, if you know what I mean. Except my sister Rita's boy, Lyndon. He went to college in Southampton to do something deep. What was it that Lyndon, Rita's boy did, Bill?'

'Engineering, he did.'

'There. I knew it was something. But not our Emily. Always a one for make-up and dresses. Natural that she should want to go into hairdressing. And she was good too – used to do all the street in her spare time. Charged them, mind. Though there's no pleasing some people, but I told them, I said if you was going over to Coleford, you'd be paying three times as much and the bus. If they didn't like it they could always go somewhere else, couldn't they? And she could cut beautifully. Course, here they wanted perms mostly—'

'Mrs Risman' – Anna cut across Joan's outpouring – 'you'll have heard about Neville Cooper's release?'

The grin slid off Joan's face. 'Why they letting him go? Can you tell me why they're letting that monster out?'

Holder kept his gaze steady. 'Because it looks like he didn't do it, Mrs Risman.'

'Of course he did it. They said so in the court, didn't they?'

'They may have made a mistake,' Anna said.

Joan's small eyes glared at her without understanding. 'How could they make a mistake about something like that? All those lawyers and policemen and specialists? How could they make a mistake?'

Anna shrugged. 'It is difficult to believe, isn't it, but the fact is that they did. The police had evidence that showed that Neville Cooper was somewhere else, but they chose not to disclose it. Witnesses saw Cooper at an amusement arcade the afternoon of Emily's death and at a cinema that evening.'

'Then why didn't they say so at the time? Why wait all these years?'

'Because…' Holder said, but faltered.

Anna glanced at him and then smiled at Mrs Risman. 'What did you think of the investigative team?'

The woman's eyes glazed over momentarily in something akin to rapture.

'Mr Briggs, he was in charge. Wonderful man. But Mr Wyngate, he was special. They both promised us the first time they walked in through the door that they would find the man who killed our Emily and put him away. And he did that for us did Mr Wyngate. He had that look in his eye, a determined look. Spent hours here, he did.'

'Not Maddox?'

'Not so much. Not one for conversation over a cup o'tea and a biscuit was Sergeant Maddox. Stern, you know?'

Any thought that Anna harboured of pointing out Wyngate's failings evaporated at that point. She didn't want to make an enemy of this woman.

'Have you met Mr Wyngate since that time?'

'Only at the trial.'

'Not since?'

'We've seen him on TV. We've watched him put a lot of villains away. A great man, Mr Wyngate.'

An electronic chirping suddenly burst from Holder's jacket. Mumbling an apology, he stood and flipped open a mobile phone.

'Hello?'

Anna watched him move out of earshot into the relative privacy of the hallway. She turned back to Joan. 'Can I ask you about the day Emily died? Did she say anything to you about what she had planned for that day?'

Joan looked up at the glass cabinet as if seeking permission to speak. Her daughter smiled back at her approvingly.

'She left for work on the Thursday morning as usual. She'd walked around with wet hair for half an hour, eaten half a piece of toast, and wouldn't listen to me telling her to wear something other than the sloppy T-shirt she slept in.' Joan shook her head. 'She wasn't a bad girl, mind you. Terrible one for boys, but then so was I in my day, wasn't I, Bill?' The last three words were delivered at a higher volume and aimed out towards the kitchen. It received an incoherent mumble from that direction in reply.

'That Thursday, she left for work at eight. She caught the bus to Coleford. Thursday was her half-day. Sometimes she went in to Gloucester, but sometimes she didn't. That day, she didn't. She left work at one and never came home again. Someone met her that afternoon, I'm certain of it.'

'There was no other way for her get to Millend from Coleford except by bus?'

'We didn't have a car, if that's what you mean. She must have come back on the bus.'

'But no one remembered seeing her get off here?'

'There was someone,' Joan protested.

'Someone said they saw her on the bus, but no one saw her get off here, did they?'

'No. No one said they did, but you don't, do you? You sit on a bus and think about your shopping. Leastways, I do.'

'Did she talk to you about her boyfriends?'

Joan shook her head. 'It was just a game for her. There was no one she was really sweet on. She didn't talk much about it.'

'What about Richard Osbourne?'

'Oh yes, we knew about Rick. Mad for him at one time she was. Wrote his name all over her school satchel.'

'Did she ever bring him home?'

'Just as far as the garden gate. Then her dad would go out and fetch her in. She was only fifteen then, remember.'

'And Roger Willis?'

Joan's brows furrowed. She shook her head. 'He was a nice boy. Always polite when I met him in the village. I could hardly credit him and Emily… Stupid to fall like that.'

Bill came back in with a battered tray laden with mugs and a steaming teapot. He poured out a dark infusion that turned a sienna colour with the addition of milk, and handed Anna a mug with a faded photograph of Charles and Diana on the side.

'Uh, thank you,' Anna said and took a tentative sip. The tannins were bitter and the liquid scalding.

The sound of a car pulling up drew Bill to the window.

''Ello,' he said cheerfully peering out, 'more visitors.'

Joan squinted above the rim of her cup and caught Anna glancing up at the photographs on the wall. Among those of Emily, one stood out. A black and white image in a black frame beneath a cross. A baby. Tiny, wrapped in shawls.

'That's Emily's sister.'

'I didn't know she had a sister?'

'She don't. She died soon after that photo was taken. I keeps her picture up there with Emily.'

'I'm so sorry…'

'Don't be. These things… they happen. Some people thinks it's to do with living here. Them pylons over at the electric station.' Anna didn't respond. She waited for Joan to continue.

'Well, it does happen, doesn't it? Mary Trimble from Hassett is convinced to this day that her trouble started with the accident she witnessed.'

'And what trouble was that, Mrs Risman?'

'You'll probably think me daft.' Joan's eyes narrowed.

'No, tell me, I'm interested.'

Joan glanced across at her husband and leaned in close to Anna, her overall straining to contain the flesh within. 'Her Jenny was born funny, you know. Bits of what should have been inside on the outside. Terrible it was. Poor little thing lived for almost five months over there in Gloucester.'

'I'm sorry,' Anna commiserated.

'She can talk about it now. She must have been five months gone when the accident happened in Hassett. Hay lorry coming down Bird Hill, lost control and went straight into the ironmonger's there. Four people there was in that shop. Didn't stand a chance. Mary Trimble was in the baker's opposite. She was almost the first there. The first to get to those people smashed up in that shop.'

'She thinks the trauma had an effect on her unborn child?' Anna's question was for her own clarification and Joan nodded, sagely.

'Stands to reason, doesn't it?'

Anna opened her mouth to speak but the words wouldn't come. She couldn't remember who said that superstition was the religion of the feeble. However arcane, it was in a way understandable in that it provided an explanation, a way of rationalising fate. It may well have been laughable and derisory, but clearly it was something Joan believed. A part of Anna wanted to pour scorn on this ignorant superstition, point out to this woman how ludicrous all this was. But the look of concern and, yes, pity almost in the woman's eyes, made her falter. No wonder she wanted to accept that Cooper killed Emily. After the media sensationalised the Woodsman, she must have clung to the idea that Cooper was guilty, and found it the only solace, the only resolution. Anna knew that two or three glib sentences would not dismiss a hundred years of rural myth. Instead, biting back her cynicism and knowing how proud Shipwright would have been of her restraint, she humoured Joan.

'Yes, it is dreadful when things like that happen.'

The doorbell rang and Bill shuffled off to answer it, just as Holder appeared in the doorway, phone still in his hand and his face troubled.

'Uh, ma'am, could I have a private word?'

Anna stood and walked into the kitchen. Along the hallway, she glanced at Bill. He stood outside on the threshold talking to someone, voices muffled through the half-closed door. Holder leaned in and spoke in hushed tones.

'That was Ryia. There's been a development in the Hopkins case. They've found something incriminating at Cooper's workplace.'

Anna stared at him.

'Cooper's in custody, ma'am, and apparently all hell is breaking loose.'

'Shit.'

Bill came back in to the hallway. Two people stood beyond the door. A woman and a man. Both mid-thirties, the woman dressed in tight black jeans and a heavy coat, the man in a dark woollen beanie and cargo pants, hauling a heavy camera bag.

'Joan' – Bill addressed his wife in a shocked voice –'it's the papers. They want to speak to us. They're saying that bastard Cooper's done it again.'

Anna squeezed her eyes shut. This was not good. Sighing, she said, 'There's nothing here for us. This is old ground. Come on.' She hurried to the living room. 'Thanks for talking to us. We—'

'Is that why you came?' Joan's voice was a hoarse whisper. 'To tell us he's done it again?'

'No.' Anna shook her head. 'This is—'

Bill's mouth hardened. 'You let him out. You let that monster get away.'

'You'll have to excuse us,' said Anna. 'We'll be in touch.'

'We trusted the police. We trusted you!' Joan's shouts followed them out as they left the house, watched with interest by the two people on the path.

'Hi,' said the woman. 'Did I just hear the word "police"?'

'Excuse us,' said Anna and walked away, Holder right behind her.

'Are you here because of Neville Cooper?' The question echoed in the still air.

Bill appeared in the doorway, his face mottled with anger. 'Why didn't you tell us he'd done it again?'

They were at the car and opening the doors. When Anna looked up it was into the lens of a very big camera pointed in her direction. She heard the ominous sound of a motor drive's rapid clicking before the engine fired and she accelerated away.

CHAPTER FOURTEEN

Anna drove hard until she reached the rear of the station in Gloucester. As soon as they were through security she could sense the electric anticipation filling the air. There were even more people there than she remembered from her last visit. Curious eyes followed her and Holder as they made their way purposefully through the building. Slack met them and took them to an anteroom next to the room where Cooper was being interviewed.

On a screen in front of her, Anna watched the scene.

Harris sat opposite two men across a table. Anna recognised one of them instantly. Cooper, the wiry youth, had grown into portly middle age. Under a faded orange T-shirt, his arms were flabby and his fingers thick. It looked like his cheeks had been ravaged by years of anti-epileptic drugs, bringing with them florid acne as an unwelcome guest. A row of brown and uneven teeth showed through behind his full, but parted lips.

If ever there had been an image that was easy to despise, Neville Cooper epitomised it. He sat with his head bent, eyes downcast and away from Harris's predatory stare.

'Who's the other man?' Anna asked.

'Howard Tobias, Cooper's solicitor,' Slack explained.

The name rang a faint bell in Anna's memory. Images of a triumphant, bespectacled face amid Cooper and his small group of supporters on the steps of the High Court sprang to mind. Now that same full face looked agitated and angry, staring defiantly at Harris across the table.

'I want fifteen minutes alone with my client, please.'

'We need to finish the interview,' Harris said.

'And I'm telling you that you're already pushing your luck. Mr Cooper has already been questioned exhaustively in my absence. Now, I'd like fifteen minutes, alone.'

Harris stood and waved away the uniformed man from inside the door.

'And I want that thing off while I have it.' Tobias waved a hand towards the camera.

Harris put a hand up and the image faded from the screen as a technician closed down the video camera. Fifteen seconds later, Harris came in, grinning.

'We've got the bastard on the ropes.' He turned to the technician. 'Gemmel, let's have a look.'

The screen filled with a poorer quality view looking down at the two men in the interview room.

'What are they saying?' Harris asked.

The sound of Tobias's entreating voice emerged from a speaker above them.

'You've got nothing to worry about, Neville. They're intimidating you to try to get you to say something you don't mean.'

Holder exchanged glances with Anna, who rounded on Harris. 'We shouldn't be listening to this. He's asked for the camera to be turned off.'

'This is a security camera,' Harris said, turning to Anna and frowning, as if registering her presence for the first time. 'And why are you even here?'

Anna turned to Slack, who kept his eyes averted and shifted uncomfortably. Holder just shook his head.

Harris watched their reactions in turn with a defiant grin before motioning to Gemmel. 'Turn it off. Apparently, it's offending these officers.'

This man is a power junkie.

'You've filled in Inspector Gwynne, Sergeant?' Harris asked. He delivered 'Inspector' again with sardonic emphasis.

'The basics sir, yes.'

Harris turned to Anna, his lids at half-mast. 'Then there's no reason for you to stay, is there?'

'I'm still unclear on several points,' she said.

Harris didn't reply right away. But she could see he was pumped and confident enough to indulge her.

'You found something at Cooper's workplace?'

'In his locker at the feed mill. Bloodstained tape. Blood that matches Nia Hopkins' type,' Harris informed her. 'DNA will take a day, but in the meantime, it was enough for a search warrant of Cooper's home.'

'And?'

'And in his dirty little garage, among the dirty little rags he cleans his dirty little bike with was a pair of women's underwear. Bloodstained knickers.' Harris's enunciation was full of that irritating defiance.

'Is that it?'

Harris snorted in disbelief. 'Nia's mother has confirmed that they are very likely the missing pair.'

'Very likely?' Anna repeated.

'What more do you bloody want?' Harris's eyes bulged.

Anna ignored his belligerence. 'How did he react when you arrested him?'

'Did two cartwheels and a forward roll. How do you think he reacted? He almost crapped himself. He started shaking because he knew we'd got him this time. And this time there will be no mistakes. No bullshit.'

'Like that you mean?' Anna glanced over at the now empty screen.

Harris smiled and shook his head. 'That was just a bit of fun. Sorry that you don't see it that way. It's obvious that your little investigation hasn't produced much of a result for you. I could have told you that it was a complete waste of time. You're looking for something that doesn't exist.'

'You know that for certain then, do—'

Harris cut across Anna's protests. 'There is only one killer and he's next door with his liberal-minded, bleeding-heart solicitor.' He drew himself up. 'I don't want you here, in case you hadn't guessed. But I've been told to share intelligence, which is what I'm doing. But make no mistake, this is my case. My patch. And the sooner you get back to Bristol and sergeant status the better, as far as I'm concerned.'

'Are you married, Inspector?'

Harris smiled again here. 'Fifteen years. Second time around. This one's a keeper.'

'Cooper has been inside longer than you've been married. And possibly for no reason whatsoever.'

Harris smile turned into a sour sneer. 'I've got no time for this. You're welcome to watch, but then you can piss off down the M5.' He turned and left.

Slack waited until the door closed completely before commenting. 'You got nothing at all out of visiting the crime scene, then?'

Holder shook his head. 'Old ground.'

'I need more time,' Anna said.

'Not on DCI Harris's agenda, that.' Slack massaged the bridge of his nose.

'I had noticed.'

'In fact, the word is he's opened a book on the time it takes.'

'For what?'

'For him to get a confession out of Cooper.'

'A confession? He can't be serious.'

'Wait ten minutes, you'll find out.'

'Is he going back in there?' Anna asked Slack.

As SIO, Harris's job was to coordinate the investigation. Interviews were normally the role of operational officers like Slack or a DI.

Slack shook his head. 'I don't know anyone in this station with the bottle to tell him to stay out.'

'But normally—'

'Normally is a ship that sailed a long time ago in this case, ma'am,' was all Slack could offer by way of explanation.

Harris recommenced exactly fifteen minutes after he'd walked out of the room.

'Time is five thirty p.m., Gloucester police station, interview room three. Present are DCI Alan Harris, Neville Cooper and Howard Tobias. Neville, I'm going to make this as simple as I can. Now that Mr Tobias is here, are you prepared to answer my questions?'

'Yeah. Yes, sir.'

Harris smiled. In charge. Back in the driving seat. 'Good. So, can you tell me how it was that we found duct tape in your locker at the feed mill?'

Cooper shook his head. 'Don't know, sir.'

'You're the only one with a key, aren't you?'

'I think so. Yeah.'

Harris kept it light. 'So, you have the only key and you don't know how the duct tape got there, have I got that right?'

'I don't know—'

'We found blood on that tape, Neville.'

Cooper looked up, frowning. 'I didn't put it there.'

Harris waited a beat, changed tack. 'How do you get to work, Neville?'

'I've got a motorbike now.'

'I thought epileptics weren't allowed to drive?' Harris turned to Tobias.

'Neville hasn't had a fit for six years. He passed his test a month ago. First time.'

Harris turned back to Cooper. 'Where do you keep the bike, Neville?'

'At home, in the garage.'

'Keep it locked up, do you? Not outside where everyone can see it?'

'Yes, sir.'

'Like working in the feed mill, too, do you?'

'Yes, sir.'

'What sort of work do you do there?'

'In the warehouse. Making sure the bags are stacked OK.'

Harris nodded. 'Good job, is it?'

'I've got some mates there.'

'Ever see the boss there?'

'Sam's my boss.'

Harris consulted some papers. 'Sam? He's the foreman, isn't he?'

'Yeah, Sam.'

'I don't mean Sam. I mean the big boss, Mr Hopkins.'

'Sometimes. I see him sometimes.'

'Does he ever come in with his family?'

Cooper concentrated. 'I saw him once with his kids. He had a big car, pulling a horsebox.'

'So you saw the kids, did you?'

'Two girls and a boy.'

'You go out for spins on your bike, Neville?'

'Sometimes. On weekends.'

'Only on weekends? I would have thought you'd be itching to get out there?'

'I would but... my mum isn't well.'

'I'm sorry to hear that, Neville. So on the night Nia Hopkins was abducted, you were at home looking after your mother?'

'Yeah. Yes, sir.'

'Didn't go out for a ride after she'd gone to bed?'

'No, sir.'

Harris leaned forward, elbows on the table, dropping his voice. 'See, I'm wondering if you might have gone over to visit Mr Hopkins that night on your bike.'

'No, sir.'

'Nice spin. Half an hour would it be?'

'Yeah, maybe, I'm not sure…'

'And I'm wondering if you went up there and saw a light on in the stable.'

Tobias interrupted. 'Chief Inspector, my client has already indicated that he was at home that night.'

'And I'm just trying to get everything straight in my head, Mr Tobias. See, Neville, you've got to try to see it from my point of view. Here you are, just out of prison for murder—'

Tobias interjected. 'I'm warning you—'

'Just out of prison with everything going for you, and suddenly there's another girl raped and stabbed to death.'

Cooper shook his head. 'It wasn't me…'

Harris persisted. 'Another girl stabbed to death just like Emily Risman.'

Tobias said, 'That's quite enough, Superintendent. Mr Cooper has been acquitted…'

'And then,' Harris said, loudly, 'if that's not enough, we find Nia Hopkins' blood in your locker. Sixteen, Neville. She was sixteen. How did that get there, Neville?'

'No… it wasn't me.'

'I want this interview terminated now,' Tobias said. 'These constant references to Emily Risman are intolerable.'

'The facts indicate that the two cases are linked, Mr Tobias. Am I supposed to ignore the facts?' Harris glared at the solicitor.

'I don't know how,' Cooper said.

'We've heard that one, Neville. Tell us another one. Tell us the one about you finding the girls asleep in that stable. Tell us what you did to them. Tell us where you keep the knife. Tell us, because it's the only hope you've got here, Neville. Think about what a jury's going to believe if we take this to court and you keep on denying it. Cry wolf, Neville. They're not going to give you a second chance. But if you tell us, maybe we can find you somewhere better to go to. Somewhere where they're not going to eat up child killers for breakfast.'

Cooper looked horrified. 'NO!' His denial emerged with a sob.

'No point crying like a kid, Neville,' Harris said softly.

Tobias stood up. 'That's it. I want you to be quiet. This is out and out harassment.'

Harris's tone was suddenly cold and reasonable, but his eyes were blazing. 'You want to end it. OK, I think we all know where we stand now.'

Tobias returned the glare. 'I don't want you anywhere near my client unless I'm here, DCI Harris. And I'm lodging an official complaint.'

'Lodge away.'

'I want to accompany my client to his cell.'

On hearing the word 'cell', Cooper flipped. 'Do I have to stay here? I don't want to stay here!'

Tobias tried for calm. 'It'll be all right, Neville.'

'No, it won't. They won't leave me alone! It'll be just like last time!'

'No, it won't, Neville.'

Cooper pushed back from his chair and stood up. The door opened and two uniformed officers entered. Cooper stared at them and then at Tobias. 'Yes, it will. It's happening again. Why is it happening again?'

Harris said, 'Interview terminated at five forty p.m. Time to go back to your cell, Neville.'

'I don't want to. You can't let them take me.'

'Neville, it'll be OK. I promise it'll be OK.' Tobias stood and put a calming hand on Cooper's arm.

Three policemen in the interview room, spoiling for a fight, used to restraining drunks and addicts. But Cooper surprised Anna and disappointed Harris by quietening down once Tobias spoke to him, cupping his hand around the man's ear. She could see a smug superiority on some of the coppers' faces; others showed a grudging admiration for this dignified exit. But there was something terrible in that quiet acceptance that shook Anna. An acceptance reflected in Tobias's eyes. A look that showed how Cooper had learned hard and bitter lessons in prison. He knew that there came a point where you needed to take your lumps, quell the feelings that raged inside, the indignation that burned. She found herself wishing he had yelled and screamed, clawed like a cat against his captors. It would have been an affirmation of the spirit inside. Instead, the institution of the law imposed itself upon a customer of long standing. It was a pitiful thing to behold. When she could drag her eyes away from Cooper's downcast face, she saw that Tobias's hand was balled into a fist around a scrap of paper, the knuckles white against the dark desktop.

The solicitor gathered his papers hurriedly.

'I don't want you to ask him the time of day without me here, do you understand?' He leaned in close across the desk, his face inches from Harris's.

The chief inspector smiled beatifically and said nothing. Anna got up and left the room. She needed air.

*

'He sobbed in his cell for half an hour.' Holder shook his head. They were sitting in Slack's small office, the men with their ties loose and jackets off.

'Can Harris really do that?' Holder asked. 'Can he really offer a soft option to Cooper?'

Anna and Slack exchanged cynical glances. It was Slack that decided to answer. 'There are no soft options for nonces. Cooper knows that. For a large chunk of the time he was inside, he was isolated under Rule 43 for his own protection. When they tried integration, it became very unpleasant.'

'You mean he was attacked?'

'Yes, ma'am.'

'Tobias doesn't want Harris to talk to Cooper without him being present. How likely is it that will actually happen?'

'Nothing will stand up in court unless it's recorded and Tobias is present.'

But there is nothing to stop Harris from visiting Cooper in his cell when he gets his food delivered.

She shook her head in disgust. One major criticism of the case against Cooper eighteen years before was the periods of time he'd been detained without proper access to a solicitor. Those days had long gone, thank God, but there were obviously still ways to coerce and browbeat. And, from what she'd seen, to say that Cooper was susceptible to such tactics was an understatement.

Harris's pursuit of a confession, seemingly ludicrous when it had first been suggested, now seemed all too plausible in the face of the psychological war he was waging. Yet his unsubtle approach seemed fuelled by something far less healthy than pure zealousness. He seemed driven by a resentment that was deep-seated and poisonous. A desire to incriminate Cooper at any cost. A desire to have an answer to the questions from the Rismans, the press, the public. Again.

'What is Harris trying to prove?' Anna said.

Slack shrugged. 'I don't know, ma'am.'

But that wasn't true, and Slack knew it.

'Are they talking to the press?'

Slack nodded. 'Officially in about an hour.'

'But it's been leaked, hasn't it? There were press at the Rismans' house today.'

Slack could only shrug.

Anna got up. 'Tell DCI Harris I'll catch up.'

What she really, really needed to do was to get home and, more than anything else, take a long, hot shower to rid herself of the dirt that suddenly seemed to be in every pore.

CHAPTER FIFTEEN

Anna was halfway to Whitmarsh on Tuesday morning, her brain in overdrive and still smarting from Harris's barbs, when Holder rang.

'Have you seen the news today, ma'am?'

'No, Justin. I showered and left without passing "Go".'

'Newspaper?'

'You're making me nervous. Do I need to see one?'

'Yes, ma'am. It's best that you do.'

She stopped at the next services, bought a coffee and checked the news on her phone. There, a grainy and candid image of her face, taken from outside the Risman property, stared back at her. Serious, her eyes defiant and giving nothing away, the accompanying text said it all.

INSPECTOR ANNA GWYNNE, LEADING THE INVESTIGATION INTO EMILY'S KILLER, DECLINED TO COMMENT

The article rehashed the gory details of both Emily's and Nia's murders, along with the news of Neville Cooper's arrest. All with the words that could panic the public once again: The Woodsman.

Anna shook her head, annoyed. She should be focusing on Emily Risman, not on her way to a prison to interview Hector Shaw. The sooner she got this over with the better.

*

Shaw was waiting for her in the grubby interview room. He looked the same as a week before. Anna sat, went to switch on the DIR, but Shaw shook his head.

'I'd prefer this off the record. To start with.'

Anna shrugged and sat back. 'What can I do for you, Mr Shaw?'

'No gorilla?'

'DCI Shipwright is otherwise engaged.'

Shaw smiled and crossed his arms on his chest. 'Yeah? How's your other investigation, Anna?'

'You know I can't discuss any other investigation. I'm here to talk about Tanya Cromer.'

Shaw nodded. 'The thing is, I already know what it is you're caught up in. We get the newspapers, too. Nice photo. A smile wouldn't have hurt though.'

She waited.

'Neville Cooper. The Woodsman. Did he, or didn't he? It's a real two egg question, that. If he did, the courts get yolk all over their face, if he didn't your colleagues get it instead. There'll be a ton of flak either way.'

'Mr Shaw—'

'Looking at it from the outside, or from the inside, like I do, there are too many things that don't add fucking up. I mean, it looks like the police fitted him up for the first murder. But when he's inside, there's nothing. Then, when he comes back out, *kerch-ing*, there's another fucking murder. Two plus two equals four on that one.'

She tried not to listen, tried to summon up some white noise to play in her head. But the truth was this was exactly how it looked from the outside. Exactly how the newspapers saw it.

'Unless, of course, some devious bastard wants Cooper as a double scapegoat. What do you say, Anna?'

'I'm only here to talk about Tanya—'

'Oh, we will, I promise. But for now, I want to talk about you, Anna. You and your cold case. A cold case that's suddenly on fire and burning at eight hundred degrees fucking centigrade. We both know that the easy thing to do would be to roll over and let Cooper rot for another seventeen years. That's a long time. But why not? No one gave a fuck the last time. People will love you for it. The press will love you for it. Would you like that, Anna?'

Shaw paused. He gave her one of his slow blinks, and smiled. Not the broad, dangerous smile she'd seen in the Connor video, but still feral. She felt horribly exposed all of a sudden under his oily gaze.

'But you can't, can you? It's not in your DN fucking A, is it? I think I can help you, Anna. I've had a lot of time to think about the Woodsman. Plus, I may have some… special knowledge.'

Anna felt her breath quicken and fought not to show it. This was more than likely to be nothing but a sick game. Jane Markham had warned her. And yet, damn it, Shaw was bright. Might it be possible that he did know something?

'Yeah, see, you know it. I like you, Anna. I want us to be friends.'

'I can't do that. I can't be your friend.'

'Don't say that. Not this early in our relationship.'

'Tanya Cromer,' Anna said.

Shaw let out a snort. 'We both know that Tanya isn't going anywhere.'

Something in his voice made her swallow hard. If he noticed, he did not acknowledge it.

'"The Woodsman". Pathetic name, but things were different then. Seventeen years ago, things weren't quite as sophisticated. The newspapers were powerful. Not like now where they're irrelevant to anyone under thirty-five. But then, they could really sway public opinion.'

'If you know anything…' Anna said.

Shaw nodded. 'That's the real question, isn't it? Knowing.' He blew out air. 'This case. It has so many angles. So many places you could trip up. But your angle… your angle must be that Cooper isn't guilty, am I right?'

She didn't let anything show, but Shaw smiled anyway.

'So how do you fit the evidence around that? I mean, now we're into a different kind of algebra altogether. X plus y minus z equals fucked up.'

Shaw kept talking so quickly, she couldn't shut him up.

She didn't want to shut him up.

'Say someone wants Cooper back inside, and I'm not talking about your shit-for-brains colleagues. I'm talking about someone *very* special. What doesn't make sense to you, Anna? What is it that doesn't add up?'

She spoke then, knowing she shouldn't but unable to stop herself. The same rhetorical question she'd asked Khosa after interviewing Richard Osbourne. The one that had festered in her mind for days. 'If it isn't Cooper, why have there been no other killings in the seventeen years he's been inside?'

Shaw leaned forward, his eyes intense. 'Exactly,' he whispered. 'So, hold that up to the light and look at it. What's hidden in the glass?' He paused before adding, 'What if he doesn't like killing them?'

Anna frowned. 'Emily Risman was strangled and stabbed. So was Nia Hopkins.'

Shaw nodded. 'How many times? Five? Ten?'

Anna didn't answer.

'It's in the paper. Twenty-four, *The Times* said. Twenty-four's a frenzy killing. Everyone knows that. He lost it the first time. There was too much baggage. He knew her, she knew him. His only hope of getting away was to kill her.'

'Cooper knew Emily *and* Nia.'

'We're presuming it wasn't Cooper, remember? That's your angle. So, what if before whoever this man is kills Emily, before the red mist comes down, he starts enjoying himself?'

Anna frowned. This was a minefield. But Shaw, damn him, was walking her through a process she'd struggled with mentally and had found impossible to articulate. He was asking her the questions she should be asking herself, pushing her towards establishing a pattern. It was something Shipwright encouraged her to do. Something she was supposed to be good at.

'Subdues them to semi consciousness. He likes them half-dead,' Anna said.

'Exactly. Maybe he likes to take them to the edge before bringing them back for more.'

'That's why he chokes them.' Anna nodded, but then frowned. 'But why kill Nia?'

Shaw shook his head. 'She's a casualty of war.'

'He killed her so that Cooper would be crucified again.' Anna saw it then. It was obvious, but such an alien thought, such a despicable thought that she'd baulked at it until now.

Shaw was enjoying himself. 'Come on, Anna. Follow it through.'

Frowning, she voiced her thoughts. 'While Cooper's free, people like me are a threat because we're looking somewhere else. Once Cooper is back in custody, everything quietens down.'

'And then maybe our special boy can get back to business.'

Special boy?

'What business?' Anna asked.

Shaw sat back and folded his arms again. 'Some people need to talk about their hobbies, Anna. It's part of it for them. Bragging rights. Let's just say that, at one time in my life, I became very familiar with a certain type of individual.'

'Was this when you were trying to find the people responsible for Abbie's death?'

Shaw blinked very slowly. Anna felt her pulse quicken. But all Shaw did was lower his chin and look at her. 'Once, in a chat room full of scum and detritus and the dregs of the world, someone came and went like a ghost. Untraceable, obviously. But he gave details. Details you could check if you really wanted to. He was genuine. I could always tell the genuine ones. Oh, there were a ton of chancers, wankers who got their kicks from reading about things or making crap up. But the real players, they never had to try too hard with their explanations. This one loved the outdoors. He was naive, young, I'd say. Said he liked to squeeze the apple as he made them squirm. I didn't care for him then and I don't care for him now, but it stuck in my mind, Anna.'

'Who? Who is he?'

Shaw shook his head. 'You're the detective. Assume this is all a test. A test of our friendship.'

Anna forced herself to breathe slowly. 'How do I know you're not making all of this up?'

Another slow blink.

He doesn't like his integrity being questioned.

'The one in Cirencester had roses on her dress.'

'What?'

'You're a police officer, Anna. Prove it.'

'I…' She caught herself. Remembered Jane Markham's words and the reason she was there. 'Tanya Cromer.'

Shaw tilted his head to one side. 'You were hoping for a confession, am I right?'

Anna fumbled in her bag for some paper and a felt-tipped pen. No lead pencils. No metal-tipped Biro. It had to be felt-tipped. She slid them across. Shaw picked up the pen and took a long, hard sniff. He might have been enjoying the solvents, but something told Anna it was her smell he was sensing. Something she'd left on the casing from her hand. A pheromone only he could smell. Shaw smiled before leaning forward and writing in a long, looping hand. He wrote one sentence, signed it, turned the paper around and slid it back across the desk. The prison guard watched. His expression alert but inscrutable from behind.

Anna stared at the paper. In blue felt-tipped pen Shaw had written: 'Tanya Cromer. I did not do it.'

'Lots to think about, Anna. Like the mixed DNA sample you found on Tanya.'

'If you know the answer, we need justice for that young girl. We need closure for her fa—'

'It's a mystery, right? A puzzle for you to work out, just like roses on a dress. I'd like to say take your time, but our boy has had to be patient while Cooper was out of jail. Now that he's back in, who knows what might happen?'

Anna was shaking badly by the time she got back to the car. She sat and tried to assimilate all that had happened. Took out her notebook and wrote as much as she could remember down. Had Shaw really caught a glimpse of someone online? Someone who liked to squeeze his victims' throats to the point of unconsciousness? Could someone really be re-incriminating Cooper, killing purely to get Cooper put back inside, and get Anna off his tail for Emily's murder so he could get back to doing something else? What? What else had he been doing?

Adrenalin coursed through her. The windows were fogged up. She was glad because that meant no one could see her flaming cheeks and wild eyes. Her hands were trembling badly when she gunned the engine. She'd broken Jane Markham's rule and let Shaw inside. Broken it so badly... But everything Shaw said had resonated with her own thinking so bloody perfectly it scared her. It felt so wrong and yet Shaw had lit the kindling for the conflagration that now burned and crackled inside her. Shipwright would have a fit if he ever found out.

The trembling didn't stop until she was halfway back to Bristol. By then she knew there was no way of putting out the flames unless she did something about it.

At Portishead, she called the team in for a 12.30 p.m. briefing. She'd calmed herself down, but still ideas were fizzing inside her and she knew she had to get them out somehow.

Together, they watched a Sky News bulletin from the previous evening. Harris met the press on the steps outside Gloucester police station, eschewing the clinical austerity of the press room. A variety of phones and microphones were arranged in front of him, bristling like missiles on a rocket launcher. Harris's brow glistened with sweat and the bright glare of spotlights reflected off his corneas, augmented by the odd camera flash. His statement was concise and delivered with grim but triumphant concentration.

'We can confirm that there has been a significant development in the hunt for the murderer of Nia Hopkins.'

His statement was drowned out by the clamour from the assembled press.

A single voice pierced the cacophony. 'Can you confirm that you have someone in custody?'

Harris turned towards the voice, his face serious, his tone controlled and measured. 'A man has been arrested in connection with this killing.'

Another voice shouted above the rest. 'There has been speculation that there are links between this case and the original Woodsman killing. Would you care to comment?'

'There are similarities which we are considering in our investigation.'

'Is it Neville Cooper?'

Harris's grim expression didn't fade for an instant. 'I'm not at liberty to reveal any names at this stage. No charges have been brought yet.'

'Are they likely?'

Harris fixed the new questioner with one of his looks. 'I think we're close.'

The image reverted to a newscaster wearing a Liberty tie and a suitably earnest expression, who proceeded to recap the details of both murders. Library footage of the deserted patches of woodland where both bodies had been found appeared.

'They're making a great big meal out of all this,' Khosa commented.

'It's a feeding frenzy,' murmured Trisha. 'Once they get their teeth into the story—'

Holder thrust his hand up to silence her as the screen in front of them changed abruptly.

'Peter?' the newscaster asked, addressing a reporter holding a microphone outside the police station in Gloucester. 'We've heard what the police are saying. On the one hand linking this to the murder of Emily Risman and on the other implying that the evidence is inconclusive.'

'They're obviously anxious not to say too much at this stage, but I can state that Neville Cooper is in custody here at Gloucester police station. That has been confirmed by his mother and more recently by his solicitor.'

'This case seems to be taking a very bizarre turn.'

'Bizarre indeed, in the light of recent events in the Appeal Court. There is a great deal of confusion and shock, even in police ranks. Surprise and some horror at the thought that Cooper is implicated here after the verdict in the murder of Emily Risman was judged to be unsafe. But I also sense an undercurrent of indignation at the thought that perhaps everyone was wrong, and that Cooper was capable of such an act. He is due to stand trial again, of course, for that murder in the new year.'

'Peter, thank you. Peter Glass there, live from Gloucester.'

Holder sat back and blew out air.

'None of this should come as a surprise to anyone,' Anna said, using the remote to shut down the TV.

'I've looked through the report of the search of Cooper's locker at the feed mill, ma'am, but, as you suggested, I learned a lot more from seeing for myself.' Khosa pulled up a complicated-looking layout of the feed mill on a screen. A small area was outlined in orange. 'This is the changing room. You can see it's just off the yard where all the lorries park up for loading, and it's at the rear of the biggest of the silos they use for storage. I took a walk around. Twice I walked in and out of that changing room without meeting a soul. Drivers use a toilet just off that room. The yard is busy. People constantly coming and going.'

'And that was why you went? To gauge how busy it was?' Holder asked.

'Not exactly. The other thing was the locker itself. There's a padlock. Cooper had the key. His name is on the door, but...'

'What?'

'It's a tall, cabinet-style locker with a smaller, separate lock box above for wallet and keys and smaller things. The lock box is opened from inside the main cabinet-style locker by a catch. The fact is, ma'am, it is possible to open that lock box without the key. I've seen it happen dozens of times at the squash club I play at. People forget their keys. If you can prise open the top corner of the main cabinet-style locker wide enough to get three fingers in there, you can elevate the catch and release the upper lock box.'

'Does Cooper's locker show signs of the upper corner being prised open?'

'Yes, ma'am. It's pretty battered.'

'And that upper lock box is where they found the evidence?'

'Yes. It looked like someone rammed something in there in a hurry, dragging stains all over the place.'

'That could have been Cooper himself,' Holder said.

Anna nodded. 'Or anyone else. What about Cooper's garage?'

Holder pulled up another schematic. 'Not so much a garage as an old shed he keeps the bike in. It's not locked. Access is easy over a fence at the rear.'

'You've talked to the investigating team about this?'

Holder nodded. 'Sergeant Slack, this morning.'

'And?'

'He told me to stop meddling. He said it doesn't change anything.'

Anna recalled Shipwright's words. A police mindset. Very old-school; formulate a theory and then modify the facts to fit it driven by emotion, not science. And righteousness was a very powerful emotion.

She turned to the whiteboard. Under 'FORENSICS' in capitals, Holder had written two more headings: 'Crime Scene' and 'Cooper'.

'OK. Let's refocus. Talk us through the crime scene of Emily Risman's murder, Justin.'

'It looks like a pretty thorough job. The bad news is that the "hollows"—which is what the local kids called it—was a known haunt. Before they were old enough to go to the pub, kids would go there to drink and smoke and hang. So there was lots of foot traffic, though it was dry for two days before and on the night that Emily was killed. There was evidence of forced sexual activity on Emily's body, but nothing positive on nail swab. There were some defensive wounds on both forearms.'

Khosa nodded. 'So, she knew the killer. Or thought she knew him until he turned on her.'

He knew her, she knew him. His only hope of getting away was to kill her. Shaw's words echoed in Anna's head.

Holder pointed to a photograph of a DNA blot. 'The DNA match from the foetus was positive for Roger Willis. He admitted that she'd told him he was the father, or certainly could have been, because he'd had sex with Emily more than once in the previous three months.'

'Fine. But I want everything rechecked.'

Holder nodded. 'I'm on it, ma'am. Trouble is, the lab they used no longer exists.'

'They must have archived the samples somewhere.' She looked across at Trisha, who was making notes. 'Can we leave that with you, Trisha?'

Trisha nodded.

Holder continued, 'The strongest evidence against Cooper then was the trophy underwear found on his parents' property.'

Trophy collection was classic sexual predator behaviour. Everyone knew that. With Cooper, though, stealing underwear from people's washing lines could just as easily have been something someone dared him to do. The defence barrister at the time of his trial had tried to point this out, but the jury chose to accept the behavioural psychologist who'd given expert testimony for the prosecution.

'Given that we now know he could not have been there when Emily was murdered, how do we explain this finding?'

Khosa answered for all of them. 'Either whoever did the search planted the underwear, or the real killer planted it to frame Cooper.'

Anna nodded. 'Where exactly on the property was the underwear found?'

'An external storage shed.'

'Unlocked?'

Holder nodded.

'So, we have the exact same pattern. If we accept the possibility that Cooper is innocent, then someone deliberately implicated

Cooper in 1998 and has more than likely done the same thing now with Nia Hopkins.'

'But why now?' Khosa asked.

'Belt and braces?' Anna suggested. 'Who knows? But implicating him again won't do any harm for the CPS's case in a retrial either. In people's minds, Cooper would be the Woodsman all over again.'

'But why take the risk?' Holder asked.

'Fear,' Anna said. 'While Cooper was inside the real killer was safe. With Cooper free he knows there'll be someone taking a fresh look at the original investigation. He wants to muddy the waters.'

'Ma'am,' said Holder. 'If Emily's murder was sexually motivated, and if the same thinking is being applied to Nia to implicate Cooper, I'm sure I read something about Cooper's… abilities?'

Anna blinked. 'Are you saying he's impotent?'

'I'm sure I read something but I'll go through everything again,' Holder said.

'This is good, Justin. Really good.'

'To think someone has been hiding all this time,' Khosa murmured.

'We ought to seriously consider that he's been hiding and active,' Anna said. 'I'd like to broaden the scope here. Let's get HOLMES to look at 1999 onwards. Unsolved attacks on young females over our own and Gloucester's and West Mercia's patches.'

HOLMES 2, the Home Office's large major enquiry database, was a vital tool for this sort of cross-referencing. Less exciting was the thought of trying to get information out of it using the iffy Internet access that seemed to plague Avon & Somerset's HQ.

Khosa looked at Trisha, who was already making a note. 'Yes, ma'am.'

'This is great work, both of you.'

Holder sat and Khosa took his place, pointing a pen at the images of the original investigative team. 'I found an address for

Superintendent Briggs. Maddox we know is dead. But Wyngate went abroad as a security consultant for almost ten years. Immigration has him coming back into the country in 2015, but no address yet.'

Anna nodded encouragement.

Rainsford stuck his head through the door and looked pointedly at Anna. She followed him out to his office, grabbing a file from her desk. Once inside, he shut the door. 'So, how did it go with Shaw?'

She handed him the paper with Shaw's 'confession'.

Rainsford clenched his teeth. 'Damn. I really thought he wanted to cooperate.'

'I think he still does, sir. As you know, the DNA that tagged him was from a mixed sample. More than once he's pointed that out to us.'

'Do we have a match for the other?'

'None, sir. But it obviously bothers Shaw.'

'Lots of things bother Shaw. Well, at least we tried. I'll let the CPS know.'

Anna hesitated. 'Could we hold off on that for a while, sir? It's just that I don't think Shaw's finished with this. Today…' She sighed, hesitating, toying with not saying anything to Rainsford, but it was too important. 'Today, Shaw suggested that he might actually know something about the Woodsman, sir.'

The pained expression on Rainsford's face was exactly what she'd expected.

'How?'

'I know how it sounds – and it all might be – complete rubbish, but when Shaw was trawling for information on his daughter's suicide on the dark web, he claims he might have come across information in an Internet chat room about someone who might fit.'

Rainsford shook his head. 'Chat rooms and the dark web? Not my sort of language, Anna.'

'Nor mine, sir. But I know a bit. The "dark web", the "deep web", these are tabloid names for encrypted Internet sites that are not accessible through normal search engines. The fact is, Shaw was an expert in all of this. And we also know that, typically, paedophile and other niche pornographers use the dark web in closed networks for exchange of images and information. Occasionally in chat rooms.'

Rainsford scowled. 'Why would he possibly want to give us information like that? The man hasn't said anything to anyone about his crimes in all the time he's been in prison.'

Anna counted to three and said, 'He likes me, sir. I think he identifies me with his daughter. We'd be about the same age. Maybe he likes the challenge. Maybe he's just puffing out his chest, trying to impress.'

Rainsford walked across and sat behind his desk. Despite the early hour, he looked suddenly drawn. Or perhaps it was disgust at what he was about to say.

'Jesus, Anna, you're a cool one. Shaw attached battery cables to his victims. All three. He cut their faces with a box-cutter before watching them bleed to death by slicing the major artery in their groins. He videotaped it all so that he could show what he had done to his next victim. In his first year in prison he stuck a toothbrush handle into another inmate's eye and tried to hammer it in with his palm.'

Anna knew all of this, but hearing it again made her narrow her eyes.

'Do not let him distract you. He's dangerous. And I don't want you up there alone again. Next time, if there is a next time, take someone with you.'

'Yes, sir.'

Khosa was waiting for her on her return to the squad room, looking animated.

'HOLMES came up trumps, ma'am. Thames Valley Serious Crimes are coordinating what they think might be an ongoing serial-rapist investigation involving four regions.'

'How serial?'

'Up to twenty reported cases so far, spread across the patch. What stands out is that they've taken place over a fifteen-year period.' She consulted the paper in her hand.

'What's the date of the last known attack?'

'June, last year.'

'Exact date?'

Khosa consulted the printout in her hand. 'June 7th.'

Anna nodded, trying to keep the tingle that Khosa's news triggered under control. 'That's three days before Cooper's Appeal Court verdict. And they don't think he's attacked since?'

Khosa shook her head.

'What's his pattern?'

'Targets his victims. Undoubtedly stalks. Victim configuration is rigid, although they have got older as he has, I expect. Initially they were teenagers, but the last one was twenty-seven. We know he's white, likes to subdue and then choke his victims, but never fatally. He takes trophies.' Anna's eyes lit up. 'Clothing, items. Marked displaced aggression. It's one of the reasons we've had such a high victim report rate. Over half of them have required hospitalisation. Two broken jaws and several fractured ribs.'

'They've done the profiling?'

'They have. And it's been completely useless. He's very careful. Uses a mask, which also disguises his voice. Always gloves, always a condom. Lubricant analysis is always the same brand available from three thousand pubs and motorway dispensers. Occasionally he'll change something, varying the approach, but he always waits until they're isolated and usually at an outdoor location.'

'Have they got anywhere near?'

'Not even the faintest sniff, looks like. There were three attacks in the first five years but then the cycle accelerated until June last year. And those are the ones we know about.'

Anna considered this grim news. Not all rapes were reported. Shame and fear were powerful deterrents.

'How have they managed to keep it out of the press?'

'Deliberately. Victim anonymity until or unless they go to court.'

'Do you have a case synopsis?'

'Of course.' Khosa handed over the papers.

Trisha appeared at Khosa's elbow. 'I've sent you a link to the Thames Valley file, ma'am.'

'Thanks, Trisha.'

Anna went back to the office and called up the file. Nineteen assaults, all rape or attempted rape. She noticed instantly that the attempted rapes were associated with more violence. If he failed, he lashed out. He wanted the control and compliance. All attacks were at night, in isolated spots. He was a stalker and a planner. The one unifying aspect of the MO was his predilection for strangulation.

He puts his hands around their throats while he attacks them.

Another of Shaw's sentences resurfaced from the morning's encounter. It sent a fresh spurt of electricity through her already wired system: *… liked to squeeze the apple as he made them squirm.*

Apple? Could that be Adam's apple?

Rainsford's warning rang in her ears. But this was too real to be ignored.

Anna turned back to the file. No particular month. No particular day, other than the fact that the most recent attacks over four years had happened mid-week. However, that sample was too small to be significant. The next attack could just as easily be on a weekend.

The next attack.

If this was true, if there really was someone out there who'd hidden behind Cooper's conviction, with the supposed Woodsman once again under arrest, there was a chance the real killer would yield to the urge to act again.

To attack another girl. To strangle them into unconsciousness and then revive them so that they could experience more.

Cirencester.

Anna called Trisha over. 'Can you find the forensic report on the Cirencester case from this file? Umm, 2003, I think. I want images of what the victim was wearing.'

'Just this one, ma'am?'

'Yes. For now.'

Anna scanned the archived documents again. One stood out. Megan Roberts had fought her attacker, but he'd broken her arm and she'd been forced through pain to submit. What was remarkable was the detail she'd given the police. His smell, what he'd worn… She stared at the image of the twenty-three-year-old, torn between dismissing all of this as purely a fishing expedition, with Shaw holding the reel, and following a reasonable line of inquiry driven by her instincts.

She leaned back and called out to Khosa. 'Ryia, a word.'

Khosa appeared in the doorway.

'There's a victim in the Thames Valley file. Megan Roberts. Give her a call and ask if I can speak to her. We'll go to her.'

'Yes, ma'am.'

She turned back to her computer. An unfamiliar name chimed up on her emails.

> Inspector Gwynne,
> Excuse this intrusion, but I think it would be to our advantage
> if we talked. Please ask your secretary to contact mine and we

*can set up a meeting between ourselves. I think it's important
you meet Mrs Cooper.
Howard Tobias*

It took her a couple of seconds to place the name. *Cooper's
solicitor. Of course.* She got Trisha to do the needful. Half an hour
later, they had a meeting set up for the next afternoon. She had no
idea what Tobias wanted to say to her, but it would undoubtedly
be worth her listening.

Just before five, Trisha put her head through the door. 'I've
found the report on that Cirencester rape case, ma'am. Just sending
the link through.'

Cirencester was in Gloucestershire's patch. They'd used a standard physical evidence recovery kit for fluid sampling, hair and
fibre analysis. But they would also have sent larger items to the lab.
She found what she was looking for three pages in: photographs
of the victim's clothing and jewellery. The dress was stained with
mud, torn and bedraggled, an inanimate reminder of the ordeal.
But there was no doubting the design.

A floral print. Pink roses.

Shaw hadn't been lying.

CHAPTER SIXTEEN

Megan Roberts sat in the littered annexe next to her classroom with a straight back, silhouetted against a big window that badly needed cleaning. Despite the grime, Anna could see through it to a playing field, where some boys enjoyed an organised game of football.

It was 9.30 a.m. and Ms Roberts' class in the science laboratory at Ledbourne School was being supervised by a student on teaching practice. Every surface in the annexe was covered with books, flasks, reagents and papers. The items were grouped neatly, if closely together, into an organised heap. No chaos here, only an acute lack of space.

Anna had already expressed her gratitude to Ms Roberts for agreeing to speak to her, but explained again her professional interest.

'If I can help in any way, I'll be happy to,' Megan responded. She wore a serious, shrewd expression, but Anna surmised from their initial greeting that the severity she saw there could be transformed by a lovely smile. The rape had occurred not long after she'd taken up her teaching post. Megan had then been twenty-three and she didn't look much older now. Small-boned, fair in colouring, piercing blue eyes with heavy lids adorned with little make-up, and a small mouth within a heart-shaped face. This was Megan Roberts, the teacher, blighted by an unprovoked attack. The face of bravery.

'Have you spoken to any of the others before me?'

'No,' Anna said. 'You're the first.'

'I see.'

'Megan, my involvement in this is not quite what you think it is. I'm working on a different inquiry and I think that perhaps your case might be linked to it. I can't tell you as much as I'd like to but you deserve to know something.'

'So, not rapes?' Megan asked.

'No.'

'Worse?'

'Yes.'

Megan nodded, lips tight in understanding. 'He's killed, hasn't he?'

'I think it's possible that he has, yes.'

Megan's expression softened into an ironic little smile. 'All this time I've dared to wonder if I should have played it differently, resisted more, somehow. But I always felt that he was capable of killing me. The threats were real, the knife was real, his hands around my throat... but there's always the magazine articles that tell you to reason with them, try to talk them out of it. With him, there was no talking.'

'Could you take me through it once more?'

Megan nodded. 'It was a Friday night in September. We were three weeks into the new school term. I was living in Stroud with my boyfriend, Luke. I'd called at Sainsbury's on the way home and I had three carrier bags full of food. We lived in the second-floor flat of an apartment block. There was a courtyard at the rear for parking. It was seven thirty, the light just beginning to fade, but not dark by any means. The carriers were heavy and I left my school bag in the car as I walked the twenty yards to the entrance. I had to walk past the rear of some gardens that backed on to the courtyard. I saw some movement to one side of me, half turned and then he was there, hand over my mouth, pulling me through a gate into a space. We were close to houses, but he'd found an overgrown garden. We might as well have been in a jungle somewhere.'

Anna shook her head in sympathy. 'He was behind you all the time?'

'Not all the time, but he was masked. He hit me in the stomach and then the face. It was ferocious and sudden. He put tape over my eyes and face and tied my hands. I think he went back out to get the bags because they were with me when they found me. He put his hands around my neck and squeezed. He kept warning me to be quiet. I didn't understand; I mean he'd stuck the tape over my mouth. But then he took the tape off because he wanted my mouth open… so that I could…' She looked away towards the window for a moment and made herself breathe slowly.

'Did he speak to you at any length?'

'Just threats. Warning me not to struggle and then squeezing my neck so that I knew that he meant it. He kept the mask on all the way through. It muffled his voice. I couldn't breathe, he kept squeezing here.' She pointed to just below her Adam's apple. 'I think I must have passed out.'

'Did he take anything from you?'

Megan snorted. 'He stole my phone.'

'Megan, I know how painful this is for you. If this is the same man that I'm hunting for, I need as much information as I can get. I know what you've told the police about his physical appearance, his size, his weight and what little accent you might have heard. I have all that. The fact is that it's likely he'd been following you for some time. He's not opportunistic. Had anything happened in the few days or weeks before? Anything untoward that sticks in your memory?'

Megan frowned. 'I've never thought about it that way before. Term had begun and I was in the thick of things.'

'Will you think about it? I know it's a long time ago but…'

'No, I can do that, I keep a diary. How far back do you want me to go?'

'If we said three months to begin with?'

'Fine… is it recent, what he's done?'

'Yes.'

'Is it more than once?'

'We think it's possible that it's at least twice. Probably many more times.'

Megan nodded. Short, sharp little movements.

Anna handed her a card. 'You can phone or email me here,' she explained. 'And thank you for talking to me. I know it can't have been easy.'

Megan smiled. 'In an odd way, it helps. Sometimes I think I've come to terms with it but then, no. It's still with me every day. I got over the physical hurt very quickly. The bruises faded and psychologically I was able to confront it. But I hate him for what it did to me and Luke.'

'Rape victims' partners often need as much counselling as the victims do,' Anna said, sounding rueful.

'Luke couldn't handle it. We split up six months later. He couldn't cope with the thought of what had happened to me. He used to cry when we tried to make love. We'd been together for two years. I still don't understand any of it.'

'Has there been anyone since?'

Megan's eyes bored steadily into Anna's. 'No, no one.'

A wave of unexpected sadness washed over her. Rape was always thus – an emotional landmine, indiscriminate and maiming.

A few muffled cheers emanated from the laboratory, quelled by a high-pitched beseeching voice.

'Sounds like I'd better get back in there,' Megan said, glancing towards the door.

Anna stood. 'Of course. I've taken up enough of your time.'

'No. I'm pleased to be able to help.'

They shook hands and Anna wandered between the school buildings to her car and sat for a moment, her mind full of an aching sympathy for Megan. A helpless victim. It was impossible to remain indifferent to it and she harboured a loathing for those who tried. Perhaps it was time to throw off the gloves and drag a few of those precious, insensitive beings from their ivory towers.

And there was no doubt in her mind who to begin with.

CHAPTER SEVENTEEN

There was black ice on the road the following morning. With Khosa driving, Anna took out a file she'd asked Trisha to compile on Cooper from the time of his arrest. An assortment of court orders, police charge sheets, social workers' reports and, with a Post-it note attached to make it easy to find, a medical assessment.

Holder had written a second note and stuck it on the assessment: 'This is what I'd read, ma'am.' The report said that Cooper was medicated, needing hefty doses of anti-epileptic therapy even then.

Despite having spent most of the day before pouring over everything, Anna made herself read it all again, hoping that there might be something of use. In a three-page psychologist's report, one paragraph caught her eye:

> *Cooper was reluctant to talk of his sexual contacts. Although not unusual in an adolescent of his age, he did admit to finding any talk of his 'private parts' embarrassing. He felt confused and angry by his peers' constant talk of sex and their fantasies. After much persuasion, he admitted that he felt abnormal and humiliated because he had difficulty with 'it' – his own words. He would not be drawn, and when masturbation was mentioned, drew the conversation away from further discussion. When questioned directly as to what exactly 'it' was – asking, 'Do you mean erections?' – he became agitated.*

Anna read the paragraph twice. Cooper was epileptic. An addendum to the report explained that the condition was a known and well-established organic cause of impotence. Reason enough for wanting to wreak revenge on an overtly promiscuous Emily Risman, perhaps? On the other hand, from this report it seemed as likely that thoughts of sexual contact, let alone rape, might not have entered Neville Cooper's head. Would he risk further humiliation? Had the CCRC squad known this?

Tobias had requested that they meet at Cooper's cousin's house in Churchdown, two and a half miles outside the city of Gloucester. This neutral venue had more to do with avoiding the press than anything else. Cooper's mother's house was under siege and Tobias's office was, Anna suspected, also being watched.

'Did Tobias say anything about why he wanted this meeting?' Anna asked Khosa.

'No, ma'am. My guess is he sees in you something that may be lacking in Chief Inspector Harris.'

No surprises there, Anna thought.

'I haven't told him,' Khosa said. 'But we're acting well within our remit, aren't we?'

'Of course we are. Cooper's conviction was deemed unsafe on the basis of fresh evidence. What we need to know is if that evidence, as well as exonerating Cooper, points us in the direction of anyone else. We're treading on no one's toes here, Ryia, and we need to work fast. It would be a disaster if Harris and Slack force another confession out of Cooper. Meanwhile, the real Woodsman is still out there.'

'I'm not sure Harris would see it that way, ma'am.'

'Perhaps not, but that isn't our problem. What's Harris like, I wonder? Away from work I mean?'

Khosa glanced across at her. 'Harris? Married, two kids in their early teens. He's a warden in his local church, does a bit of fishing. Doesn't drink, doesn't smoke. Lives for his job. Pretty average bloke really.'

Anna's eyebrows went up.

'I asked a mate,' Khosa said.

'Yes, well, I thought as much. There's an air of arrogance about him, constantly claiming the moral high ground.'

They lapsed into a pensive silence, which lasted until they arrived in the village. Khosa craned forward to read street signs and eventually, they pulled up outside a semi-detached grey house with yellow windows and doors, fronted by a small, neat garden guarded by a low gate.

'This is it.'

A curtain flicked back as Khosa killed the engine. 'I think they're expecting us, ma'am.'

Tobias emerged from the front door, glancing up and down the street as he held the gate open for Anna. He was tall, wearing thick-rimmed, fashionable glasses and carrying more than a bit of extra weight that a good suit, white shirt and a blue tie couldn't hide.

He greeted them with a solemn, 'Thank you for coming, Inspector. Mrs Cooper is grateful, too. I think it would be best if we go directly inside. You can never be sure who might be prying.'

Anna and Khosa shook his hand, then followed him into the house to another small living room, this one devoid of china shire horses. It was cleaner, neater and furnished in a more modern style than the Rismans'. Tobias made cursory introductions to a middle-aged couple, Anita and Joe, who had the dubious honour of being Neville Cooper's cousins. They graciously disappeared into another room as Tobias brought Anna across to an elderly woman, who sat upright in a straight-backed chair. The resemblance between herself and her son was obvious. Same small eyes and full lips, same round face. She struggled to get up and Tobias lent an arm to help her. She stood, tottering slightly, and took Anna's hand.

'Inspector Gwynne, meet Maggie Cooper.'

They shook hands and Anna moved over to an armchair as Maggie sat back down shakily. Khosa pulled out a chair from under a dining table and sat near the window.

Maggie groaned as she settled. 'You'll have to excuse me. My legs are not what they used to be.'

Anna glanced down at a pair of swollen oedematous ankles and noted the understatement.

'Heart trouble,' explained Mrs Cooper. 'I take so many tablets I rattle, but…'

They all waited while Tobias arranged himself into a seat. Outside, someone passed by in the street. Fragments of a one-way phone conversation drifted in and then away again, ending in a raucous laugh. A brash snapshot of someone else's life. Anna wondered, briefly, when anyone in this house had last felt joy like that.

Tobias cleared his throat. 'I expect you're wondering why I asked to meet you like this? Let me make it clear that I do not, Inspector, for one moment, wish to compromise your position.'

Maggie Cooper interjected. 'I saw your picture in the paper. I said to Mr Tobias, she's too pretty to be a policewoman. It was my idea to ask you here.' She wheezed as she spoke.

'Why?' asked Anna.

'Because Mr Tobias told me that you've been asked to find out who really killed Emily. That means you must believe in Neville.'

'Mrs Cooper—'

Tobias interjected. 'Inspector, we realise that reopening the Risman Case after this length of time must be daunting. Mrs Cooper felt that we might be able to offer you our services to help in any way that we can.'

'I can't take sides in this, Mr Tobias.'

Tobias didn't smile. 'That is not what we're asking. We are used to not receiving any favours.'

'Then…'

Tobias held up both hands in a gesture of truce. 'If you'll just hear me out. We were campaigning for Neville's release for seventeen years. There is very little about this case that I am not familiar with.'

Tobias's eyes locked on hers and she felt Maggie Cooper's stare burning into the side of her face.

'I'm grateful for the offer, but you'll realise that I have full access to all the police files.'

Tobias's answering smile made his face look like he'd just bitten down on a slice of lemon. He reached down and picked up two box files. 'This is a distillation of the hard evidence refuting Neville's conviction.'

'We're familiar with the case, sir,' Khosa said, and Anna sensed the mild irritation in her voice.

'Excuse me, Constable, but you are not,' Tobias said. 'You may have read the police files, but they do not represent the true facts of this case. Let's just say that disclosure was not CCRC's or the CPS's strong point. Neville Cooper was nowhere near the area on the day Emily Risman died. He was in Gloucester. We have witnesses who were previously too intimidated to come forward. Neville was with his friend William Bradley. Bradley was interviewed by police and a statement taken early in the investigation. Initially he admitted being with Neville that night, first at the amusement arcade and then in the cinema. Later he changed his statement, claiming he couldn't be sure that it was the same night as that of the murder. Bradley was on probation and was awaiting a hearing on a burglary charge. At that hearing, he was given a light sentence because he'd helped police in securing Neville's conviction. Bradley is currently in prison and has been labelled a pathological liar, yet the Appeal Court ruled his evidence as perfectly acceptable time and again.'

'Mr Tobias—'

'We have forensic evidence via ESDA, electrostatic detection testing, that Neville's confession was obtained falsely. Police wrote out the statement double-spaced for Neville to sign, and added incriminating sentences later. The added sentences indented the cover of another document that showed up last year. This was in DS Maddox's hand. Neville insisted he was in Gloucester and that he and Bradley hitched a lift back that evening in a white van. The driver was never traced, but we found a scribbled note – again in Maddox's hand – indicating that a witness reported seeing two boys being picked up on the ring road at a little after ten p.m. that night. A witness statement was never taken or followed up.

'The police searched the Coopers' property twice before the bloodstained underclothes were found during a third search, supposedly hidden under some coal. It will come as no surprise to you to learn that the officer who found this item was DS Maddox. Despite being suspended five years later for misconduct in another case, the Appeal Court judges consistently ruled that there was no reason to doubt his propriety in the Woodsman investigation.'

'I understand that DS Maddox is no longer with us,' Anna said.

'No. And I, for one, do not regret his passing,' Tobias said and didn't wait for Anna to respond. 'You have no idea what these people did in the name of "justice". Maggie found a cinema ticket in Neville's coat with the name and time of the film he had seen on it. Maddox denied ever receiving it, although there is mention of a "ticket" in the evidence book at the station where Cooper was held. Maddox claimed that this was an old bus ticket, which was never produced in court. Maddox had bragged and bet that they would get Neville convicted.' Tobias stopped, his lips a thin angry line. 'These facts will re-emerge at the retrial. I am going to make sure of that. But there is still evidence that we haven't seen.'

'You're not suggesting that there's still a conspiracy?'

'I'm not suggesting anything. But I know that if Neville is charged a second time, for the murder of Nia Hopkins, the retrial will turn into a farce and there are some people, some very high-ranking people, who would welcome that.'

'Such as?'

'The prosecuting barrister in the original case was a QC called John Jeavons.'

'I know that name, don't I?'

'You should. His career blossomed following Neville's conviction. He is the Sir John Jeavons who now sits in the High Court of Justice. If we can prove that the cinema ticket existed, that would bring into question just how much the prosecution knew and chose to withhold from the defence. It could prove to be a very embarrassing few days.'

Anna nodded.

'We don't talk to the Gloucester police any more,' Mrs Cooper said with surprisingly little bitterness. 'That was why we wanted to talk to you.'

'All we want,' added Tobias, 'is a fair hearing now. Neville's defence team behaved in an inexcusably heavy-handed manner. They ran an alternative defence, without Neville's permission, seeking to limit the damage by suggesting that Neville was in a state of mental confusion after his fits – ignoring his alibi and the retraction of his confession. The defence barrister is now a judge on the Queen's bench. He's not going to relish the criticism that's bound to come his way either. It looks like the bugger rolled over and played dead at the end.'

'Do you have any children, Inspector?' Mrs Cooper asked.

'No.'

'I didn't think I'd been very lucky with Neville. I had him late and he was a difficult child with his fits and all. But he's still my boy and I've had cause to be very proud of him over these last years. I told him never to give up, never to stop believing in himself. We have to stop them doing this to people.' She looked pointedly at Anna. 'What if it's your child next time?' She hesitated and began to cough; a bubbling bark that left her gasping for breath.

Tobias looked across. 'OK, Maggie?'

Mrs Cooper sat with a handkerchief over her mouth and nodded weakly. The spasm took the colour from her face, her lips aubergine against the pallor.

Tobias sighed. 'I knew this was a bad idea. We'd better get you home. Inspector, I'm sorry to have to cut this short.' He pulled out a card and handed it to Anna. 'My numbers. Home and office. Ring me at any time, if you think I can help.'

Anna watched as the two cousins came back in and began fussing over the old lady. Anna excused herself and went to the bathroom. When she came out, Tobias was hovering near the front door.

'Sorry about this. She isn't very well. Having Neville in jail was the last thing she needed.'

'It must be hard.'

'She doesn't care much about herself, only Neville. Look, I hope you haven't seen this as a total waste of time.'

Anna shook her head and conceded. 'I'm sure I would need to talk to her at some point. At least this way she knows who I am.'

Tobias hesitated with his hand on the latch. 'What I really want you to take away from here is the certainty I have that there is other evidence out there somewhere. Things we haven't seen. Things that not only exonerate Neville but implicate someone else…' He caught himself. 'Neville's been in and out of a secure unit for the last two years. Depression mainly. Seventeen years have taken a significant toll. More than anyone should have to bear. Three weeks ago, I went in to a travel agent and booked a holiday for the family. I thought that we were out of the woods at long last.'

If Tobias had intended a pun, he showed no sign.

When Anna reached the gate, Tobias said, 'With your permission, I'll send you a file of what we've found. It makes for very interesting reading.'

They returned to the car and Anna drove away in silence. A numb dull anger thumped away inside her. She tried very hard to quell it with some deep breaths. It was essential that she remain dispassionate, but it was becoming increasingly difficult.

'It's hard to believe, isn't it, ma'am?' Khosa's candid assessment echoed her own thoughts.

'That it is.'

'I can't see it happening today though, can you?' Khosa asked.

Anna didn't answer immediately. She liked Khosa. She was pleasant, helpful, and keen to learn and observe. She didn't want to mar her enthusiasm with too much cynicism.

'I'd like to think so, but if the circumstances arose and public pressure was great enough…'

'You don't think Cooper's guilty, ma'am, do you?'

'No.'

'I spoke to Cooper's cousin while you were in the loo. He was laying it on thick about how awful it has been for Cooper's mother. Did you know that the house they owned in Millend was burned out three months after he was sentenced? There was no question that it was arson. The old lady was lucky to get out alive.'

Anna didn't respond. A depressingly familiar story. The stigma was real. The finger constantly pointed.

'I think I need a drink, Ryia.'

Khosa turned to her phone and started texting. They were on the outskirts of the city by now. It was already dark. Khosa finally spoke, 'My mate, the same one who had the skinny on DCI Harris, says there's a place near Gloucester. It's a coppers' watering hole though. If you don't mind that.'

'Anywhere will do.'

*

They ran the gauntlet of a dozen smokers to enter the Rock and Fountain's bar. Anna slipped Khosa a tenner and the DC ordered. Her white wine spritzer came in a tall glass, nicely chilled.

Anna scanned the room over the rim of her glass, froze as she clocked a familiar face, and pivoted back towards Khosa, who handed over her change. 'Tell me that's not who I think it is in the far corner.'

Khosa looked over her shoulder. 'It is, ma'am.'

Anna groaned. 'I don't suppose we could quietly slip out the back, could we?'

'Too late, ma'am. He's coming over.'

'A little after-work refreshment, ladies?'

Anna turned towards the voice and looked up into DCI Harris's face with what she hoped was a look of surprise. 'Just called in on our way back to the station, Chief Inspector.'

'Got a minute, have you?'

'Actually—'

'Won't take a second. I want you to meet an old friend of mine.'

He led the way through the crowd to a corner table. There sat a balding, squat, powerful-looking man with no neck and a pair of dark brown eyes under hooded brows.

'Anna Gwynne, meet John Wyngate.'

Anna muttered a hello. Wyngate made no effort to return the gesture.

'We were just reminiscing,' Harris said. 'John and I both worked with Ewan Briggs during our formative years.'

Wyngate drained the remains of his pint in two swallows and pushed the empty glass towards a loitering Khosa.

'Get the gentleman a refill, Constable, will you?' Harris said.

Khosa looked at Harris despairingly, the muscle of her jaw working as she ground her teeth.

'My shout,' Anna said, and handed over another twenty.

Shaking her head, Khosa took the empty glasses to the bar as Wyngate watched in dour silence.

'I was telling John of your involvement with our Woodsman,' Harris said.

'Really.'

Wyngate sat back and put an E-cigarette to his lips. 'Must be a bastard after this length of time.'

'It isn't easy.'

'Never is. Just you and Catwoman, is it?'

'There are others, but we're a small team.'

'Quality, not quantity, eh?' Wyngate did nothing to hide the heavy sarcasm in his voice.

'Someone must think so.'

Wyngate's gaze never wavered from Anna's face. 'You sure you're going to be able to stay the course?'

Anna opted for silence.

Khosa came back and Wyngate reached for the full pint without a thank you.

'What brings you to Gloucester, Mr Wyngate?' Khosa asked. She made it a blunt, direct question. The sort she'd normally reserve for suspects.

'Old friends,' Wyngate said. Only his eyes were visible behind the pint glass raised to his lips. Anna hoped he wasn't smirking. She wanted to believe this man had a little integrity left.

'You won't be staying long then?'

Harris sat back and sipped lemonade, watching the exchanges with an odd, detached amusement.

'Don't fence with me, girlie. I've had more college shits like you crying in the bog than you've had chicken baltis,' Wyngate snarled.

Khosa stared back defiantly.

'Now, now, you two,' said Harris.

'Have you any regrets, Mr Wyngate?' asked Anna.

'About what?'

'Neville Cooper. The Appeal Court's decision that his conviction was unsafe must have grated.'

Wyngate took a long drag on his E-cigarette before answering. 'It was the court that put him away for seventeen years, not me.'

'But you still feel that's OK?'

'Your heart's bleeding all over your shirt, Inspector. I was a copper that ran on instinct. What we did was standard practice at the time. We didn't have the benefit of help from clever people like you then.' He turned to Harris. 'Makes you wonder how the hell we managed, doesn't it?'

'It seems you *managed* to convict the wrong man,' said Anna.

'I didn't question what went on. The CPS were convinced we had enough to nail him, so that's what we did.' A slow smile appeared on his lips and he looked across at Harris. 'My boss at the time didn't encourage discussion of the finer points of police work. You just got on with it.' His smile vanished and he glared at Anna again. 'We gave everyone in that community peace of mind for seventeen years. That may not mean a lot to you, but as far as I'm concerned it's what being a copper was all about.'

'Of course. I mean, why let the truth get in the way of peace of mind?' Anna said.

Wyngate frowned. But Anna kept her powder dry on the rape cases. This was not the right place for that.

'Any scapegoat in a storm, is that it?' Khosa said.

Wyngate shook his head. 'I was only interested in putting away the nonce that killed Emily Risman. If it turns out that Cooper really is that nonce, let's just say I won't be too disappointed.' His smile revealed a row of small and widely spaced teeth.

'What if he isn't?' Anna said.

Wyngate shrugged and lifted the full glass to his lips, but his eyes never left Anna's.

Khosa looked at her watch. 'We should be getting back, ma'am. The meeting was for six thirty, wasn't it?'

Anna embraced the lie. 'Sir, Mr Wyngate, you'll have to excuse us.'

Anna stood and followed Khosa to the door. Halfway there, a peal of brassy laughter burst from Harris's table and she turned to see the men almost doubling over in glee. There was no way of knowing if she was the butt of their joke; the chances, however, were high.

Khosa stared openly at Wyngate. 'What a prick,' she said.

Anna kept on walking. 'Come on, Ryia, let's get out of here before I throw up.'

CHAPTER EIGHTEEN

He watched the woman push the stroller while her partner walked ahead, kicking at stones, smoking, the tattoos on his hands and neck clearly visible. The man wore tracksuit bottoms and a light, unzipped fleece, defying the cold as if he was trying to prove something.

Idiot.

The woman wore a puffer jacket and tight jeans and a beanie hat, her bottle- blonde hair spilling out from beneath it. She was pretty, even from forty yards away. She talked to the little girl in the pram, who was swathed in a warm coat and mittens, pointing out the trees and the ice still covering the puddles.

She might do. She might well do.

He breathed in and out slowly, savouring the delicious anticipation. He'd missed this. So much.

He let his mind stray towards how it might go with her and he knew that it would be difficult now to stop at the red line. He'd squeeze until she couldn't move. Squeeze until she passed out, but… he'd liked the sound of the knife and the way the last girl's body had bucked with each thrust.

Liked it a great deal.

He knew which car the woman and the child and the tattooed man had arrived in. A Subaru with a spoiler on the boot. He'd watch them for another two hundred yards and then double back to the car park, out of sight, and park so that he could watch them leave without them seeing his car. Then he'd follow, confident that they'd drive to a nearby town or village. They were not dressed for hiking. They had not come far.

He toyed for a moment with what he might take from her, what would be the most precious thing? The child, perhaps. He'd never contemplated that before. He liked the way the thought uncoiled. He let it marinate in his brain.

Everything was falling into place. The police and now the press had taken his offering and Cooper was in custody. They'd believed, once again, that they had the Woodsman, when nothing could be further from the truth. He'd watched the police run around like ants, clueless insects. Watched the press like wild dogs snapping at everything.

Even the pretty detective, the one who looked like she was smiling but had ice in her eyes, couldn't see what was in front of her face.

So be it.

The child made a noise, a bored cry. The tattooed idiot kept walking, not his job. The woman bent over to tend to the child, revealing a tight round bottom in the jeans. She was very shapely.

Shapely enough.

He moved, invisible to the strollers, and turned back towards where he'd parked the car. He would not wait for them to complete their walk. The child was getting restless. The idiot had his hands in his open jacket pockets, refusing to yield to nature, but cold, no doubt. They would return to their car soon.

He'd follow. Find out where they, or perhaps only she, lived. Watch and return, perhaps for several weeks until the moment was right, when she least expected it. Savour the watching. The stalking. Until he could stand the pressure no more.

He knew, by the time he'd stripped off his camouflage and sat in the car, that this time would be different. He'd crossed the red line with the Hopkins girl and it had filled him with ecstatic energy and light.

Now, there was no going back.

CHAPTER NINETEEN

Rainsford was knotting his tie in front of the bedroom mirror when he took the call on his mobile. The dispatcher from Portishead explained that she'd been contacted by the governor of Whitmarsh Prison. He'd left a number and a request that Rainsford ring him back urgently. Hair wet, Rainsford wrote down the number and dialled. He stood at the window watching the grey shapes in his garden develop in front of his eyes as morning light leeched into the day.

'Thanks for ringing. Sorry about the early hour,' said the voice that answered. Rainsford recognised it. They'd spoken previously when they'd laid the ground for Shipwright and Gwynne's visit after Shaw's DNA lit up on the national DNA database. George Calhoun had a Scottish burr and a no-nonsense attitude. Even so, anxiety gnawed at the superintendent. A seven-thirty call hardly ever meant good news.

'What can I do for you?'

'Shaw,' Calhoun said. 'His lawyers have been in and out the last couple of days. This morning I found out why.'

Rainsford waited, his pulse thick in his throat. He hoped this was not another complaint. Something Gwynne or Shipwright had said or done. The usual BS, no doubt. But he was not prepared for what Calhoun said next.

'Shaw wants to show you where he buried the body.'

Rainsford sank heavily on to the edge of the bed as Calhoun's words thudded home. 'What?'

'Exactly. But don't crack open the champagne yet. This is Shaw we're talking about. There are caveats.'

'What does he want?'

'Seems he's taken a shine to your girl Gwynne. He'll only do this if she's there.'

Rainsford was silent. There was no denying that this was a real coup. He was also very aware that allowing Shaw to manipulate the situation carried risks. But assessing risk against benefit was why he was in the job.

'You still there, Superintendent?' Calhoun's voice broke the silence.

'Yes, still here. And she's Inspector Gwynne now.'

'At this rate, she'll be in your job before you turn around twice.'

Rainsford laughed politely at Calhoun's stab at humour. But it felt hollow. He'd already made his mind up. They had no choice but to comply with Shaw's demands and there was nothing at all funny about that.

'Oh, and he'll only do it if it can be done today.'

'What? We'll never get the paperwork done in time.'

Rainsford knew that the police had no right to have prisoners transported from prisons to external locations, though this was commonly done in order to take part in identity parades, further lengthy interviews, or to identify premises or deposition sites in connection with investigations. But such requests were normally done on Ministry of Justice CID 25 forms at least seven days in advance.

Calhoun was ahead of the game. 'I've already spoken to the Home Office. They're prepared to give special dispensation under the circumstances, if you think we should go ahead.'

'Do we have any choice?'

There were always choices, of course, but both men knew that for the relatives of missing victims these choices were few and far between. If there was an opportunity for Shaw to cooperate, it needed to be seized with both hands.

'No,' said Calhoun. 'None that I can see. Shaw says this is a one-time offer. It's this or nothing.'

Rainsford looked in the mirror and the face that stared back knew that Calhoun was right. 'I'll get it set up.'

Anna took Holder and made him drive. She wanted time to think. Rainsford's call had taken her completely by surprise. She was annoyed that this was taking her away from the Risman case, but she also acknowledged that she needed to put all that aside temporarily. Ideally, she would have wanted to involve Shipwright. Talk the scenario through with him. But he was still in intensive care. A difficult-to-control heart arrhythmia was delaying his recovery and his advice was still very much off limits. That left only one other person she could think of to contact for advice. She put the call in at five minutes before nine and got through after three rings.

'Professor Jane Markham.'

'Jane, this is Anna. Anna Gwynne.'

'I take it this is not a social call?' A background hum suggested to Anna that she too was using a hands-free system and was probably also driving.

Quickly, Anna explained the circumstances. The static hum diminished and Jane Markham's voice became steady and clearer. 'You realise that by pandering to his demands you are reinforcing his belief that he is in control?'

'What choice do we have?'

'None. But be warned. He'll be getting a huge kick out of this. He's been prevented from doing whatever he wants to do in prison. Now he's trying the next best thing by invoking uncertainty and anxiety in others. Specifically, you.'

'You mentioned his serotonin levels. I presume he'll be having treatment.'

'SSRIs—'

'Jane, I'm not a doctor.'

'OK, serotonin modifies aggression. It's a neurotransmitter, but it doesn't hang around once it's done its job. It's reabsorbed by the nerve cells. Selective serotonin reuptake inhibitors work by slowing down that reabsorption, allowing serotonin to stay around for longer and elevating levels. They are widely used as standard antidepressants but also to reinforce cognitive behavioural therapy.'

'So, in Shaw's case, they would help?'

'Undoubtedly. Though he'd need a hefty dose, given the very low baseline levels he demonstrated. Why are you asking?'

'I'm wondering if he's stabilised enough to genuinely want to cooperate,' Anna tried for reassurance.

'I doubt it. Don't forget, you are also a woman and, like it or not, his next victim.'

'I won't let that happen.'

'It already has. You're already doing something you do not want to do.'

'I'm a police officer, Jane.'

'He won't see it like that. Do not underestimate this man. Even if his aggression is lowered, his needle's hovering just a notch below red.' She let out a small, harsh laugh. 'His programming skills were phenomenal. His supervisor in GCHQ was genuinely sorry to lose him.'

'But he has given me something already. He thinks he's come across the perpetrator in a case I'm working on while he was hunting for his daughter's killers.'

'Do you believe him?'

'It checked out so, yes, I do. But I don't know what he wants in return.'

'*He* knows even if he hasn't told you yet. Shaw lives mostly inside his own head and is more than happy to be there. Whatever script he's written here it will be calculated.'

'You make him sound like some all-seeing monster.'

'My impression of him hasn't changed since I first came across him. And it won't until the day he dies. My advice would be not to go anywhere near him, but I know that's impractical. Instead, go with your guard up and be very careful.'

'We'll have armed support.'

'I know. But you're on Shaw's radar now. You need to tread carefully wherever you walk. And any time you need to talk I'm more than happy.'

Anna ended the call with thanks.

Holder had been listening and now he turned to speak with a disbelieving frown. 'She's a bit dramatic, isn't she, ma'am?'

'Professor Markham's an expert, Justin. And she knows Shaw's mind better than most.'

'Even so,' Holder scoffed.

But Anna wouldn't yield, and Holder's frown, as he turned back to monitor the road ahead, deepened.

Shaw was already in the interview room at Whitmarsh when Anna and Holder arrived.

'You could save us all a journey and tell us where to go, Mr Shaw,' Anna said.

'Please, Anna. Call me Hector.'

'You could save us all a journey and tell us where to go, Hector.'

'What, and ruin a good day out? I hope you've brought the boiled sweets.'

Three prison guards hovered, keen to get on. 'The escort's waiting downstairs. We'll take him down.'

'So, what are we waiting for?' Shaw asked. He turned to Holder. 'New gorilla. Rangy fucker, aren't you? I expect labouring is in your genes, right?'

Anna touched Holder's arm before he could say anything.

'That's good,' said Shaw to Holder's departing back. 'Because we're going to need a shovel.'

The address he eventually gave Anna, written on a piece of paper, was North Wales County Asylum in Denbighshire. She passed it on immediately and Rainsford arranged for some local uniforms to secure the area and for a cadaver sniffer-dog unit to meet them there as well as a local plant-hire company to provide a mini digger. Shaw was in a police van, handcuffed, with two armed officers as escorts. Anna and Holder followed, with Anna driving. They took A roads and the journey seemed never-ending. Two and half hours after leaving Worcester they arrived.

'Jesus,' Holder said as they approached the long and winding drive up to the hulking building. Built of pale sandstone in a Tudorbethan style, what little glass the mullioned windows contained looked like broken teeth in the battered, Gothic façade. The asylum had stood on this site for almost two hundred years. At the time of its construction, it took only two doctors' signatures to have an inconvenient wife confined. A place where the unwelcome, or the different, or the simply unwanted were dumped. Where the vulnerable faced unimaginable treatments in the name of ignorant science. Toxic mercury for the hysterical, antimony for the uncontrollable, designed to induce constant nausea to keep the worst of their insanity subdued. Lobotomies and electro-convulsive therapy followed. This place was no stranger to misery and horror. It came as no surprise to Anna that Shaw might have chosen such a place to bury a body.

The thick iron sheet welded over the entrance looked to have failed completely as an anti-vandal measure. Many of the windows were boarded up, fires had gutted whole wings. Unkempt lawns had given way to bracken, and moss was reclaiming the tarmac drive. The building and its surroundings exuded a dank foreboding that seemed to suck the joy from the air.

'Held two hundred patients at one time, apparently,' Anna said.

'It looks like Arkham. When did it shut?' replied Holder.

'In 1995.'

The police van drove around the rear and parked. The building was dilapidated and its outbuildings in an even worse state.

Shaw got out of the van and made a show of stretching his legs. He was still handcuffed. The police officers with him asked him something, but Shaw shook his head and nodded towards Anna's car.

'What does he want?' Holder asked.

'Me, I expect.'

'Ma'am, I don't think that's a good idea.'

'I'm not going to hold his bloody hand, Justin,' she snapped. 'But if there is even the slightest chance that he's brought us here for a reason, and not just to go up some blind alley, then I will happily walk with him.'

'Then I will, too.'

'You'll walk behind, as we agreed. He'll be flanked by the two uniforms, both of them armed, and I'll be next to them.'

Holder shook his head and exhaled. 'Sorry, but this is fucked up, ma'am.'

The day was blustery and grey but there was, thank God, no rain. They'd given Shaw a padded jacket to wear and he stood, sniffing the air as if it were a fine perfume.

'Smell the snow from Snowdonia here,' he said, as Anna approached.

'Come on, Hector. We've done our bit.'

'Yeah, you have. Trouble is, this place has gone to the dogs. It's been a long time.'

'If you can't remember, just say and we'll all go home.'

'Home?' Shaw repeated the word.

'You reap what you sow, Hector.'

Shaw nodded. 'Very poetic. And ironic coming from you, Anna.'

'What do you mean?'

'Having your picture in the paper means lots of people see it. People like the Woodsman… and people who think they have a connection. They like to touch the flame.'

'Hector, we need to get on—'

'Did you know your ex-boyfriend was inside?'

Anna stopped walking. The wind was bitter, but Shaw seemed not to notice.

'Ah, a surprise. Tim Lambert is doing a four-year stretch for intent to supply. He's not with us monsters in Whitmarsh. Nah, they put him in Chelmsford. But he's been telling everyone about your… connection. The story is that he's swapping details for a pinch of Spice.'

It took two thrumming beats of her heart before she could answer. Should she be surprised that Shaw knew? Lambert was the skeleton in Anna's cupboard that would not stop rattling. Her mother and now Shaw. Worse was that Shaw's barbs had the sting of truth attached.

'Tim Lambert has nothing to do with being here and you know it.' The wind whipped her words, weak as they were, away into the ether.

'He almost cost you your career, didn't he? Storing gear in your flat when you were applying to the force. You did the right, thing, Anna. To get rid of him.'

'Hector, we've come a long way for Tanya—'

'I've seen Spice dropped from drones over the prison wall. Seen it arrive between the pages of *Men's Health*. I thought that was funny. You know about Spice and Black Mamba, Anna?'

She knew. The synthetic cannabinoids were highly potent and a curse of prisons. Addictive, constantly modified, and difficult to trace in the blood stream.

'I've seen men killed because of it, and for it. Some people say it would be safer to supply cannabis.'

'Hector—'

'I wouldn't want him sharing those details. Not if you were my daughter.'

'I'm not your daughter, Hector.'

Shaw turned his face to the wind. 'Did you know that when they built this place infidelity was considered a mental illness? You could lock your wife up here if you caught her giving the gardener a blow job. Or, in Edwardian times, even a steamy glance.'

Anna looked back at Holder. He wore a grim, sceptical expression.

Shaw continued, 'Maybe this is where they should have put your ex.'

Anna dragged her mind back to the moment. 'We could get a search team in if you can't remember.'

Still Shaw kept his face up to the elements. 'I didn't say I couldn't remember, I said this place had changed. Look at all these crumbling buildings.'

He turned, orientating himself, and nodded towards what looked like a small chapel with boarded-up windows and a roof in dire need of some slate.

'Thing is, I reckon they used to bury their patients here. That's why it was chosen for Tanya.' He began walking.

The two armed police officers exchanged a look and followed, keeping Shaw between them.

'Now, if I remember rightly, it was west-facing. So that she could feel the sun in the afternoon.'

He pointed with both hands to a spot ten yards from a corner of the building.

They signalled the digger and waited for it to trundle across and bury its bucket into the hard earth.

Shaw watched impassively for several minutes until he frowned. 'Wait. That is west, isn't it?' He looked up at the horizon. 'Anyone got a compass?'

Holder had one on his phone. He turned to face the direction Shaw was indicating. 'No, it's north.'

Shaw made some reprimanding clicking noises with his tongue. 'Wrong corner.' He began to walk anticlockwise around the chapel and then stopped. 'Mind you, shame to waste the hole. Looks about your size, Justin.'

Holder, to his credit didn't lose it. Instead he said, 'Maybe we could cuddle in there together, Hector.'

Shaw smiled. He looked as terrifying as the buildings. When they arrived at the western elevation, he paced out ten yards and nodded. The digger driver repeated the performance. All through it, Shaw kept his eyes on Anna, barely blinking. The sniffer dog and his handler stood closest and, after the fifth scoop, the dog became agitated, barking and straining at the leash. The handler considered the hole and waved at them. Anna and Holder walked across as a very pale and very human-looking bone poked through the black earth.

'Hello, Tanya,' said Shaw. 'I see the diet's worked.'

Anna knew she wanted nothing more than to set the big German shepherd on Shaw, as he watched all this, orchestrated all of this, but she stepped on her anger and spoke in a flat tone. 'Get a forensic team out here. It's North Wales' patch. Let them do the donkey work.'

'Yes, ma'am,' Holder said. He didn't look up from the grave as he put his phone to his ear.

Anna turned and walked back to Shaw. 'Something tells me that you think I should be thanking you, but I'm worried that if I do that, I'll throw up.'

Shaw nodded. 'Tough gig, this. But you're tough, Anna. Or at least you think you are.'

'What I can do, and with the utmost pleasure, is to ask my colleagues to throw you back in the van and take you back to Whitmarsh.'

'But if I leave now, you won't get the bonus ball.'

'What do you mean?'

'I didn't put Tanya here, Anna. Someone else did.'

For a moment, the wind whipping the long grass was all that Anna could hear. Eventually, she found her voice. 'Who?'

Shaw tilted his head, looked at the chapel and walked around to the eastern side. Anna nodded at the armed officers and they followed once more. Rubble from a crumbling storage shed spilled over the earth, but Shaw walked to the corner and counted out eight steps, before he came to a standstill looking down into the ground beneath his feet.

'You could ask him, but I don't think he'll answer. Though he made enough noise when I put him in there.'

Anna's pulse hammered at her skull. 'Him? Are you saying there's another body here? Who is he?'

Shaw looked up and gave one of his slow blinks. 'You can find out, Anna. You already have his DNA.'

Quickly, Anna made a cairn out of the rubble to mark the spot. Despite her persistent questioning, Shaw would say no more. They put him back in the police van while the digger continued. This time the body was wrapped in black plastic. There would be more remains. More for forensics to deal with.

An hour later, tents were set up around the crime scene. Anna decided to try one last time to get Shaw to talk. She spoke to him through the window of the police van. It was cold in there and they'd left the window open a crack and hadn't turned the heater on for him. Like they might with a dog. He looked pale, the dark stubble on his head almost blue.

'Whose is the second body, Hector? Did you do this to Tanya together?'

'I can see how you might think that, Anna. That's why I'm not angry. But I'll let you think it through. It'll be something for us to talk about.' It was then that she registered the change in his face. No, not his face, his eyes. Something flared there. An animal intelligence that had no right to be there. 'I've enjoyed our day out, Anna. Next time we'll make it summer so you can wear something nice.'

'We won't be meeting again. There won't be a next time,' Anna said.

'No? Not even if I tell you where I've hidden another body?'

His words, so nonchalant in their delivery, jolted her like a blow to the solar plexus. She took a stuttering step back to steady herself.

'Yeah,' said Shaw, 'there's more buried treasure. So, I get to come out to play, and we get to be pals all over again. But, I want it to be warm. I want to be able to smell your perfume, or your nervous musky sweat.' He paused, still grinning. 'That is, of course, if you pass your test.' He delivered the last word with slow emphasis, letting the sibilant 's' linger. He moved back into his seat, allowing the darkness of the van's interior to swallow him up. It left Anna looking at nothing but two pinprick reflections of light on his corneas. It made him look like he was made of smoke.

'You any closer to him, Anna? The Woodsman?'

'We think we are, yes.'

'Good. I'm glad. Because he's not going to be happy with you, is he? I reckon he's going to be mightily pissed off, in fact. Who knows what he might do, eh?'

It was difficult to know if he was smiling or not.

She had to ask. 'You know the investigation is still ongoing. Why today? Why did we have to do this today?'

His voice came to her out of the shadows. 'It's Abbie's birthday today. I couldn't give her a present, Anna. But I could give one to you.'

Unnerved, she turned quickly away and walked back to Holder. When she turned back, the van was pulling away.

Afterwards, even after several strong drinks, Anna still couldn't sleep with the light from the sodium lamps in the street outside leeching into her bedroom. She knew why. People aren't designed to live their nightmares. That's what the subconscious is for. Experiencing them without the buffer of dreams is like drinking surgical alcohol and tonic. It has the same effect as gin but without the camouflage of flavour. She lay in bed, emotionally raw and mentally discomfited from her little jaunt with Shaw.

They'd taken the corpses to the big forensic unit in Birmingham and were yet to confirm identity. One would not be difficult, since they'd keyed up dental records for Tanya Cromer. If it was a positive match, someone was going to have to speak to her parents. She wondered if that would have to be her. She hoped it would be Rainsford. He'd be good at that with his earnest delivery and eye contact. As for the second corpse, the pathologist could tell her only that it was male, thirties, evidence of significant trauma with leg fractures and facial mutilation. It would take an autopsy to ascertain cause of death.

She got up at 11.45 p.m. and made herself a hot chocolate; she tried to read some pages of a novel by an Icelandic writer that Kate had recommended, but gave up after reading three pages twice. Nothing wrong with the book, this was all about concentration.

A little after midnight, she rang Jane Markham, knowing she was a little drunk, but needing to offload with someone who understood.

'He actually showed you two bodies?' Jane didn't mention the lateness of the hour. Maybe she had demons of her own.

'I'm sure one of them is Tanya's.'

'How do you feel?'

'Filthy. Like I've had to lie in a cesspit to hide while the storm troopers pass.'

'Did you have someone with you?'

'My DC. But Shaw knew all of the buttons to press with him too.'

'It's never easy, Anna.'

'The other body… Shaw said it wasn't a body when he buried it. He said it was alive—' She caught there, unused to the tightness in her chest, conflicted by the relief she felt at feeling something but still not quite understanding what it was and why. It had always been this way with emotions. This struggle to understand them in herself, the irritation of how irrational they were. Her voice, when it spoke next, was more controlled. 'He wants to do it again. Wants to show me more of his… treasures.' She snorted. 'Listen to me. This is *so* not me.'

'Anna, it's OK to feel like this. You're grieving and you've been abused. Just because he didn't touch you, it doesn't mean he didn't harm you. You ought not to be doing this alone. I can help.'

'No,' Anna said. 'He insists on it being just me. And I can do it alone. I'm better alone.'

'Who told you that?'

Anna didn't answer. She was angry for letting her emotions trip her up.

Blame the alcohol.

'Anna?' Jane's voice brought her back.

'I did. I gave myself permission.'

A silent beat followed as both women analysed the lie.

'Is there anyone there with you?' Markham asked.

'No.'

'Is that by choice?'

'For now, yes.'

'You don't give of yourself very easily, do you, Anna?'

'I've never felt the need.'

'Some people are like that. But sometimes other people are all that is needed. I'm here if you need me.'

'Thanks,' Anna said, ending the call. She sat and finished her hot chocolate, pondering Jane's words for long minutes. She fetched her iPod from where she kept it next to the turntable and picked a playlist that she found comfort in. Old tracks; the things she'd listened to in the car with her mother and father and Kate; songs to sing on holiday trips. Often this music was as good as having other people around and had the added advantage of never leaving wine stains on the coffee table.

ELO's 'Mr Blue Sky' began and she caught her breath because it was the song she remembered best.

Hot chocolate had been a comfort since childhood and, in combination with the music and Jane's penetrating insight, she dredged a memory up from the silt in her mind. A birthday party when she was ten. She had not wanted to go. Her mother and sister had wanted to dress her up, but she'd opted for unfussy jeans and a T-shirt, already knowing that after an hour and a half she'd be bored rigid, looking for things to do away from the inane noise, craving a few moments of solitude.

Her father had driven her to the party and, as always, he'd sensed her mood. 'How many parties is it this year?' he'd asked.

'Six,' she'd said, sighing.

'But you like Gemma, don't you?'

'Ye-es.'

'And what about your other friends?'

'I like them too. But it gets weird after a couple of hours.'

'It?'

'OK, *I* get weird. It's OK at school 'cos there's lessons and stuff. But after a while it's like everyone's talking at once and I can't shut out the noise. I start to feel really tired and I—'

'Wish there was a cupboard to hide in?'

She'd looked across. He wasn't laughing. 'Sort of,' she'd said softly. 'Do you feel that way too, Dad?'

'Sometimes,' her father had said. 'In crowds.' Recognition and sympathy had registered in equal measure on his face.

'So, it's not just me?'

'No.'

'So, I'm not weird or anything?'

'Oh, I wouldn't say that.'

She'd punched his arm and he'd laughed. 'Anna, you are the least weird person I know.'

'Mum and Kate think I'm weird.'

'Different is a better word.'

She'd stored it all away. But he'd still made her go to the party. Ninety minutes in, she'd been in the garden alone, pretending to look at flowers, when Gemma's mum had called her. 'Anna, your dad's here.'

He was in the hall; Gemma's mum was holding her coat.

'I'm so sorry to hear about your Aunty Louisa. I'm sure she'll be better soon. Do you want to take something from the party for her? Do they even allow sponge cake in hospital?'

Anna had looked confused. Her dad had shaken his head. 'Best not to.'

And then they were in the car.

'Are we really going to the hospital?'

'Waterstones,' her dad had said, deadpan. 'Fantasy for you. Detective and crime for me.' He'd grinned then and relief had flooded through her.

He understood.

'Does Mum know about Aunty Louisa?' she'd asked, confused.

'Good Lord, no. Why should she? She's *my* aunty.'

She'd hugged his arm and almost made him swerve. 'Mr Blue Sky' was playing in the car and she'd started singing along.

Aunty Louisa became their safe words. Hers and her dad's secret words. Anna had never told her mother, but she knew now that she'd found out. Secrets were dangerous things. This special thing between her and her dad might even have explained her mother's unfathomable cattiness. Might even have been the thin end of the wedge that grew between her parents. A wedge that her feckless mother used to push him away, and which Anna found the most difficult thing of all to forgive.

But that all came later.

Her dad, that day, had made it OK for her to need her own space. To deal with crowds on her own terms and, when gatherings became like a roaring waterfall, she knew that it was OK to walk away. OK not to be a part of the herd. Her dad, and later Myers and Briggs, said so.

Shame they hadn't announced it to the rest of the world.

She was up at dawn on Sunday, running through the park, the leaves wet beneath her feet, sucking the ozone-sharp air into her lungs with gusto.

She ran for far longer than usual, twice around Badock's Wood, craving the endorphins and the immediacy of putting one foot in front of the other so that it became all she needed to think about. By the time she got back to Horfield Common an hour and a half later, the dog walkers and drone flyers had arrived.

When she was a child her father would sometimes take her and Kate to the wide-open moorland on the edge of the Brecon Beacons on Sunday afternoons. There, enthusiasts would fly huge, remote-controlled planes, some with four-foot wingspans. Her dad loved to watch the aerobatics executed by these skilful amateurs. Now, the lovingly crafted Hurricanes and Spitfires had given way to quadcopters and multirotors hovering over the trees, flipping and zooming in and out of the branches. Nothing like as elegant, but much easier to fly. Technology marched ever onwards and yet Anna wasn't sure her dad would approve.

She did her stretches on a low wall within sight of her front door, accompanied by the barking of dogs and the high-pitched waspish drone of miniature electric motors, then finished the last of her water and, refreshed, put Shaw back in the locked drawer of her mind. Time to go to work once again on the living.

CHAPTER TWENTY

Tobias's file was waiting for her the next day. He'd seemed convinced that there was more evidence exonerating Cooper. But Anna wanted to know if there was evidence implicating someone else buried in the file, too. It lay open on her desk at Portishead and she read through it avidly. The top five sheets were poor photocopies of what appeared to be itemised evidence lists. All five had the same date of 10 March 1998 and all contained roughly the same content. The numbers 1 to 5 were ringed in another hand at the bottom. The sixth sheet was a copy of a typed letter from a company called Nordoc Document Laboratories. Anna turned back to the lists. They each contained several scrubbed-out entries. The signature at the bottom of each page belonged to Maddox.

Khosa came in with two mugs of tea and caught Anna shaking her head as she thumbed through the papers again.

'Interesting reading, ma'am?'

'You've seen it?'

Khosa nodded. 'Glanced at it. Trisha made a copy.'

'Multiple lists?'

Khosa shook her head. 'I asked Tobias. It's one list. The same list, in fact, modified and rewritten at least half a dozen times. Maddox was writing all this in his notebook to include or exclude whatever evidence was thought to be helpful to the investigation.'

'Like no cinema ticket?'

'Exactly. And he was a great one for lists was Maddox.'

'I presume Tobias asked for the ESDA test as part of the appeal?'

Khosa nodded. Electrostatic imaging for indented writing often revealed a great deal more than what was actually written down. Anna'd researched how the detection analysis worked; by stretching Mylar film over an indented page and picking up the difference in electrostatic charge between the indented paper and the background. It varied with the type of paper, the type of pen or pencil or stylus used, humidity, the number of sheets between the actual page that was written on and the page the indent was being read from. It was clever science and very damning evidence. Nails in the coffin of the Crown prosecution's case against Neville Cooper, if Tobias could get the jury to accept it at retrial, she was sure.

The reports and the files made compelling and harrowing reading, but they still weren't exactly what Anna was after. She busied herself with trivia and came back to the file at lunchtime. Between mouthfuls of an overpriced ham and mustard on granary bread, Anna sifted through sheaves of photocopies and a flotsam of unrelated items. On each page, Tobias had carefully stapled a brief explanatory note to himself, indicating source and occasionally a cursory explanation or query.

Anna sipped her tea, flicking through the file until a police fingerprints report caught her eye. She called Khosa back in to her office.

'Is this the mysterious cinema ticket?'

'As mentioned,' Khosa said. 'Maddox covered his tracks expertly. He submitted a false witness ID and a different scenario to the lab when he asked them to report on the ticket. The report confirms that the prints on the ticket are Cooper's, but the ticket itself is missing. This was Maddox camouflaging their paper trail.'

'So Wyngate knew exactly what was going on?'

'Maddox was his protégé. It's difficult to believe otherwise. I'm trying to pick out stuff that's relevant, ma'am,' Khosa said as she headed back to her desk. 'Slim down the file.'

'That's a really good idea, Ryia,' Anna called after her.

*

It was Khosa who finally found something. Another piece of revealed writing in Maddox's, by now recognisable, hand. The explanatory note said: *Maddox's daily notepad – torn sheet*

The ESDA method had revealed a list of witnesses who'd purportedly seen Emily Risman in Coleford on the day of her murder: a woman who had spoken to her as she left the hairdresser; a shopkeeper who had sold her a salad roll; a list of hairdressing colleagues. It looked very much as if this sheet was the page of Maddox's notepad he'd used on a visit to Coleford – a list of potential witnesses who would be contacted later for statements.

Khosa brought it through to Anna who peered at the indented image of the fragment. It was a brief entry – a name and a scribbled note.

Mr J Stanton, van driver. Car park at approx. 3.15-3.30.
Blue saloon
tel. 38517

Odd that this should have been torn out. It was an anomaly, because Anna had seen witness statements from everyone else on that list but not from any van driver called Stanton.

Ann walked out into the squad room with Khosa and on the whiteboard, she wrote:

Cinema Ticket
Coleford
Van driver witness

She asked Trisha to contact the DVLA about any Stantons owning a van in and around the patch.

On the way back to her office with Khosa, Anna was buttonholed by Holder, looking unhappy.

'Slack rang. Neville Cooper's in hospital. Tried to hang himself.'

'Oh, no,' Khosa said.

'Christ,' said Anna. She knew it happened. They all did. People tried to commit suicide in detention and prison all the time. 'At risk' prisoners were put on suicide watch. Obviously, Neville Cooper had not been. Knowing that did little to numb the shock. 'When?'

'Last night.'

'OMG,' Khosa muttered.

Anna immediately rang Harris but got no answer. Slack, too, was unavailable. Frustrated, Anna stayed late at Portishead, writing up the report on Shaw's disclosure, but it was a struggle because she kept being distracted by Tobias's file and a burning anger over what had happened to Cooper.

There was a growing conviction in her mind now that Emily Risman's and Nia Hopkins' killer was linked to the serial rapes. Shaw, damn him, had planted the seed with his enigmatic online encounter with the chat-room ghoul who'd known about the dress with the floral rose print. Nia and Emily had marks on their necks consistent with non-fatal strangulation. Megan Roberts had told her how her attacker had 'put his hands around my neck and squeezed'. And the other rape victims who'd come forward told the same harrowing story. But it was what Shaw had said, in his inimitable way, that she kept coming back to.

Maybe he likes to take them to the edge before bringing them back for more.

There was a pattern here. A very obvious one. All she needed was that one little piece of the jigsaw to make the picture whole so that everyone else could see it, too.

*

Despite ringing twice more, Harris was still not answering his phone so Anna turned again to Emily Risman.

The police had traced her movements from the hairdresser in Coleford to a bakery, where she had bought a sandwich on the day she was killed. After that the trail went cold until her body was found in the Forest of Dean. Was it that easy to disappear?

The prosecution witness the Crown produced made a statement saying that Emily Risman boarded a bus to Millend at 2.05 p.m. on the day of her murder. This was the Monmouth to Lydney bus, which would have taken twenty minutes to get to Millend from the square in Coleford. The defence questioned the witness's memory. She had been a seventy-five-year-old commuter from Yorkley, a village two stops down the bus route from Millend, who travelled in to Coleford every Thursday morning for a weekly shop and returned home again at lunchtime. In her testimony, she remembered Emily Risman as a regular traveller who sat at the rear of the bus reading magazines. The very regularity of this journey was the flaw that the defence went after. How could she have been sure that Emily had been on the bus that day? The bus driver, another regular on the route, had not been able to swear that Emily had been a passenger. As a result, the jury saw no reason to doubt the prosecution's contention that Emily had met Cooper in Millend.

They might not have been so quick to think this had they been shown another witness who may have seen Emily getting into a car in the car park that afternoon. And Maddox had conveniently torn out the entry in his notebook regarding that witness.

Anna groaned. She was tired. The more she read, the more disgusted she became. The whole case seemed mired in filth. She closed the file and left, hit the gym and had an early night. All she wanted was a few hours of not having to think about Emily and Nia and a man who liked squeezing apples. But even in sleep, she knew that the algorithm in her head was still running.

*

In the morning, Anna's phone rang early. It was an unfamiliar number, but she recognised the animated voice as belonging to Tobias.

'You've heard about Neville?'

'How is he?'

'A mess.'

'What happened?'

'What happened, Inspector, is that Chief Inspector Harris appears intent on trying to send my client to an early grave.'

'That's a bit strong, isn't it?'

'You be the judge. And I am telling you this because I'm certain that Harris wouldn't volunteer this information. Yesterday afternoon, I was with Neville. He likes me to call, bring him news about his mother. We talked in a seminar room. He was feeling well and buoyed by me telling him that you were also on his team.'

'I don't know about—'

'Let me finish. We left together. Me to my car, Neville to go back to his cell. There was someone in the corridor with Harris. Does the name Wyngate mean anything to you?'

'Yes.' The word hissed out of Anna's mouth like steam from a kettle.

'Obviously, Neville recognised him. When he did I saw him tense. I saw his whole demeanour change. He looked terrified. As we passed, Wyngate said something. Neville didn't respond. But I saw he'd gone very pale. I asked him if he was OK and he said he was, but I knew something was wrong. An hour later I get a call to say that Neville tied his shirt to the metal legs of his bed and tried to strangle himself. Wyngate is a bogeyman from Neville's past.'

Anna shut her eyes, her imagination working overtime. 'What was Wyngate even doing there?'

'I don't think it was a coincidence,' Tobias said.

'A set-up?'

'My money is on that.'

She exhaled loudly. 'God, you'd think they'd learned their lesson, wouldn't you? Thanks for letting me know.'

Tobias's tone was grim. 'Believe me, it gives me no pleasure at all.'

Anna grabbed her coat and went directly to her car. She headed north for the M5, phoned HQ and left a message on Trisha's answerphone.

'Anyone asks, I've had to go to Gloucester.'

It wasn't strictly true. But Harris wasn't answering his phone and what she had to say to him would undoubtedly be better done face to face.

Slack pretended to hide behind his computer screen in the squad room at Gloucester.

'Where is he?' Anna demanded.

'Just come out of a roasting with the ACC. He isn't talking to anyone.'

'He'll talk to me,' Anna said.

'Ma'am, it might be better to wait until tomorrow—'

'I think we've waited far too long already.'

'We've had orders that he's not to be disturbed,' said Slack. Anna read it as more of a show to the others in the room than a real warning, especially as he made no move to stop her.

Harris's office was at the very end of the large squad room, which was filled with desks and filing cabinets. Five sets of eyes looked up as Anna walked by and the subdued buzz trickled to silence as they tracked her progress to the glass-panelled door at the end.

Harris looked up as she knocked and entered without waiting for an invitation, his face dark with a brooding anger. On recognising her, the anger died to a sullen defiance.

'What do you want?' he asked, shuffling the papers on his desk.

'Guess,' Anna said, folding her arms and standing with her back to the door.

'Look, I didn't plan for Cooper to end up in the bloody hospital.'

'No? Then what did you plan for, Chief Inspector? Or was Wyngate there by pure coincidence?'

Thunder gathered again on Harris's brow. 'Be careful, *Acting* Inspector Gwynne.'

Anna shook her head, walked across the room and sat opposite Harris, matching his glare with one of her own.

'I'm not really interested in your motives, *sir*. I can almost begin to grasp the vague idea that you, or Wyngate, may have suggested that letting Cooper see him might just scare him enough to…' She shook her head again.

'You think you're so bloody smart, don't you?' His belligerence said it all. *It had been his idea.*

'I had you down as misogynistic, patronising and bloody-minded, but not stupid,' Anna said.

The skin on Harris's neck turned an ugly shade of purple. 'Who the hell do you think you are—'

'Everyone's been telling me that you can be a pious pain in the arse, but beneath it all a good copper. That's why I can't believe you'd do anything so crass as goad Neville Cooper like this.'

Harris's lips kept opening and shutting like a fish out of water. Whatever words he was searching for seemed stuck in his throat.

Anna leaned in close. 'Wyngate has his own agenda, which has nothing to do with the truth.'

'Cooper is still our prime suspect.' Harris remained defiant, but it was almost as if he was appealing for understanding rather than trying to shout her down.

Anna's hands came up to the side of her head as if she were about to tear out two clumps of hair. She exhaled loudly before speaking with exaggerated calmness. 'Cooper did not kill Emily, but it is very likely that whoever did kill her also killed Nia. In arresting

Cooper, you're simply chasing your own tail. Whatever misguided loyalty you feel for Briggs or Wyngate, or whoever else you were buddied up with, you have to walk away from it.'

'You don't know anything.' He dropped his gaze and began massaging the back of his neck.

'I know enough to see a good officer's reputation going down the toilet.'

Harris's head snapped up, ready to protest, but Anna quelled him with a sweep of one hand.

'This stops now. We have two choices. Either I walk away and let you handle this your own way, which, as far as I can see will be a disaster. Or, I can tell you what I think should be done and we remain on the same team.'

'And you think *I'm* bloody arrogant?'

'Call me what you want, the choice remains the same. Like it or not, I still have a brief and either you come with us on this or you don't.'

Harris stared.

Anna cocked her head, cheeks burning, her pulse throbbing in her throat.

Harris said, 'I'm listening.'

Anna nodded. A small, barely perceptible movement. 'Try to take a small step back for a moment. Let's take it as a given that Cooper did not kill Nia Hopkins. Accept that and you must also accept that someone wants very much for us to believe that he did by planting evidence at Cooper's workplace.'

'Who?'

'The same person that planted Emily Risman's underclothes eighteen years ago.'

Harris considered this thought for all of two seconds, before anger once again erupted. 'If you believe all the press are saying, that could have been the CCRC.'

Anna shook her head. 'Wyngate and Maddox and Briggs were responsible for many unforgivable things, but I don't think they did that – even if Maddox was Tonto to Briggs' Lone Ranger.'

'John Wyngate isn't like that.'

Anna held up one hand, palm open towards him. 'At least accept that someone planted evidence. It's inconceivable that Emily's undergarments were only found on the third search of Neville Cooper's property in 1999.'

'You have a name?'

'Not yet. But whoever it is, he's played you and Wyngate like an expert fisherman with an irresistible lure. He's relied on the fact that the police were willing to make a case against Cooper once – so why not again? Now he'll be praying that the case sticks. So, here's the choice we must make. I'm asking you to perpetuate the lie. That way we can continue the hunt in the faint hope that he might be slightly off his guard. It's the stealthy approach and definitely the one I'd prefer.'

Harris let out a mirthless laugh. 'Stealthy? Yeah, right. I've just had my arse kicked from here to Sunday by the ACC and she has very sharp boots. What's going to happen is that I have to call a press conference with me eating a two-hundredweight slice of humble pie and releasing Cooper from custody. At least while he's in hospital. The ACC says it'll show compassion.'

'I really don't think that's a good idea.'

'No?' Harris's mock surprise was pure am-dram. 'And there's me thinking you'd be applauding the loudest.'

'I'm sure it would be good for Cooper, but it's asking for trouble.'

'What trouble?'

'It's too provocative. With Cooper still under suspicion the real killer feels safe. Take away that safety net and who knows what he'll do.'

'You don't think that flushing him out is an option? Isn't that exactly what we want?'

Anna recoiled. 'No.'

Harris's eyes were shining now. 'Why so negative? I thought you'd jump at the chance?'

Once again, she found Shaw's words fuelling her train of thought.

And then maybe our special boy can get back to business.

She felt trapped, like a thumb in a vice. She didn't want him to 'get back to business' if the business meant stalking and raping. She hated the thought of it. But contemplating the alternative made something reptilian coil and uncoil in her gut.

'I despise the fact that Cooper's been targeted by you again, but if you let him off the hook, it's likely the killer will panic. This man has killed coldly and cynically to keep himself free. He picked out Nia Hopkins for maximum effect because of her link, through her father, to Cooper. I think he's capable of anything and I don't want to be responsible for that. Frankly, it smacks of real unfettered malevolence and it scares me silly.'

Harris stood up and crossed to a large pinboard, which was covered by the monstrous collage of photographs, drawings and details that told the dreadful story of Nia's murder. When he spoke he was still facing the board. 'John Wyngate made a promise to Emily's parents that he would find the killer of their daughter. He's still driven by that promise. We all learned a lot from Briggs. He's the sort of boss that commanded fierce loyalty. They were desperate for a result.'

'Desperate enough to plot a confrontation that put Cooper in hospital?' Anna knew she shouldn't have, but the words slipped out anyway.

Harris pivoted, his face flushing a dusky red. 'Wyngate just asked him how his mother was.'

Jesus. Anna shook her head.

'It was only meant as one more little turn of the screw, that's all.'

She rounded on him. 'God, don't you get it? It's not enough for us to find the guilty. We're here to protect the innocent as well.'

For the first time since she'd met him, the fierce conviction left Harris's face, to be replaced by... what was that? Doubt? But this was Harris. It didn't last.

'The ACC hasn't given me any choice. We go ahead with the press conference.'

Anna rolled her eyes.

Harris said, 'And she wants you to be a part of it.'

'I've just told you. I think it's far too dangerous.'

'I heard you. But she wants to show solidarity.'

'Who are you doing this for? Yourself or Wyngate?'

'This is all for Nia. Believe you me.'

'The answer's still no.'

CHAPTER TWENTY-ONE

Cooper's attempted suicide made the News at Ten. She watched, mulling over the events that had followed her meeting with Harris. She'd spent an hour with Tobias and the assistant chief constable and both, for very different reasons, refuted her argument and insisted on the conference.

On screen, yet more library Woodsman footage and lurid Nia Hopkins details were churned out and Anna watched as her own face was paraded as the detective re-examining the evidence in the case of Emily Risman. Harris's delivery was deadpan, devoid of anything but the most essential background information as to Cooper's state of mind. When asked if he was still in police custody, Harris trotted out, 'Neville Cooper is still helping us with our inquiries. However, he has been released from custody and we are exploring other lines of inquiry.'

There was, as expected, no mention of Wyngate. Anna'd fought the suggestion that she should take part in this little fiasco and had won that small skirmish. But they'd filmed her leaving the nick and her hurried exit was tagged on to the report, making her look like a fleeing suspect in her own right. Watching it in her flat, and feeling the misgivings rumbling in her gut, she knew it had been the right thing not to appear at the conference. She did not want to be associated directly with Harris and his squad. It didn't feel right.

The nagging certainty that she knew the answer to all of this itched in an unreachable place inside her head. The pattern was here and all she needed to do was see it. Anna was convinced that something set up an auto-search function in her head for unanswered conundrums. Eventually, it would complete its search and present the memories to her, fully formed as an answer. But whereas, in most people, this happened silently, in Anna her right brain algorithm fluttered constantly like a damaged moth against a lit window and there wasn't much she could do about it except get on with the day to day and wait for it to break through.

Her eyes drifted from the screen momentarily to the room around her. One of millions in which the images were being viewed. In one of those rooms this throw-away news item was going to cause irritation in the killer's mind, and possibly something much, much worse.

One of her phones woke her some time during the night. She fumbled for them both, saw it was non-work and picked up in a semiconscious stupor. She croaked a hello, but heard nothing except muffled sounds and static in reply, before the ring tone mercifully intervened as whoever was on the other end killed the call. She didn't even open her eyes to look at the clock.

In the morning, she half believed she'd dreamed it, but her call log showed the number to be a landline. When she arrived at Portishead, she gave it to Trisha to run, but the analyst frowned and said, 'I know that number.'

'How?'

Trisha consulted her screen and nodded. 'There. It's in the file, ma'am. The address is Beacon Cottage, Alburton.'

'Charles Willis?'

'That's right. Would you like me to ring it, ma'am?'

Anna nodded, mind whirring.

After several seconds, Trisha shook her head. 'Engaged, ma'am.'

'I've tried twice already, too.'

'Phone off the hook?'

'Possibly.'

'You sound a little anxious, ma'am.'

'Do I? I don't like calls at two thirty in the morning. In my experience, it usually means bad news. Keep trying, Trisha.'

Once Khosa and Holder arrived, Anna summoned them to the whiteboard.

'OK. Let's consolidate. Shaw has been too big a distraction. Justin, where are we with forensics?'

'We've managed to trace most of the samples, ma'am, though there was nothing on the nail swabs or on Emily's clothing. No blood or semen. Little or no fibre contamination.'

'But we know Roger Willis was not surprised to learn that he was the father of Emily's unborn child, am I right?'

Holder nodded. 'Given Emily's history, we know there were other possibilities but, as I said, the DNA matched up with him.'

'Let's get confirmatory testing done on that. In-house if possible, but use Chepstow if needed. And go and knock on Forensics' door. We need all this pushed.'

Holder nodded.

'OK. Ryia, I want you to concentrate on the van driver's statement that was never presented as evidence. The one we found in Maddox's handwriting on the torn sheet in his notebook. We need to find that man, if he's still alive.'

Khosa nodded.

The whiteboard was filling up, arrows branching off from the main photograph of Emily Risman in a network of interconnected threads.

'And, of course, there's Wyngate.'

Trisha shook her head. 'I've been unable to contact John Wyngate, ma'am.'

'What a surprise.'

'But I do have an address for Briggs.'

'Good. I'll need to speak to him at some point, too.'

Trisha picked an envelope off her desk. 'Oh, and this came for you yesterday, ma'am.'

Anna took the large manila envelope addressed in a firm neat hand and opened it. Inside was a handwritten note and two pages of typed A4. The note was brief and to the point.

Dear Inspector Gwynne,
As requested, I've looked through my diary and jotted down the events that were not routine. That means I've left out trips to Sainsbury's and concentrated on things that I deemed note-worthy. As you suggested, I've written them out and signed the note. I hope it helps. If you think I ought to go back further, just let me know. It's less tedious than marking year nine projects!

Yours sincerely,
Megan Roberts

Anna took the sheets out and forced her brain to concentrate. There were trips to the cinema, restaurants, dentists, shopping in Bath, and hiking trips on two of the Sundays in the twelve-week period covered. Megan Roberts had copied her entries verbatim and the term she used to apply to these trips were 'jaunts'. It was the second of these that drew Anna's attention.

Sunday, 15 June. Up with the sun this morning for our jaunt to the Forest. Luke made egg and bacon but managed to burn the toast. Away by seven thirty on a beautiful morning…

As she read this simple account, Anna's pulse began to pick up. There were a hundred forests Megan Roberts could be referring to and yet…

We arrived at Wenchford at 9 and despite the fine morning found it deliciously deserted. We decided to do the walk in reverse, for the hell of it, and stood on the Drummer Boy Stone for a 'photo op'. Luke tripped over the stile but had recovered by the time we'd climbed to the viewpoint, which overlooked the Blakeney Straits. We could see Blakeney village and the Cotswolds clearly in the distance...

Blakeney. She'd seen signs for Blakeney when they'd visited the Rismans. She googled it and found it easily. Blakeney was exactly where she'd thought it to be. Less than two miles from Millend, on the edge of the Forest of Dean.

Face flushing, she read on. There was little or no further reference to any place names, just a small essay on how much Megan and her boyfriend enjoyed the day. But there was enough for the germ of an idea to take root in Anna's head and turn the fluttering disquiet that had not left her since reading Tobias's file up a notch.

'Ryia, have a word with the Thames Valley team investigating the rapes. Find out if any of the victims visited the Forest of Dean in the three months before their attacks. No, make it six months. See if they got within half a dozen miles of Blakeney.'

Khosa wrote something down and nodded. Anna told them about the phone call in the night. Neither of them had any real explanation. She tried the Willises' number again on her mobile. A call to BT confirmed no fault on the line.

'Well, there's only one way to find out why they called,' Anna said. She grabbed her coat and, pondering Megan Roberts' information, headed north.

Anna arrived at the Willises' cottage at 11.20 a.m. The scene, as before, was idyllic. The day had mellowed and the backdrop that nature had painted made Anna think of old chocolate boxes. Clouds raced overhead against a robin's-egg blue sky, the breeze ruffling what little foliage was left on the trees. Once again, the adjacent farm's contribution to the day was less than ideal, with a fresh pungent bouquet of sprayed slurry hanging in the air.

Anna noted that the Isuzu was missing, though the Astra was parked in front of the garages. Three milk bottles stood on the step inside the porch, together with half a dozen eggs in an open, torn, cardboard egg carton. Most of the eggs were covered in feathers and dark material, which could, in Anna's opinion, have been almost anything.

It's called the countryside, Anna, she reminded herself.

She rang the bell and stared down at the eggs with a grimace. When no reply came with the third ring, she followed some crazy paving around to the rear, impressed again by the neat garden. She knocked firmly on the back door. It made the latch rattle. After three knocks, she put her hand on the handle and opened the door. Silence, dense and complete, was all that met her straining ears.

At first, all she did was to lean in and sing out, 'Hello? Is there anybody home?'

When no one answered, Anna stepped into the narrow hall, mentally preparing a little apology for when Willis or his wife would appear.

From the hall, she could see into the kitchen at an acute angle. She caught sight of a small spill of flour on the surface of the butcher's console. Spilled flour wasn't something you left lying around unless you were in the middle of baking.

She sang out another greeting. 'Hello? Anyone home?'

A waft of breeze from the open door behind her caught the flour and sent a powdery spiral into the air. Anna took a step forward into the kitchen with her hand outstretched as if to try to catch the plume. A sizeable mound had spilled and accumulated on the floor beneath the block. Her eyes followed more abandoned things; a broken plate, an overturned knife block, something dark on the wooden floor. It looked like spattered liquid. Oil, perhaps. Not much, but Anna stepped over it, her awareness ratcheting up. The door leading out to the workshop and back garden stood open and she stepped through.

The workshop door was slightly ajar. She crossed to it, poked it open with her foot and froze. The room had been trashed. Shards of pottery littered the floor, shelves had been ripped down, Gail Willis's delicate creations now nothing more than rubble and dust. But it did not look like anything systematic. More as if some awful violent storm had visited this space and left a trail of mayhem.

Anna stepped quickly back out into the garden. Outside, all was quiet except for the noise of her heart hammering in her own ears.

An overwhelming sense of foreboding overtook her. She needed to call this in. Get some uniforms over and…

She saw it then. At the end of the garden, where it led to open fields. A patch of lawn and beyond that a bed that in the spring might harbour flowers, but now showed only the desiccated yellow stalks of sedums, and… something beyond… incongruous, blue, extending out of the black earth to a point where it was covered by an arrangement of branches and sticks.

Anna took some quick steps along the edge of a sodden path, signs of something heavy dragged along the ground evident in the flattening of the grass. She got to within six feet and stopped. He hadn't tried too hard to hide the body, but he had done enough to leave his trademark arrangement. The clumsy tent of sticks and branches, which she'd seen in the SOC photos old and new, bore no relationship to the careful and elaborate arrangement that sat on the earth. The whole thing was held together by a woven circlet of long twigs. It looked symbolic and arcane. She had no idea what it meant and guessed that its true meaning might only be known to one mind. One very disturbed mind. Trembling, she let her eyes drop through the gaps in the wooden totem to the horror beneath.

Gail Willis lay on her front, half out of the shallow grave he'd dug for her, one hand resting on the earth. Just like Emily Risman and Nia Hopkins.

All the air escaped from Anna's lungs in a rush. She turned away, retching drily, tears of horror and rage springing to her eyes and coursing down her face. The dull roar of a transatlantic jet high overhead was the only sound. Even the birds were quiet. Anna looked up, acutely aware that she was alone in this garden but convinced all of a sudden that she was not. The Woodsman had been to this cottage and he could still be here, watching, waiting. She sucked in oxygen, her mind incapable of coherent thought, as the instinct to run as far away as possible kicked in.

She turned, stepping madly to one side, not wanting to contaminate the crime scene any more than she had already. She walked around the outside of the cottage, heading for her car, unable to wash out the stench of slurry that clung to her nostrils, that she would now always associate with violent death. Yanking open the car door, she clambered in and rang Holder.

It was then that she thought of Charles Willis. She'd run away without even finding out if he was still alive, or perhaps injured. The dreaded prospect of having to go back and search the house brought out, to her consternation, an involuntary moan of denial. But what if the Woodsman was still there? Stalking her, waiting for his chance. Sense, that rarest of commodities, finally took charge. She was alone and unarmed at a murder scene with the real possibility that the killer was still in the vicinity. It would be foolhardy to put herself in danger.

Shipwright's voice echoed in her head. *Do not fly solo, Anna.*

She found a foothold on that treacherous slope of shock she'd been sliding down, put the car in gear and drove out, retracing the two miles to the turning off the main road where she parked on the verge. A part of her knew that her reaction, as weak as it seemed, was normal and human and the correct thing to do. And this iota of insight provided a crumb of comfort. But fear still prickled the hair on her scalp and made her glance in the rear-view mirror every couple of seconds, hissing like white noise in her head.

When, several minutes later, blue lights danced on the distant horizon and the strident siren's wail reached her, relief washed over her like a warm bath. Anna flagged down the patrol car, flashed her warrant card and led them back to Beacon Cottage.

Holder and Khosa came later, after the local uniforms and local CID, and Anna let them take the weight until Harris arrived with his posse of serious crime officers to take over. After watching the white-clad CSI team crawling over the place like white-suited ants, Anna called her squad together. It was getting dark now and the temperature was plummeting. They sat in her car and she switched on the engine to try to get some heat working, but in the light from the harsh xenon lamps that lit up the house like an airport runway, their breath plumed out like word balloons as they spoke.

'There is no sign of Charles Willis, ma'am,' Khosa said.

Anna sighed. 'I'm not sure if that's good or bad. Is it possible he got away?'

Holder shrugged. 'The Isuzu is missing and the workshop is a complete mess. But there's also blood in Willis's office.'

'When I let myself imagine what went on there… Charles Willis is almost blind.' Anna shook her head. 'He can't have taken the jeep. Are there signs of forced entry?'

'No,' Khosa said.

'So, who rang me last night?'

Khosa shrugged. 'Yours was the latest entry on the electronic phone book on his PC. Your number was still up on the screen. Perhaps he got through in desperation and was then caught.'

Anna shivered.

'And there's one more thing, ma'am,' Holder said. 'It seems Osbourne didn't go home last night.'

'Osbourne?' Anna looked from Khosa to Holder. Neither of them offered an explanation and so her imagination filled in the blanks. 'We should have been more careful. We should have played this another way.'

'How could we have, ma'am?' Khosa asked.

'I don't know. But if Osbourne's involved… why take Willis?'

'That's one on a list of a dozen questions I've got, ma'am,' Khosa replied.

Holder stared at them. 'Hang on, are you saying that Osbourne did this?'

Anna shrugged. 'Perhaps. Or perhaps whoever did do it has taken Roger Willis and Osbourne, too. But I think our priority has to be finding Osbourne, and quickly.'

Khosa shook her head. 'But why did he have to do that to Gail Willis?'

That was a better question. One that Anna considered carefully before answering.

'Who knows. Perhaps he can't help himself now. Killing Nia to re-implicate Cooper had a kind of twisted logic to it. Thanks to Gloucester's heavy- handedness Cooper's in hospital, but he's no longer in custody. That's not helping because it means our killer's plan isn't working and he may be getting desperate. But we shouldn't make the mistake of trying to apply logic here.'

Holder shrugged. 'It's as if he wants us to know he's out there.'

Anna nodded.

Holder banged his hand down on the dash. 'How the hell did they miss this bastard the first time around?'

Anna didn't answer but she risked a glance at Harris outside in the harsh lights, his gaze anchored firmly on the cottage. He'd not spoken to her since he'd arrived, preferring to use Slack as his go-between. She knew why. He was fearful of being ridiculed, of her crowing, 'I told you so.'

She didn't pretend that it hadn't crossed her mind, but she'd dismissed it instantly. A woman had died here. Anna had no appetite for one-upmanship or copper banter. But Harris was a different breed.

'Are we any further forward with anything else?' she asked.

Khosa answered. 'Trisha is still trying to trace the van driver, uh… Stanton. We've tracked him to two addresses but he's moved on. I'll get on to it again tomorrow.'

'There is one other thing. I think it would be wise to liaise with the rape team. I think we may have found their serial attacker.'

Holder and Khosa both snapped their heads up.

'I know how this is going to sound, but it's possible we may be looking at the reverse of the usual pattern. Let's go with Osbourne for now. If it is him, we know he killed Emily in a rage. She'd been having intercourse with him from a young age. If she said no to him, for whatever reason – the pregnancy maybe – he could have lost it and killed her. He got lucky, Cooper was an easy scapegoat, but Osbourne's pattern of behaviour might have been set in that one incident with Emily. Perhaps he thinks he's lucky, is being protected by a higher power, who bloody knows what's going on in his head. But he's been attacking women since that time. And instead of letting it escalate, he's controlled himself, avoided killing until he really had to.'

'But how does that explain Gail Willis?' Khosa looked confused.

Anna sighed. 'I don't know. Maybe he's finally lost control. Whatever the reason, he's out in the open now. And we need to stop him before he does this again.'

'We should try to correlate the rapes with Osbourne's known movements,' Holder suggested.

'I'll see to it. I'll get an APW out for Osbourne nationwide,' Khosa said.

'So, Emily Risman's pregnancy…?' Holder let his words trickle out as a question.

'Might have been the final insult to Osbourne,' Khosa muttered.

Holder thought about it and then nodded slowly. 'That would fit. But it still doesn't tell us why he's taken Willis.'

'That one I can't begin to answer. Possibly he's doing it because of something Willis knows, or even some sort of distorted revenge for what his brother did.'

'Should we be concentrating on airports, docks, that sort of thing?'

'We shouldn't ignore them, that's for sure.'

'You don't sound convinced, ma'am?'

'Don't I?' she said. Holder was right. There was something else here that she was missing, but it was so far out of reach there was no point articulating that niggle. Not yet.

'What are the chances of us finding Willis alive, ma'am?' Khosa asked.

'There is still a chance.' Anna tried to put a positive spin on it. She needed to convince herself as much as anyone else. 'The very fact that he wasn't killed in the cottage is in our favour. And there won't be a sexual motive there, but then again, who knows what's going through this bloke's mind.'

Slack's face appeared at the car window, his nose and ears purple from the cold. 'Thought you ought to know that Cooper's condition is stabilising. It looks like he might be OK.'

'Thank God for that,' Anna said. 'I don't suppose there's been any sign of Wyngate?'

'No, ma'am.'

'Is someone looking?'

Slack shrugged. 'Been so many other things going on.'

Anna shook her head. 'I'm uncomfortable with him out there, not knowing what he's up to, because I'm sure he's up to something.'

Slack glowered. 'If it's any consolation, I think DCI Harris would set the dogs on John Wyngate if he turned up, that's for sure. What a total bloody balls-up.'

CHAPTER TWENTY-TWO

From high in the hide, he'd watched her arrive. The good-looking one with ice in her eyes. Through the binoculars he'd seen her enter the cottage, step out into the garden and find the body. All nicely laid out for her. Her reaction impressed him. She hadn't run, though she'd moved pretty quickly once she'd realised what he'd left for her. He'd laughed at that. His Bushnell binoculars were fitted with a camera and he'd look at the photographs later.

Now the cottage was swarming with police and he needed to move. He had another one in the van who was trying to attract attention by kicking at the panels. He still had some of the vet's drugs. He'd use some to shut them up. But he didn't want to use it all. He needed to keep some for later.

He put the binoculars away and climbed down from the tree.

He realised now how everything had changed once the detective started poking her bloody nose in. He knew it was over. His carefully constructed life. There was nothing he could do to change things back. But he'd leave his mark before he went. He wanted to show her. Wanted her to feel his power and know that he was better than her. Fucking arrogant bitch that she was.

Time to go to ground.

She had no chance.

CHAPTER TWENTY-THREE

The dream was vivid and all the worse for her stark and recent experiences. She was in a dark, damp place, with moisture dripping off the leaves of gnarled trees in a strange woodland, on a sunless winter's afternoon. Hurrying, vaguely aware of something in pursuit. Whenever she stopped and looked behind her, there was nothing to see except an impenetrable gloom between the endless trees, and nothing to hear except the echoing cawing of rooks perched high in the branches. She was alone and filled with dread, because there were things in the woods that she didn't want to look at. She kept her head down, not wanting to confront, not wanting to see. But the voice, when it came, made her look up.

'Take your time, look around.'

It was Gail Willis's voice, calm and untroubled, floating down in the stillness. But there was something very wrong with the placid calmness in that voice, something wrong with the way the words emerged as if through gritted teeth. Anna stared up and understood. Stared up into Gail's swollen, blackened face and bulging eyes, as they peered down at her from forty feet above, dangling by the neck from a tall branch. There were more bodies, all hanging from the trees above, black blood dripping from their swaying feet. Waiting, like dreadful fruit, to fall or be picked at by the circling rooks.

'Take your time, look around.'

Words from their first meeting in Gail's workshop, now tinged with some other meaning that Anna couldn't fathom. Behind her, a twig snapped before another rook cawed, and Gail began her automaton message again.

Anna slipped on a wet leaf, her knee meeting with the soggy earth, her hands sinking in to the ground that should have been hard but had the springy consistency of flesh.

'No, no, not now.' Her own voice in the dream. A voice full of dread. Ahead of her stretched a path that wound upwards on a rise towards a lighter sky. She dragged herself upright, her head pivoting around to the noise of yet another twig snapping and the unmistakable rustling of dry leaves spared the dampness of the rain of blood. Some movement in her peripheral vision brought her head back around. The bodies were descending. Everywhere, clones of Gail gradually floated down to the woodland floor as the ropes lengthened.

'Take your time, look around.'

Behind her, the rustling of leaves became rhythmic, the noise of footfalls gathering speed. She stumbled towards the path, her gut churning as all the bodies reached the ground and stood, turning dead eyes full of accusation towards her. The rustling became a stampeding drumbeat of feet as she stumbled and clawed her way forward on the path, certain now that something was behind her, almost upon her. A hot, animal breath seared her neck.

She came awake confused and disorientated, sweat beading her forehead, exhausted. The lurid dream left her aching and tired and she toyed with turning over and seeking refuge in a doze. But she knew it was not going to happen. A fear of revisiting that subconscious charnel house would keep sleep at bay. She switched on the light and got up, acutely aware of one thing and one thing only.

The Woodsman was off the leash.

Harris's team convened in the conference room at Gloucester. Two sets of photo-boards were now set up, one for Nia and one for Gail. They sat in a semicircle around a raised dais on uncomfortable plastic chairs, each with a wooden fold-up writing table. Out front stood Harris, tie done up, his face moist with a rubric glow of dull anger. Anna looked from him to the photo-board. It was the first time she'd seen crime-scene photos of Gail, and the sight triggered fresh memories of her lying in the garden. One of the images hung awry and it was all she could do to stop herself from getting up and adjusting it. It seemed somehow disrespectful.

Despite experience, she knew she'd never get inured to violent death. It screamed horror at her. As if the dead were crying out for help. And yet the feel of a murder scene, the sense of desolation and desecration it imparted, were somehow necessary for her to get a handle on things. Gail's was the first body she'd ever found. Not an experience she wished ever to repeat, but realising, once she'd thought it, how empty a hope that was. Harris had told her she didn't need to be there, but that was simply out of the question. She flicked her gaze back to the DCI and concentrated on his voice.

'Forensics are still at the cottage, but from the amount of blood and the initial assessment it seems that Gail was attacked inside the house and then taken outside, choked to unconsciousness, sexually assaulted, revived, and then stabbed to death.'

Out of the corner of her eye, Anna caught Slack standing against a wall, folding his arms over his chest, the fingers on his biceps white and tight with tension.

'Stab wounds are from a four-inch blade. There's little doubt that the weapon will be the same as that used on Nia,' Harris went on.

'And on Emily Risman,' Anna said. 'That's been confirmed.' Her voice drew half a dozen glances, including a venomous one from Harris. But he nodded slowly.

'We estimate time of death was between two a.m. and four a.m. Since Inspector Gwynne received her call at two thirty, we can assume that the murder was a protracted affair, and that it took place after this time.'

A voice from the floor piped up, 'Any evidence of forced entry, sir?'

'No. Either the doors were unlocked or he was let in.'

'Is it likely they'd open the door to someone at two in the morning?'

'He could have been there all evening, for all we know.'

'What about Osbourne, sir?'

'As of this moment, finding him is our top priority. We've traced Osbourne's movements up to the afternoon. He left work at three p.m., telling his workmates he had a business meeting. We found his car yesterday in a public car park near Blakeney, and a stolen pushbike was found abandoned in woodland half a mile from Willis's cottage.'

'And the night of Nia's murder, sir?'

Harris motioned to Slack, who pushed off the wall and moved to the front.

'We have a statement from Osbourne's partner saying that he was with her at home that evening.'

'You believe her?'

Slack shrugged.

'You're bringing her back in for questioning, I take it?' Anna asked.

'On the way,' affirmed Slack.

Harris turned back to face the audience. 'Just to remind everyone, the vehicle stolen from the Willis property needs to be found. An Isuzu four-wheel drive, registration number as on the board. We need ANPR reviewed for all major roads leading out of the forest. We also need a thorough search of Osbourne's property. Interviews with co-workers, background information. We need to find out if there is anywhere he might go, somewhere quiet he frequented where he might have taken Willis.'

There was a measurable silence until someone asked, 'Is it likely that Willis is still alive, sir?'

Harris fidgeted and glanced at Anna before replying.

'I don't know the answer to that one. If it is Osbourne, we don't know why he's taken Willis. If he wanted him dead, why not finish it at the cottage? As far as I'm concerned, Willis is still alive until we find a body.' He paused, letting his eyes engage as many in the room as he could in a direct challenge. 'I want them both found. Inspector Gwynne's cold case team has been re-examining the Emily Risman murder. In the light of recent events all the evidence suggests that the same man killed Emily, Nia and now Gail Willis. This would be a good time to be brought up to speed on their progress.'

Harris sat and Holder went up front and briefly ran through the main points of their investigation, before fielding a few questions from the floor. When he'd finished, she watched Harris's team file out, flipping shut notebooks and muttering to one another. Eventually, with only Anna, Holder and Slack left, Harris came over to them.

'Any thoughts on why he took Willis?' Harris asked.

Anna shook her head. 'Gail Willis's murder, according to the pathologist, was protracted. Could have been a vengeful act. Willis told us there'd been bad blood between his older brother and Osbourne.'

'Grudges don't end up with people being stabbed and—'

'A grudge to us may have been something very different in the mind of this killer.'

'Do you have anything else?' asked Harris.

'Only the car park witness from Coleford on the day that Emily Risman was killed. Something never properly followed up,' Anna said.

Holder sighed despondently. 'That's proving a bit of a thorny one, ma'am. I've been helping Ryia and Trisha. Two addresses and a dead end so far.'

'Keep trying,' Anna said.

'There'll be a daily conference,' Harris announced. 'Any contribution you have will be very welcome.' He allowed his gaze to linger on Anna's face. She wondered if his officious statement was an olive branch or a warning. In return, she gave him her unflinching attention, knowing full well he would not be able to stand it. He looked as if he wanted to say something but was too embarrassed or proud to do it. Not in this company. Instead, he lifted his chin, gave a barely perceptible nod and turned on his heel.

'Do I detect a certain thawing of Arctic ice?' Holder said when Harris finally left.

'You've got a bloody sensitive thermometer if you have,' muttered Anna.

'Things are on the line for him, now,' Slack said. 'The knives are well and truly out.'

Neither Harris nor Slack had mentioned Cooper in the briefing. Anna suspected it was deliberate. Humble pie, in her experience, was always a difficult swallow.

On the way to the car, Anna confided in Holder. 'I'd much prefer them as allies, but I'm not sure they see us that way.'

'They've got no choice now, ma'am.'

'Agreed. But it still doesn't feel like it.'

It had become a desperate fight to stop more mayhem for both Harris and Slack. Their approach might have been very different to hers, but somehow, she sensed that both men lay awake at night thinking of Nia and her parents.

Khosa was waiting for Anna when she arrived at the squad room, looking animated. 'Just had a call from Thames Valley, ma'am. You've hit the bullseye with your suggestions on the rape cases. They were well impressed.'

'They were?'

Khosa nodded. 'They've canvassed over half the victims and asked them to itemise visits they'd made to tourist locations in the year prior to their attacks.'

'What's the link?'

'Approximately half mentioned the Blakeney area and the remainder were unable to remember exactly where they went, though they do remember travelling to, or through, the Forest of Dean.'

A spurt of electricity shot down Anna's limbs. 'He was there, watching them all.'

'Oh, and one of the victims is a vet. She stopped her van on a regular route because she'd noticed a sheep in distress. Leg tendons cut with a Stanley knife. The sheep was a sacrificial lamb, if you'll excuse the pun, ma'am. The attacker pounced on her once she was out of the vehicle. But the point is, later, she reported that the van was missing several drugs, surgical instruments and a dart pistol. Included in the list of missing drugs was ketamine and thiafentanil.'

'Bingo,' said Anna softly. This was it. The jigsaw piece that finally made the picture whole. The same man who'd attacked the vet had abducted and murdered Nia Hopkins. The only thing that stopped her punching the air was the stark awareness that her instinct about Shaw had been spot on. He had given her this information. But at what cost?

'They're going to put some manpower into canvassing locals about frequent visitors and they'd like to meet up with you whenever it's convenient,' Khosa added.

'That whole area is criss-crossed by old disused railway lines and forestry access roads. My guess is he's got his own way in and out,' Anna said.

Khosa nodded. 'I'll tell them that. Maybe they'll enlist some local help. Anyway, they want to buy you a drink.'

'Great. At least that's some progress.'

'Osbourne and Willis are still missing then?'

'They are, Ryia. And I have no idea where to start looking.'

*

Anna had got halfway through rereading the SOC report on Gail Willis when Holder, looking even more sheepish than usual, put his head round the door. 'Ma'am, I think you ought to see this.'

'What it is?'

He held his phone out, screen first. 'Twitter. A friend of mine sent it to me as a joke. Umm… It's you, ma'am.'

Holder pressed a link and the small screen filled with a message.

Fed up of being Fucked by the Police? Here are some Cops I'd like to Fuck.

Beneath it in large letters was the acronym:

CILF

Short, ten-to-fifteen-second video clips of policewomen walking along the street followed. All were attractive, and from several countries, judging by the uniforms. One was of a training session on an obstacle course, with the inevitable clinging mud, and one was of a woman in skin-tight running gear doing stretches, her ponytail swinging as she reached down to her ankles to touch her toes, the muscles of her thighs and buttocks tight under the clinging material.

'That's me,' said Anna.

'I know, ma'am.'

'That's me last Sunday in the park after my run.'

The footage ended with Anna jogging the last few steps to her door. 'What the hell is this?'

'Someone's bad idea of a joke.'

'Jesus, isn't anything bloody sacred any more?'

'You say this was in a park?'

'Yes, and there was no one near me—' She stopped, realisation thudding home with sickening understanding. 'Drones. Bloody drones everywhere.'

Holder's expression was a picture. 'Sorry, ma'am. I thought you'd want to know. In case… I don't know.'

'No, you're right, Justin. How many times has this been retweeted?'

Holder winced. 'Three thousand times, ma'am. And counting.'

'OK. If you see someone sniggering and then looking at their phone you have my permission to taser them. And could you send me a copy of this link?'

Holder nodded and ducked out.

She looked at the clip another four times, shaking her head with each viewing. There were comments that went with it. But she gave up after reading, 'I would with a truncheon' and 'Woodsman whacker is a beauty.'

She decided to file it away as nothing more than a perverted geek's sexist distraction. There was no room in her life for any of that.

CHAPTER TWENTY-FOUR

The custody suite in Gloucester looked somehow smaller as Richard Osbourne's partner, Sue Donaldson, sat with her hands clasped together on the table, staring at her thumbs with her head angled. She was there voluntarily, a thin, anxious woman, her hair highlighted with copper-coloured streaks and cut in a combed-back, boyish, feathery style. She wore faded jeans and a blue fleece waistcoat over a white T-shirt. She seemed relieved to see Anna as she entered, but the anxiety returned when Slack came into the room and took off his jacket. He sat next to Anna and opposite Donaldson, and took the lead. This time there'd been no quibble over Anna's request that she sit in.

'Thanks for coming in, Miss Donaldson,' said Slack.

Sue Donaldson's fingers had a life of their own, constantly working at the skin around her nicotine-stained nails. When she spoke, it was with a smoker's rumble.

'Any sign of Rick?'

'Not yet,' said Slack.

'I don't understand. It's so unlike him.'

'What is? He's never gone off like this before?' Slack kept his tone even and sympathetic.

'Never,' replied Donaldson.

'Not even the odd night? He's never stayed out?'

'Once or twice with his darts team, if it's someone's birthday.'

'What did he say to you the other night, when he left?'

'Said he wanted to drop off an estimate for some work. Left at about eight. Said he'd be an hour.'

'And you've heard nothing from him since?'

She shook her head. 'His phone's off.'

Slack nodded. 'How long have you and Rick been together?'

'Six years.'

'But you're not married?'

'Rick wanted to. I preferred to wait.'

'For anything in particular?'

Donaldson's eyes dropped to a ring on her finger. She withdrew the digit into a clenched fist. 'I've been married before. It didn't work out.'

'But you consider your relationship with Rick a permanent one?'

'Yes, I do. We've been trying to have kids for a couple of years.'

'Trying?' asked Anna.

'Yes. We've had tests and… it's Rick. Motility problems they called it. They say it's improving.'

'Who are "they"?'

'The infertility clinic at Oxford. We were up there three weeks ago. We're on their IVF programme.'

Anna wrote something down on the pad she'd brought in with her.

'Why would you want to know that?' Donaldson's gaze flitted between Anna's pen and her face.

'All routine,' said Anna. She found a reassuring smile from somewhere and countered with another question. 'Rick never mentioned a Charles or Roger Willis to you?'

'Yes, he did. After you lot came to visit him. We talked about it… Emily Risman, that is. Talked about what happened.'

'You talked about Emily Risman?' Slack leaned forward.

Donaldson nodded. Small, rapid movements. 'Rick wanted me to know. He said it had been a bad time back then. A horrible time.'

'Did Rick mention anything about Gail Willis?'

A look of dull horror spread like a stain across Donaldson's face. 'Who is Gail Willis? I thought I was here because Rick's missing?'

'You are,' said Slack.

Donaldson's chair scraped back and she stood abruptly, walking away to the far wall, her hand massaging the back of her neck as she pivoted to stare at the police officers. 'What's going on?'

'Sit down, please,' said Anna.

'Has something happened to Rick?'

'If you'll just sit down.'

'Tell me what's going on—' Donaldson shook visibly, imploring Anna, her lips trembling on the edge of hysteria.

'We don't know what's going on. That's why you're here.'

'Please sit down,' requested Slack.

Still trembling, Sue Donaldson sat. She picked up the polystyrene cup of water they'd given her and sipped, held it in both hands when she returned it to the table. Squeezing it. Anna didn't give the thin material much chance of surviving.

'We're simply trying to get as much information as we can to help us find Rick,' Anna said.

Sue Donaldson nodded jerkily. She looked up at Anna with her chin down. A haunted look, with her pupils like huge unfocused chasms.

'Has Rick ever said he'd been in contact with Charles or Gail Willis?'

Donaldson raised her head.

'Did he?'

'I don't know. He was upset after you'd called to see him. He wondered if you'd been to see Willis, too. He was angry because he felt that this was all behind him.'

'Did he know where Willis lived?'

'He said he'd been over that way once for a job, but—'

'Did Rick have a computer?'

Donaldson frowned. 'Yeah, of course we have a computer. I do the books.'

'Did he have a laptop?'

'A laptop and iPads. We both do. Doesn't everyone?'

'Is Rick good with computers?' Anna asked.

'Average, I'd say.'

'Does he spend much time surfing the net?'

'A bit. He likes YouTube. Has a bet now and then…' Donaldson was getting more and more concerned with this line of questioning. 'Why?'

'Sometimes search histories and emails can tell us a lot. You won't mind if we have a look at his laptop?'

Donaldson shook her head, blinking rapidly, trying to process what any or all of this really meant. 'Of course not.'

'I've written down some dates.' Anna spoke slowly and clearly. 'We'd like you to try to remember exactly where you and Rick were on those dates. We'd also like you to write down where Rick liked to take you. Any beauty spots he particularly favoured.'

Sue Donaldson looked bemused.

'Then we want you to write down exactly what happened the day Rick disappeared, from the minute you got up to us contacting you, OK?'

She shook her head. 'No. I'm not OK. You're scaring me. I really need a cigarette.'

Slack nodded. 'I'll get one of the officers to take you outside.'

Anna smiled. 'Do you want some coffee or tea?'

'Coffee. Coffee would be nice.'

'Someone will get you one.'

When Anna re-entered the room thirty minutes later, she could smell the smoke leaking out of Donaldson's clothes. She didn't mind. It reminded her of Shipwright.

'I've done what I can.' Sue Donaldson looked up, calmer now, anxious to please. 'Some of the dates…' Her hands fluttered up in a gesture of hopelessness.

Anna scanned three neatly handwritten sheets. There were gaps in the dates they'd asked for, but Donaldson and Osbourne had a weekly routine. At least it was something to work with.

Anna focused on places Osbourne liked to visit. The forest wasn't mentioned. Osbourne's fancy was boats. Inland waterways and seaside holidays had been the order of the day. After a few moments, she handed them to Slack to read and then asked Sue Donaldson to sign the statements.

'You're free to go now,' Slack said.

A look of panic flared briefly on Sue Donaldson's thin face. 'What about Rick?'

Slack nodded. 'We've got your phone number. I promise we'll let you know if we find out anything.'

'Couldn't I stay for a while? I feel a bit, I don't know, queasy.'

'Yes, of course you can stay until you feel OK. That'll be fine,' Anna reassured her.

Outside, in an adjacent room, Slack's face bore a questioning look.

'Why are you so interested in Osbourne's computer skills?'

'Curious, that's all.'

She wasn't going to tell him about Shaw and the person he'd come across in a chat room all those years ago. Digital forensics would take Osbourne's laptop and she'd find out soon enough if he'd been capable of entering the dark web.

Slack looked at the monitor set up to feed in images from the interview room camera. It showed Donaldson still sitting, sipping nervously at another coffee, the WPC talking to her gently.

'Don't you think that's odd, not wanting to leave? Most people we have in there are almost running out the door when they get the nod.'

'It's not so strange,' Anna said, but didn't elaborate. She glanced up at the monitor. Some time in the next half-hour Donaldson was going to have to go to the lavatory, thanks to the two coffees and the water she'd drunk. That was when her real ordeal would begin. When she'd be confronted by her own image in the mirror. Then she would begin to wonder who that person she'd slept next to for all these years really was. She would begin to wonder if he had secrets, if she'd lied to herself about him for all that time. If there was something she should have seen and acted upon. It was a devastating process mentally.

Anna wasn't the slightest bit surprised that Sue Donaldson wasn't keen to leave. But there was nothing more to be gained by interviewing her further. That was not true of someone else, though.

It took them half the day to find Wyngate. It was Khosa's idea to target his car. Eventually picked up on an ANPR camera on the M5, at Junction 18 heading north, he was pulled over by a police motorcyclist, who escorted him back to Bristol. With an inevitable disinclination to cooperate, Wyngate insisted on his solicitor being present before he would answer any questions.

'Some poor git he has over a barrel, I expect,' had been Holder's acid comment.

The 'poor git' turned out to have a practice in Wolverhampton and it was almost five before they sat down together in an interview room in Portishead, not unlike the one they'd sat in with Cooper and Tobias in Gloucester just a few days ago. It suddenly seemed like an age.

Thinking of Cooper brought a pang of leaden guilt to Anna's tired brain. It seemed impossible for her not to stare across at Wyngate with anything but loathing for what he and his squad had done. But for their lies and fabrications, Cooper would not be in hospital and Gail and Nia might be alive. It was a fruitless, judgemental exercise and one she suppressed. Yet, not for the first time, thoughts of Cooper brought with them the unwelcome idea that he might have been better off succeeding in his suicide attempt. That way he'd never have to wake up to a world that had so cruelly and cynically crushed his hapless life.

Anna sat with Holder. Wyngate wore an indifferent expression, his gaze neutral, flitting between Anna and Holder. It was a copper's stare. Unsubtle and intimidating. It always struck her as a particularly inelegant way of getting anything meaningful out of a terrified prisoner.

As Holder began the interview, thanking Wyngate, with blissful irony, for coming in, the ex-copper kept his eyes on Anna. But it was the solicitor, Saunders, a bespectacled beanpole of a man, who spoke in response.

'My client wishes to cooperate, of course. Is this interview under caution?'

'Not yet,' Anna said. 'We thought we'd keep things informal. Of course, we could be looking at a case of obstruction and conspiracy to pervert the course of justice. We can go down that route…'

'You're very generous,' said Saunders, writing on a legal pad. He remained inscrutable behind the glasses and Anna couldn't tell if his statement oozed sarcasm or not.

She turned to Wyngate. 'Whose idea was it to talk to Neville Cooper?'

'No one's idea. That was a pure accident.'

'*Force majeure.*' Anna nodded. 'Just an amazing set of coincidences. Like the lost evidence from Cooper's first trial.'

Wyngate laughed. 'Jesus, you're like a bloody stuck record.'

'A cinema ticket with Cooper's fingerprints on it? A witness who saw Emily Risman get into a car in the car park at Coleford on the day of her death? Ring any bells?'

'I knew about the ticket, yes. But only later. Maddox fudged it. When we did find out about it, it was clear that ticket could

have been from any time that week. There was no date stamp. I
showed it to the CPS and Briggs. It was they who decided to hold
it back, not me.'

'So, you're trying to tell me that the people who were working
with you had autonomy. You didn't know what was going on?'

'Spit it out,' Wyngate hissed.

'I'm interested in the car park witness. Maddox interviewed him
but never followed it up.'

'Dave Maddox wanted a result more than any of us. He was a
good cop who went off the rails a little.'

'A little?'

'Listen to me. I had nothing to do with that. You need to know
about evidence before you can suppress it.'

'I want to know about Osbourne. Your impression of him.'

Wyngate frowned. Anna could see suspicion driving the wheels
and cogs behind his eyes.

'Osbourne was a bit of a lad. Had the car and a bit of cash. He'd
been dating Emily for a couple of years but had known her longer.
He was terrified we were going to throw the underage book at him.
Fancied himself, but he was harmless enough.'

'Did you establish his alibi?'

'We talked to his foreman. Osbourne was a jobbing carpenter.
Worked alone a lot of the time. He was miles away when Emily
was murdered.'

'And you established that?'

Wyngate's frown deepened. 'He was hanging doors alone but
someone saw him lunchtime eating his sandwiches on site. We
didn't press too hard. We had the trophies in Cooper's possession
and his confession.'

'His confession was fabricated and withdrawn.'

Wyngate shook his head. 'Is Osbourne a person of interest here?'

'One of several,' Holder said.

Anna shot him a pointed look, but too late.

'Several, eh?' Wyngate smiled.

Anna said, 'Did you examine Osbourne's computers, his PC or laptop at the time?'

'No, we had no reason to. I don't even think he had one.'

'Do you have any evidence that you found at the time that might now shed a different light on things?'

Wyngate sat back, impassive. 'If I did, do you honestly think I wouldn't give it to you?'

Anna snorted. 'Tobias has a file of undisclosed evidence. Aren't you even the slightest bit nervous of what's going to emerge at the retrial?'

Wyngate smiled. His eyes were like coals in the snow. 'Jesus, what it is to be righteous. You're a hard woman, Inspector. But we weren't all extras from Life On bloody Mars back then, you know.'

Outside, Holder and Anna both exhaled at once.

'Do you believe him, ma'am?' Holder asked Anna.

'I don't know, Justin. For some reason I find myself wanting to, but I'm beginning to wonder who the true nutter is in this case.' Half to herself, she murmured, 'Why is he still up to his neck in all of this? The fact that he was around Harris right from the start of the Nia Hopkins investigation doesn't make any sense.'

'Could be guilt,' Holder said, and then laughed at his own suggestion. 'Doesn't come across as very remorseful though.'

'From what we already know, it was Maddox that did most of the dirty work. Ideally, he would be the one to talk to, but we can't do that.'

'Unless you've got a Ouija board, ma'am.'

'What about Briggs?'

Holder smiled. 'Ryia's found him. Last thing she said as I left this morning. He's seventy-six now. Lives alone in Tewkesbury.'

'You have the address?'

Holder nodded.

'How long would it take us to get there?' Anna asked.

'Depending on traffic, an hour from here, I reckon.'

'Then let's do it, Justin.'

'Should we run it past the Super? Briggs was quite senior.'

'And his team was corrupt. Screw protocol. I've had it up to here with playing nice while some killer walks about looking for someone else's neck to put their hands around.'

After fifty-five minutes, driving through surprisingly heavy traffic, they reached the outskirts of Tewkesbury and a village called Fiddington.

Briggs opened the door of a modern, immaculately kept bungalow on a street with smart gardens and clean pavements and lamp-posts sporting neighbourhood watch stickers. He stood, stooping slightly, peering out over a pair of half-glasses at Holder as he proffered his warrant card. He then raised his eyes and his stern gaze took in Anna. She returned it, noting the slack flesh of his jowls and the thin moustache. He looked like someone who'd lost a lot of weight too quickly. An image of the portly form that had bustled his way confidently through a dozen TV interviews during the original Woodsman monster hunt sprang to mind. Something was eating, or had eaten away at Briggs. The question remained as to whether it was something physical or mental.

'What do you want?' Briggs asked, his voice was soft.

'A few questions regarding retired Chief Inspector Wyngate,' Anna said.

Briggs looked hard at her, giving nothing away. 'My supper's in the oven. It'll be ready in eight minutes. I'll give you till then.' Briggs turned and walked inside, leaving the door open. Holder shrugged to Anna and followed the old man into a small parlour. Briggs didn't ask them to sit. Instead, he stood in the centre of the room, hands clasped behind his back. Behind him on the walls were framed photographs of himself in the force, receiving handshakes and praise.

'Constable Holder and I are part of—'

Briggs stopped her with one wave of his hand. 'Give me some credit. I know who you are, I know why you're here.'

'Do you? Then I'll get to the point. It can't have been easy facing all that criticism when Cooper's conviction was quashed. Mr Wyngate seems… reluctant to accept it. In addition, he's been involving himself with DCI Harris in the Nia Hopkins investigation.'

Briggs grunted. 'Get to the point.'

'Why do you think Wyngate is so interested in Cooper still?'

'Why shouldn't he be? The case made him.'

'Like it made you, you mean?'

'Not quite. I wasn't looking for any promotion but I was commended. So was Wyngate.'

'What about Maddox?'

Briggs rolled forward onto the balls of his feet. 'I won't have you disparaging a good copper like Dave Maddox in this house. He wasn't scared to get his hands dirty when the going got rough. He did as he was told. That's all you want in a DS.'

'I'm intrigued as to why he wasn't commended, that's all.'

'If they'd have listened to me, he would have been.'

'Why didn't they listen? Did it have anything to do with the fact that his methods were less than scrupulous?'

Briggs's voice hardened. 'You know nothing at all about Maddox.'

Anna wanted to push him on this. 'I know he was disciplined for actions likely to pervert the course of justice.'

Briggs stuck his chin out. 'Maddox was a good copper who put hundreds of villains away. Villains who wouldn't think twice about robbing you or raping you, or worse.'

'We have proof that Maddox concocted evidence, suppressed evidence, basically made it up as he went along. Wyngate won't talk about it and I'm wondering if he really knew about it at the time. From what I've learned, Maddox answered only to you.'

Briggs's mouth cracked open into a wintry smile. 'Let me tell you what I told the CPS. Intelligent discrimination is what clears up cases. Discrimination that comes from experience.' He shifted his gaze deliberately towards Holder. 'You catch muggers by targeting little shits with pit bulls and bloody tea cosies for hats. You find drugs in hippies' backpacks. Those are facts.'

'That's an abuse of Stop and Search and you know it,' Anna said.

Briggs shook his head. 'You go after targets with your mind fixed, knowing you'll find something. And if they know you know they're guilty, it helps a lot.'

Next to her, Anna could sense Holder seething.

'The press were on your back. You'd have had pressure coming from above. You couldn't have been far off retiring. It must have been tempting to go for the easy target.'

Briggs shook his head, but his eyes were telling a different story. Ragged, the lids blepharitic and swollen, they stared back at her with defiance. Or was that guilt that she read there?

Anna shook her head sadly. 'Wyngate had doubts, didn't he?'

Briggs continued to wear that icy grin.

'And Maddox did all your dirty work for you.'

From somewhere in the house a buzzer sounded.

'That's my supper,' Briggs said. He walked back to the front door and held it open for them.

'You realise that you're going to have to face all this once we find the killer.' Anna couldn't resist the taunt.

Briggs didn't reply but the whole building seemed to shake from the force with which the front door was slammed in their faces.

*

The driver of the 21.05 Paddington to Swansea train reported seeing what he thought was a mannequin hanging from a bridge near Magor. He was about to commence his deceleration on the approach to Newport when it appeared in the lights.

He caught no more than a glimpse in the front beams and then heard the thump as the train struck. *Kids*, he thought. *You'd have thought they'd have got Guy Fawkes out of their damn systems after Bonfire Night.* It shook him quite badly to think of kids out at that time at night. Especially kids throwing things off bridges.

He called his superiors and the transport police were informed. They sent a team out to investigate, but it was almost 7.30 a.m. on Thursday when Anna took the call from Holder.

'It looks like they've found Charles Willis.'

'Is he OK?' Relief surged through her, but evaporated on hearing Holder's next sentence.

'No, ma'am. He's strewn over a quarter of mile of railway track on the main Paddington to South Wales line.'

CHAPTER TWENTY-FIVE

It was a steel-grey morning on the other side of the Bristol Channel, heavy with the promise of rain on a chill sea breeze. Anna met Holder and Khosa on the approach to the bridge near Magor where the train had struck the body. She'd crossed on the second Severn Crossing, coming off the motorway at Junction 23A, and had driven along the winding lanes that divided the flat landscape of the estuary. Now she parked at the end of a line of police cars and, walking up, she could see that it was a thirty-foot fall to the tracks beneath the bridge. A young uniform stopped her at the police cordon, but Holder emerged from behind a white Scientific Support Unit van and waved her through.

'Morning, ma'am,' he said, with little of his usual joviality. 'I'll take you up.'

At the parapet, Anna looked down on a small army of white-overalled CSI officers combing the tracks, with uniformed transport police in the hedgerows searching for clues.

'They've bagged fourteen separate body parts so far,' Khosa said as she joined Anna.

'Has there been a formal ID?'

'Pathologist says it's impossible. The head and upper body are unrecognisable. He was corkscrewed under the wheels. We're relying on document ID and clothing for the moment,' Holder said.

Khosa shivered.

A uniformed officer approached and Holder stepped to one side to speak to him.

'Driver's quite shaken. Thought it was kids messing about,' Holder said, turning back to Anna.

She grimaced. 'Can't have been pleasant.'

'Bound and dumped in front of an Inter-bloody-city. Bastard.' Khosa glowered.

The area was surprisingly built up. Half a dozen houses nestled within a stone's throw of where they stood, screened from the five lines of track by a tall line of trees. From their vantage point, Anna could look east towards the swollen river, where it ballooned out towards the channel. A quarter of a mile further on and the houses petered out to be replaced by fields and hedgerows. To the west, new estates had sprung up in what was the newest part of the M4 corridor. She peered down the railway track itself. This section had several bends. To the north and south, it was a bare four hundred yards before the line curved out of sight, but she could see four bridges from where she stood, some designed for traffic, others mere footbridges.

'I can't believe no one saw anything,' she said eventually.

Holder pointed to some scaffolding poles that stood proud of the parapet towards the edge of the bridge. 'They're repairing the supports. It's like a hide under there, look.'

Anna and Khosa followed Holder thirty yards to the west. He leaned over a fence so that he could look back at the bridge. 'There. See that tarpaulin? The workers leave it hanging up as protection against the weather.'

Anna followed Holder's pointing finger and took in the flapping grey-green sheet hanging under the bridge. The scaffolding extended across in a spindly framework beneath the whole span. He was right. It was perfect camouflage. They went back up and stood for a while, watching, until they turned away collectively, letting the specialists do their job.

'We found the Isuzu in a side street two hundred yards away. There are no security cameras,' Khosa said. 'But Osbourne's fingerprints are all over the steering wheel. He nicked the jeep, hid up somewhere and drove Willis to this spot last night after…'

She didn't need to say it. They were all still raw from what had been done to Gail Willis.

Holder shook his head. 'We need to find this bastard.'

'Where's Harris?'

Khosa pointed a thumb over one shoulder towards the line. 'Down there somewhere. I'd say this has become something more than personal with him.'

And so it should, Anna thought. She'd warned him of the consequences of showing his hand regarding Cooper too early. Harris knew he should have taken her more seriously. Now they had two more murders on their hands and being right held little consolation for her. She'd give anything to have been wrong and still have the Willises alive.

Holder shook his head. 'What's Osbourne going to achieve by all this except to make us more sodding angry? It's like he doesn't give a toss any more.'

'It could be just that,' Anna said. 'This has all been brewing for seventeen years, remember. But you're right. The sooner we find Osbourne, the better.' It sounded reasonable, and everything pointed to Osbourne as their perpetrator, but she had to admit to herself that she shared Holder's confused consternation as to what was going through this man's very disturbed mind.

The rain started then, spitting out at them on the gusting wind, cold and lancing. 'Look, there's very little we can do here.' Anna turned her back to the wind and pulled her coat about her. 'Can we get out of this?'

'Of course, ma'am,' Khosa said.

'I'd like us to sit down and go over the who, what and why of what we actually know.'

Holder nodded. 'Sounds a better idea than hanging around here, ma'am.'

'If they find anything, I'll make sure they let us know immediately. It's Gwent police's patch,' Khosa added.

Anna glanced around once more at the toiling men below.

'Don't feel sorry for them, ma'am. At least they're alive to complain about the weather,' muttered Khosa.

Back at Portishead, they'd barely had time to sit down before Trisha took a call. 'DCI Harris has called a conference for two p.m.'

'Fine. That should give us enough time,' Anna said, hearing her own words bounce around in the echo chamber inside her head and wishing she could believe them. She needed to bring the team back into focus. The key to the horrific events of the present lay in the past and she needed them all to concentrate on what had happened right at the beginning.

Patterns and habits. Everyone had them. People lived by them. Emily Risman worked, and travelled, and did things that she would have been unaware of, that would have been invisible to her but not to other people. And Anna liked patterns. What detail had they seen and ignored since they'd opened this cold case that held the code to unlocking the door?

She was supposed to be good at this stuff, wasn't she?

Anna squeezed her eyes shut before looking at the whiteboard once again. 'I know that what happened last night has distracted us so I thought we ought to review what we know.'

She ran through everything, her memory detail-perfect, revisiting Emily's movements on the day she went missing.

Holder and Khosa both nodded along.

'So, what about contradictory evidence?' Anna asked, her abrupt question taking the other two by surprise.

'Mr Stanton, the van driver,' Holder said triumphantly, 'I know Ryia ended up going down a few blind alleys, but it was Trisha who finally tracked him down.' He nodded towards the analyst who smiled. 'He is now a resident of The Meadows nursing home in Kidderminster,' Holder continued. 'Had a small stroke five years ago but he's still pretty switched on. I spoke to him last night and he remembers Maddox interviewing him quite clearly. In fact he even remembers being pretty cheesed off that no one came back to him for details.'

'Does he remember what he saw?'

Holder riffled through his pad. 'He was sitting in his van reading the paper and eating a sandwich in a corner of the car park. He watched Emily Risman walk across to a dark blue saloon that then drove off.'

'Can he remember the make of car?'

'He thought it was an old… umm… Cortina?' Holder held up a printed image of the model and pinned it to the board.

'What was Osbourne driving at the time?'

'A blue Escort.' He flourished another image and pinned it up next to the first.

Anna looked hard at the cars. 'How far away was Stanton?'

'Seventy odd yards.'

'So even though the make is not quite the same, it would do for Osbourne's car?'

'The old Escorts were pretty boxy at that time.'

'Did you suggest to Stanton that it might have been an Escort?'

'Yes. He admitted it could have been.'

'Good. And Emily stepped into the car of her own volition?' Anna asked.

'Yes. Obviously knew the driver.'

'OK,' Khosa said. 'So, Osbourne met her and took her back to the forest that afternoon.'

Holder took up the ball and ran with it. 'He takes her to the woods, comes on to her and she says no because she's having a thing with Roger Willis. Is, in fact, pregnant with Willis's kid. Osbourne loses it and kills her. He panics, tries to bury her, is disturbed.

Waits for the police to sniff around, twigs that they like Cooper, and plants the underwear.'

Khosa nodded. 'It also maybe explains why he's gone after Charles and Gail. Grumbling resentment for Roger Willis getting Emily pregnant?'

'It's a stretch, but I suppose resentment could easily brew into hate,' agreed Anna.

'Right,' said Holder, holding his palm out in front of him with the fingers splayed and squeezing his eyes shut in a gesture that said he'd just remembered something important. He slid across to his desk and came up with some stapled sheets. 'Accident reports from France. I've had these for almost a week but they kept slipping my mind.'

Anna took them and scanned them quickly.

'The gist of it is that Charles Willis was driving, lost control on a bend and went down an embankment into a river. He got out, his brother didn't.' Holder said.

'Not alcohol related?'

Holder shook his head. 'Wet night. There were dozens of accidents, apparently.'

'Nothing to indicate mechanical failure or sabotage, or them being forced off the road?'

'You don't think that Osbourne…' Holder let his sentence hang.

'Just a thought,' said Anna. 'Worth checking on Osbourne's movements at that time. Was he in the country? And the same applies to the serial sexual assaults. Ryia, set up a meeting with Thames Valley. Let them know what we have.'

Khosa nodded.

Holder was looking chirpy. 'So, it's looking good for it being Osbourne all the way through, isn't it?'

'It is,' said Anna with little enthusiasm. 'Doesn't help us get anywhere nearer him though, does it? We can only hope that he's not harbouring a grudge against anyone else.'

'I can't see us second-guessing this bloke at all.'

'Agreed. We need to go over everything again today. Emphasis on the original interviews and what information Sue Donaldson has given us. See if there's anywhere that he could have gone to ground or if we can get a handle on what his next move is likely to be. The area where Nia was found had been searched two days before her body turned up there. He had her hidden somewhere out there in the woods, I'm sure of it.'

The idea of a lair crept into her head and wouldn't leave.

'You won't be going to the conference then?' Holder asked.

'Not this time,' said Anna. 'I'm sure you two can handle it perfectly.'

'Won't be the same, ma'am,' Holder complained.

'You'll survive, Justin.'

Anna read and reread her notes until her eyes burned with dryness. Outside, through the window, the day descended into a colourless drizzle and then heavy rain. Her journey home was an unpleasant, gloomy trip through a constant wall of spray. The drive demanded all her concentration and the unanswered questions thrown up by her endeavours simmered on the back burner of her consciousness, fighting with the droning buzz of that enigmatic certainty she had that the answers were all there, but hidden under a morass of superfluous information. She got home at four, changed into joggers and braved the rain for the retail delights of Waitrose.

She could, she knew, have gone to Gloucester and listened to the theories, but she didn't need that. Didn't want that. What she wanted was some time alone inside her head.

There was a reason, albeit twisted and pathological, for Osbourne's seemingly mindless violence against Gail and Charles Willis, just as there was a link between what had happened to Emily and the rapes he had been committing. Those certainties plagued her. But she'd spent too much time focused on the hard-boiled facts of the problem. What she needed to do now was give free rein to her imagination to allow it to make that empathic leap and try, for one moment, to truly think like Osbourne did. Like Shaw did.

She wasn't psychic and the effortless way TV sleuths managed to 'become' the killers they were chasing always filled her with amusement. But she had learned techniques; ways of divorcing herself, of taking on board the extreme aspects of the human condition that went beyond the normal bounds of behaviour. She needed to try and understand the subjective state of the killer at the time that he committed his crimes.

That process had begun on her way back from the railway tracks in Wales. This was also the main reason for her wanting to be away from the frenetic intensity of the station. Khosa had seen and understood it, Holder had not.

Anna bought groceries and took them home to the kitchen. It was about time, she reasoned, that she cooked something decent. But it was also part of the process. Food preparation relaxed her, occupied her, let the right side of her brain do its thing.

She made mustard chicken pie, with mangetouts and a pasta salad. She ate, drank water and found a Deezer playlist on her iPhone. This stuff was a country mile away from her father's music. Beyond the Wizard's Sleeve, Midlake, London Grammar; folk rock psychedelia to free her mind and let the nuggets of that day's conversations mingle with the stark and dreadful images she kept in the lock box of her professional mind. Anna sat on her sofa and tried to wind down.

Gail Willis loomed large, as did the Hopkins family; the railway bridge a new and oozing wound. Wyngate hovered in the wings, and the outliers – the things that had nothing to do with the Woodsman – buzzed in and out like irritating flies that needed swatting: her CILF images and, of course, Shaw. Bogeymen that simply wouldn't go away. And try as she might to push them to the back of her mind, and concentrate instead on Osbourne and where it all began – in the depths of an ancient pagan forest and its silent watching trees – a collage of horror remained. Emily and her dead beseeching hand; Gail's bulging eyes; Nia; and Megan Roberts' damaged life, all swirled around like leaves in a drain, blocking out any clear thought.

Anna tried to force it. It still troubled her that she didn't have the whole picture about Osbourne. What had triggered this need for murder? Where did his ability to meld into the environment come from? Everything pointed towards him, and his skill with wood had a kind of resonance with the awful sobriquet. Yet there was something she could almost touch that bothered her, but that wouldn't crystallise into anything solid, and so she was left with a vague awareness that scratched away inside her head.

Intuition, Anna?

That thought brought with it the realisation that everything was on the line. Rainsford had trusted her to clear up this case, and so far all her efforts had drawn a blank. It seemed to her that Shipwright's trust and belief had all been misplaced, too. Perhaps she should go back to being the sergeant and let someone else take the weight. Someone like Harris.

The idea made her cringe.

At a little after eight, her work phone rang. Holder's mobile number. The background drone told her he was in a car on hands-free.

'How was the meeting?' Anna asked before he could say anything.

'Nothing new, ma'am,' Khosa said now. 'They're tracing Willis's relatives. There's an aunt somewhere. I'm not sure why. There's not enough of Willis's head left to identify. It'll be dental records, once they find all the pieces for a reconstruction. They're still out there looking, apparently. Slack had Sue Donaldson back in but she's a wreck.'

Holder said now, 'No point you being there, ma'am. Waste of time. They're no further forward.'

Khosa once more: 'What about you, ma'am? Any joy?'

'No. Nothing. You two get home. We'll have a fresh look in the morning.'

She put down the phone and tried to marshal her meandering ideas. Something Holder had said a long time ago snagged on a niggling thought. But it vanished almost as soon as she became aware of it. She needed to organise her head before it would come back to her. She was surprised by how confident she was that it would.

Vengeful, that was the word that sprang to mind. First Gail, then Charles had met a brutal end. And there was no doubt now that Gail's murder had been carried out maliciously. If Osbourne had committed all the sexual assaults, then doing what he'd done to Gail was a big departure. She didn't fit the profile of the rape cases. It meant that he was no longer differentiating. Whatever survival instinct had held him back from killing before had gone. Firstly with his willingness to coldly implicate Cooper by killing Nia and then a malignant resentment festering over eighteen years finally unleashed as hate with what he'd done to Gail.

Yet, Charles's death was something else again.

Such a ruthless destruction of another human being smacked of vindictive malevolence, a need to finally wipe Willis off the face of the earth. There would be nothing left except mangled flesh and bone and the torn remnants of the clothes he was dressed in. Why was Osbourne so intent on ridding his world of any trace of the Willises? What had happened between them all those years ago to engender such hate?

Could Osbourne have taken offence to Emily's pregnancy and transmitted blame to Roger Willis's brother? Had Gail been simply collateral damage?

It didn't quite fit. Would a nineteen-year-old have been troubled by an insult to his manhood in such a way? Most nineteen-year-olds she'd dealt with possessed no paternal aspirations whatsoever. Unless there was another element. *Osbourne was infertile but what about impotence?*

Psychosexual dysfunction in a normal setting could escalate towards an aggressive reaction aimed at the partner, or if you extrapolated it, victim. But Sue Donaldson had mentioned only infertility and they'd need to ensure Osbourne's movements did fit with the rapes and attempted rapes.

And all the while he was still out there, running, looking for somewhere to hide in all that vastness—

And there it was. The thought that Holder's words had snagged on. Something he'd said right at the beginning when they'd visited the forest… its remoteness… about the fact that the only way to get around was with a car… Anna stood up, blowing out air as if she'd just finished a round of press-ups.

The writhing, twisting tentacle of an idea reached out from the murky waters of her mind to strike. It floated tantalisingly close before drifting away. She stood stock-still, as if she'd been hit by a gorgon's stare, waiting for it to drift back again. It did and she felt her pulse tick in her throat the second before she had it.

The reason Willis had *to be annihilated.*

She held the idea up for inspection, took it apart, looked at it from all angles, shone the brightest light of doubt she could muster on all of its facets, and knew, with a dread certainty, that it worked.

This was a clever, devious and troubled mind they were dealing with. A mind that contemplated eventualities for eighteen years and emerged with a dreadful, cynical, sickening strategy. It was such an abhorrent idea that she struggled not to shy away from it, unwilling to accept the harrowing implications. But it fitted. All of it.

She glanced at her watch and realised that it was almost ten already. She'd been worrying at this case for hours. Nevertheless, she reached for her phone and dialled Slack's mobile; the background chatter that accompanied his greeting hinted at a social setting.

'Evening, ma'am.'

'Sergeant, I realise it's late.'

'An hour to closing time. Not late at all.'

'I've just got off the phone with Holder. He briefed me on the conference.'

'I've been in better meetings,' Slack said.

'I've had some new thoughts. They may sound totally off the wall, so I need you to do something for me before I run off at the mouth and end up in that place where they wear the nice white coats with the buckles in the back.'

'I don't follow you, ma'am.'

'I want you to get hold of the specialist that runs the infertility clinic where Osbourne and his wife are patients.'

'Uh…. do I have a reason for doing that on a Friday night, ma'am?'

'Yes, Sergeant, a very good reason.'

She explained to Slack as briefly as possible. He listened without comment, whether it was through respect or frank disbelief, she wasn't sure.

Anna tried reading in the hope that it might lull her to sleep. But at midnight, she was wide awake, unable to do anything but wonder how successful Slack was at twisting a few officious arms and frustrated at knowing he would only get back to her in the morning. She went into the kitchen and made some hot chocolate, took it back to the living room and watched her current TV fix. By one, she'd numbed her brain enough with the vicissitudes of fiction to feel that sleep would come and took to her bed to await whatever the dawn might bring.

CHAPTER TWENTY-SIX

The same midnight hour under the same November sky. And in this place, too, this stone chamber carved out of the rock beneath the earth, a mind sits preoccupied with its own thoughts, waiting for the dawn in hungry anticipation.

He'd found it years before during one of his expeditions into the forest; the place where he felt, like any animal, most at home. He'd met some cavers setting off to explore the old stone mines. Curious and fascinated, he'd watched them being swallowed up by the ground. He'd come back to the spot, had found another entrance and below it the chamber. Inside there'd been crockery, crates for sitting on, old newspapers. He'd concluded that this must have been a rest area, hived off from the main shafts. A staging post for workers, now long since dead, to enjoy their tuck and tea.

The mine had closed a century ago and the entrance from the chamber to the main shaft was half blocked by rock fall. He'd completed the job, hauling pieces in from the large chambers beyond. Above ground it had been easy to conceal the entrance, so no one but he would know of its existence. And then he'd made the chamber *his*. Literally somewhere he could go to ground.

He could live there for days. Enough air from above found its way into the mine and through gaps he'd left in the walls he'd constructed. He'd bought a battery-operated lamp, which provided light, and warmth if needed, though he didn't find the cold to be a problem. He hunted rabbits in the forest. Cooked and ate when he could. Hunted other prey when the need took him, subdued them, *squeezed* them. And from them he procured his trophies. He tried to take things that were important to them, that they'd feel the loss of. Like the vet. He'd watched her limp back to the van. Saw her scream and cry in frustration at what he'd done. He'd loved that. And her trophies proved to be useful as well.

But tonight, in the light of the battery lamp, he knew it was the last time he'd spend any time in this place. He picked his precious prizes up in turn, handling them tenderly, remembering each girl with the touch. He thought about enjoying them once more, but decided not to. He'd save himself for the task in hand. And perhaps, if it all went well, one day he would return. Stronger, more powerful even than he'd become already. He looked forward to that day. It buoyed him.

There was one more piece of the poison that had tainted his existence to cut away. He'd bought himself some time. Not much, but enough. Tomorrow he would be reborn once more. One final act before he could change, transform himself. He'd need to leave his hiding place and his forest for a while, but he could do that. Needs must. He turned off the lamp and sat in the complete darkness, letting it flow over him. He'd let his eyes adjust before leaving, though he didn't need to. His hearing and smell and touch would find the way through the dark forest. Like any good Woodsman could.

CHAPTER TWENTY-SEVEN

Anna awoke, after finally falling asleep at around 2 a.m., to cold sunlight streaming in through a chink in the bedroom curtains. She squinted at the bedside clock and, not seeing it clearly, pushed herself up, brushing hair away from her eyes and face.

7.10 a.m. She never slept beyond six thirty. She pushed her hair back and checked her phone. No messages, but her news feed had a headline from a red-top that caught her eye.

WOODSMAN KILLER IS SERIAL RAPIST

Gloucestershire police refused to comment last night over allegations made by sources close to the investigation that the killer of eighteen-year-old Emily Risman, butchered in a beauty spot in the Forest of Dean in 1998, and more recently sixteen-year-old Nia Hopkins, was also a rapist they had been hunting for eighteen years. Last week, Thames Valley police revealed thus-far-withheld details of a serial rapist who had committed twenty brutal attacks in four counties. Sources confirmed last night that they were investigating the possibility that one man was responsible, but refused to elaborate.

The authorities' failure to comment in a case that has captured the public's imagination is bound to fuel further speculation. With the man known as the Woodsman, Neville Cooper, stable in hospital after an abortive suicide attempt while in police custody, sources have also refused to rule out the possibility that Cooper, awaiting retrial for the murder of Emily Risman, may not have been acting alone.

In a new twist, the identity of a body found on the main railway line between South Wales and London has been confirmed as that of Charles Willis, husband of Gail Willis, who was found murdered in the garden of her own home just days ago. Police have released the name of a man wanted in connection with the rapes and murders of these three women. Richard Osbourne is thought to be dangerous and the public are advised not to approach him if sighted.

A candid photograph of Osbourne took up one column. The journalists had chosen the image for maximum effect. Taken at work, Osbourne was smiling, a hammer in one hand.

This new connection provides yet another bizarre twist in what has become a cause célèbre for the Southwest Major Crimes Review task force, who have been re-examining the Woodsman killings following the release of Neville Cooper.

Anna scrolled down to find her own face staring back at her from a grainy black and white portrait taken years before. Beneath was a caption: *Inspector Anna Gwynne, leading the investigation.*

She groaned. Another leaked story to the press they could have done without.

Photographs of the victims stared back at her accusingly: Emily, Nia and Gail were the silent witnesses with all the answers. She read on with growing incredulity as her theories were expounded in black and white. Someone, somewhere, had tipped them off. She read the article again, the flush rising from her chest to her neck like warm water.

Fucking press.

Even now they would not let Neville Cooper off the hook. And linking the rapes to Nia's and Emily's murders was something she had hoped to avoid, but with Willis dead and Osbourne on the run, it was unlikely to cause much damage. Indeed, there was very little there that truly jeopardised the investigation, but seeing her face splashed all over the news made her cringe. On edge and needing to find an outlet for the frustrations, Anna threw on her running gear and set off with a small backpack containing only water and her phones.

She'd gone with her intuition in asking Slack to find out about Osbourne's clinic visit. He may, or may not, have taken her seriously. Harris's team did not have a good track record when it came to that. She allowed herself a little rueful snort. She wanted so much to believe that it would yield results. Wanted desperately to know that by trusting in herself – this strange alchemy of analysis and instinct that had, so far in her life, caused nothing but angst – it might once, just once, come up with the goods. Never mind the plaudits, never mind the glory. She wanted to nail this monster and, if nothing else, to at least justify her dad's belief in her.

She'd ring Slack as soon as she got in to the office. It was too early to do it now. And if it all came to nothing, she'd console herself with knowing that she'd at least given Tobias a chance to finally clear Cooper's name. But Anna knew that would not be enough for her. Even thinking these thoughts brought a wave of guilt. Shaw had seen through her and tapped into her ambition. He'd seen how desperate she was to prove herself worthy of those who believed in her, even if she sometimes didn't believe in herself. But none of this was about her now. Her hunger was driven by a need to stop this man from ruining another life. Murder was the ultimate crime, but rape could desecrate a life in another kind of way just as easily.

Better that she release the tension that was wound so tightly in her head with a run.

*

Mist had rolled up the channel during the night and, though the sun was up, grey murk hung over the city's rooftops and the naked branches of the trees on Horfield Common. Street lights were still on, glowing like miniature suns, each surrounded by a soft halo of water vapour. Even the usual hum of traffic seemed distant and strange as cars rolled by, slowed by the conditions, their lights looming out of the fog, their engine noises oddly subdued, rubber tyres on wet tarmac hissing like snakes.

Anna crossed the common and hit the damp streets, letting her mind beat its own path, praying silently that her efforts and those of everyone else involved in the horror that the Woodsman case had become would finally pay off. In the mile and a bit to Badock's Wood, she passed commuters muffled against the chill mist. When her eyes met theirs for the briefest of moments, in the split second it took for her to pass, she read wary acknowledgement.

In the summer, she was often met with smiles. But winter had arrived and with it the knowledge that every one of these people would face their journey to and from work in the darkness for another three months. If they'd seen the news that morning they'd know, too, about what the Woodsman was capable of. Fanciful though it might be, Anna found herself easily believing that she saw some of the horror of his actions etched on every face she passed. Few, if any, welcomed the coming winter, their moods a slave to a wired reaction shared with ancestors as old as the hills. An irrational fear perhaps, but one that most people were helpless to resist and augmented by knowing there was a monster in their midst.

Even in the twenty-first century, warm-blooded animals all knew that things hunted in the dark.

CHAPTER TWENTY-EIGHT

He'd stolen the bicycle from a side street off the Gloucester Road. Bolt cutters dealt with the puny chain easily. He'd chosen this one because there'd been a helmet as well and he wanted to blend in. He'd made passes on the bike, past where she lived, biding his time in the cold damp morning on the common, letting the hunger grow, embracing it, allowing it to become him and him it. He cursed the weather. He hated the wet, preferred dry conditions for his work, but today there would be no choice. And the poor visibility would undoubtedly play to his advantage, blurring details, favouring stealth. Eventually, his patience had been rewarded in spades.

He'd toyed with the idea of confronting her on her doorstep. Now he knew exactly where she'd be. A risky gambit still; even this early there were too many people on the streets. But she'd emerged dressed for running. He smiled. It was all coming together. There'd been an inevitability about it ever since he'd first watched her; her and the other detective. He'd even showed himself, his ghost self, up on the ridge. He'd thought she'd seen him. He'd wanted her to see him; his form in the woods. She'd given no sign other than to pause and peer. But he knew. The connection was made. The deal sealed there and then.

Now, in the damp morning air, he followed in silence, stalking her, keeping well back, his keen eyes on the prize. He was good at stalking. Good at watching and waiting. Ever since his brother made him wait in the woods until he'd finished with Emily all those years ago, because he'd needed help to get home through the darkening gloom even then. But he did more than wait. He *watched*.

Watched his brother and Emily at it. *Watched* and felt his groin stir. Knowing instantly he wanted it, too. He'd waited for his chance, plied Emily with cider one early evening and she'd laughed when he'd suggested she let him do it like his big brother. He hadn't liked the laughter. He did it anyway with her trying to fight him off. But he'd been too strong for her even at just over fourteen. She'd stormed off afterwards, calling him names. But when, four months later, she'd arranged to meet him, he'd brought condoms, convinced that she'd relented.

But she'd wanted to meet him to talk about something else. Three months pregnant and about to start showing. Threatened him with all sorts if he didn't sort it. There was a clinic over at Gloucester but she'd need money. If he didn't get her the money then she was going to the police to tell them what he'd done. Him and his blind brother could go fuck themselves.

That was when he'd lost it. He'd wanted her to shut up. Wanted her to stop the threats and the taunts. He'd put his hands around her neck just to stop the words more than anything. There'd been no planning but when he saw them there, they looked so cool in the Oakley gloves he'd nicked from the cycle shop in Coleford. She'd struggled mightily, but he was strong from helping his father in the woodland. Before his accident, Willis's father could cut down a forty-foot pine with twenty strokes on a good day, and Charles was a quick learner. His fingers were long, his thumbs meeting in the middle over her larynx as he squeezed the apple. Emily fought, but he squeezed even more and, to his surprise, she passed out. For a moment, he thought she was dead, but when he stopped she coughed and sucked in air.

It thrilled him.

Emily Risman, moaning, half choked, lying there just waiting for him. He'd never felt so excited, never felt so hard. This time he did wear a condom. Kept his hands on her neck as he rode her, squeezing whenever she started to fight.

And that moment shaped him. Became the mould that he was poured into, where he hardened and cured to the beast that would always need feeding.

He finished with Emily and rolled off. Got up and adjusted his trousers. She'd moaned again, but she was breathing. He reached down to retrieve his school backpack and, when he turned back, she was sitting up, glaring at him, horror and disgust written all over her face, her own hands over her livid, bruised neck. It was then that she'd started to scream.

He'd tried to stop her, tried to tell her that it would be OK. But she was hysterical, terrified of him, pushing herself away on her backside to get away. The knife was in his backpack. Something he always carried, not because he wanted to use it on another person, but because it was a tool of his father's trade, the trade he was likely to go into.

He'd hoped that showing it to her might stop her noise, but all it did was make it worse. *People would hear her. People would come.*

After he'd used the knife a dozen times, she'd stopped screaming. He'd added a dozen more to her belly just to be sure. He'd tried to hide the body as best he could, finding a natural hollow, meaning to completely cover her, but he'd heard voices and had had to abandon it. Yet not before he'd noticed the way she looked. A nymph, half covered by leaves, so still, as if she were emerging from the earth and the trees.

So beautiful.

Afterwards, he was scared. Scared enough to tell his brother what he'd done. Adding a small but important lie. That he'd done it because Emily had told him that the baby was Roger's and that she was going to ruin his life.

They'd hatched the cover-up between them, used Cooper as the scapegoat. And, after a while, Charles Willis forgot about the screaming and the blood. But what he didn't forget was the way that Emily had lain there for him. Quiet, submissive, semiconscious from *his* power.

He saw her in his dreams.

His brother Roger was weak. A bleeding heart. It would have done no one any good for the truth to come out. The river had been an obvious answer.

And still he dreamed of Emily. Quiet Emily, his first one.

After a while, he made the dreams a reality again.

Just as he was about to do with this one.

CHAPTER TWENTY-NINE

She entered Badock's Wood at Lakewood Road along the hard tarmac path. The weather and the hour meant that few had yet ventured out. She passed two dog walkers and a few cyclists, crossed the River Trym and took a right along the river path, settling in to her rhythm, enjoying the wood and the freedom it represented. Such a welcome haven in the heart of this city, Anna thought. Others had found this space of significance over the millennia. A Bronze Age barrow in the northwest corner attested to that. They'd brought their dead to this sacred place, but Anna relished it because it allowed her the space to feel alive.

She'd completed two-thirds of the loop, and was on the return leg along a soft woodland path, when her phone rang. Unslinging her backpack, the ring tone told her it was her work mobile. Panting, she accepted the call.

'Hello?'

Slack answered. 'Morning, ma'am.' He paused, hearing her breathing. 'Is this a bad time?'

'No. Morning run. Need I ask if you've seen the newspapers?'

'Uh, yes, ma'am.'

'Any ideas as to who did it?' She stood on the deserted path, gazing up at the few leaves clinging on to the branches, waiting for Slack to explain.

'Someone in Thames Valley let it slip, ma'am. Some reporter contacted them claiming they had a source from inside prison who'd tipped them off about a likely link.'

She lifted her face to the sky. 'Shaw. I might have bloody guessed.'

'You know who this is?'

She snorted, and when she spoke her words were bitter as acid. 'I do, Sergeant. And God, do I keep underestimating him.'

'I do have one bit of good news. Your hunch. You hit the jackpot with the infertility clinic. You were right, they did have frozen semen samples. For legal reasons, they do genetic work-ups and a full DNA profile as a matter of course. They've had one or two problems of disputed paternity. You know – a redhead in a family of blonds – that sort of thing.' Slack sounded jaunty. 'They didn't like releasing the information, but the DNA from Osbourne's semen matches the DNA from the corpse found on the railway line.' Anna squeezed her eyes shut to relish the electric surge that pulsed through her. His words confirmed what she'd dared to believe. Words that changed *everything*. They'd been wrong. All wrong right from the start.

She dragged her tumbling thoughts back to the moment as Slack continued. 'I got the result five minutes ago. Superintendent Harris is with me but—'

'But what?'

'But what does it mean?'

'Isn't it obvious?' Anna started walking, her breathing gradually becoming easier, but her head whirling with the consequences of Slack's news.

'Not to me. Osbourne kills Emily, Nia and Gail and then decides to top himself. It doesn't make sense.'

'It makes perfect sense if you're Charles Willis.'

'*What?*'

She spoke quickly, wanting him to understand. 'What was left of the corpse we found on the railway line belonged to Osbourne. But we were made to think it was Willis. That's why Osbourne's in a hundred pieces, to make the ID nigh on impossible. The killer knew we'd go for the clothes and wallet. He knew we'd think it was Willis.'

'Then where is Willis?'

She looked up as a cyclist approached, stepped to one side to let him pass. 'Good question,' Anna replied.

'Hang on,' Slack said as a new thought solidified. 'I thought Willis was blind?'

Anna almost laughed out loud. 'That's what he wanted us all to think. And why shouldn't we when it's a hereditary condition that his brother most certainly had? But what evidence did we have except for what Charles Willis chose to show us?' Anna walked slowly on, pausing now and again along the path, turning, seeing the trees and the meadow beyond, but not seeing them either, wanting Slack to see what she had finally understood.

'But you saw the computer and that screen for magnifying things at Willis's house, yes?'

'Exactly. What better way to be the lie than to live it. The inheritance in the Willises' disease is X-linked, also known as sex-linked because it's carried by the X genes. The genes that determine the sex of the individual. It means their mother was a carrier. But Charles Willis was by no means sure of contracting the condition.'

She waited for Slack to comment but the stony silence that followed was not encouraging.

'God,' she said. 'It'd be easier if I could draw you a diagram. Look, X-linked disorders are carried on the X chromosome, of which you have one and I have two, being a female. Female carriers of X-linked conditions have an abnormal gene on one X chromosome, which is counterbalanced by a normal gene on the other X chromosome. The normal gene suppresses the effect of the bad one. You with me so far?'

'Keep going,' Slack said.

'That's why carriers generally don't manifest the disease. But male children of female carriers will inherit one of those two X chromosomes from their mothers – they inherit the Y chromosome from their fathers and that's what makes them boys.'

'Right, I can see that.'

She stood aside as a jogger hurried past, before continuing. 'So, obviously, they have a fifty per cent chance of inheriting the faulty gene from their mother, but it's an equal chance each time.'

'The Willis brothers had an equal chance?'

'Yes. One could be affected, the other had just as much chance of not being affected. The other could be entirely normal, is what I'm saying.'

'You mean Charles Willis was faking it? All of it?'

'Why not? He'd get sympathy from friends and lovers and help from the state. Anything he did off his own bat would be looked upon as a spectacular triumph. He'd seen his brother from close quarters. He'd know exactly how to behave. He had all the equipment.'

'But he was registered as blind. We found documentation with his name on it.'

'That means nothing. Registration involves a form filled in by a busy doctor who, more often than not, does it from a set of notes. Charles Willis could have modified any of his brother's documentation.'

She didn't think twice when the cyclist that passed her earlier turned around and stopped. It drew her attention momentarily. She watched him take off a backpack and remove something from it, vaguely registering the fact that it wasn't a water bottle but something else altogether. A camera maybe? The woods were always full of twitchers.

She turned her back on him, her mind on Slack, and took a step.

Slack said, 'Christ, that puts a whole new twist on things.'

'I know…'

A dull thud on the tree just to her left drew her attention. She looked up and then around. Had something fallen from a branch?

Her eyes clocked something on the floor. Long, a steel needle, with a plastic cylinder and a bright yellow tufted end. She reached down and picked it up. A dart? She pivoted. The cyclist was still there, twenty yards away, pointing something at her. *Something with a long barrel.*

She stared, momentarily uncomprehending, a frisson of fear squeezing her heart. She felt a sharp, bright stinging in her upper thigh and fell away from the impact, dropping the phone, her hand brushing at a point on her leg and feeling something hard quivering. Her eyes followed, seeing the dart, watching as her hand struck it, reacting as if it were an insect, pulling it out and letting it fall. It looked identical to the one she'd picked up near the tree. Long, a plastic barrel, a fluffed yellow stabiliser tail. But this one looked different, the barrel shorter from having discharged its load. The sting became a burning pain. Dark blood bloomed through her running pants on the front of her leg. She looked up again.

The bicycle was on its side off the path, the cyclist on foot, moving towards her purposefully, tearing the helmet off his head.

His head. Him. The Woodsman.

Slack's voice from the phone on the floor, tinny but urgent. 'Ma'am? *Inspector Gwynne?*'

She turned and ran, up off the path, towards cover, towards the trees. Up the slope, directionless, hearing him behind her, knowing she was quicker than him, trusting her body. If she made the top of the slope, she'd turn left. Back towards the burial mound and beyond it another entrance, a sports centre, people. No more than two hundred metres.

Easy. She was fit.

The pain in her leg slowed her down, altering her gait, but adrenalin was driving her, pushing blood through her heart and muscles. Bringing oxygen and glucose where it was desperately needed. But bringing, too, the veterinary grade ketamine and thiafentanil cocktail from the site of its injection deep in her quadriceps. It reached her brain just as she reached the top of the slope and Anna's world changed.

Time froze and her legs stopped pumping, her will and her power leeching away in a cloud of opiate-induced wonder. She was near a large tree. Waves of warmth oozed out of it. She stopped to touch it. It felt… wonderful. Anna's gaze drifted to the first unspent dart still clutched in her hand, its yellow tufted stabiliser looking suddenly and astonishingly vibrant before she leaned over and threw up. But her stomach was empty, and even the nausea didn't seem to matter.

Noises behind her.

She turned. He was there. Closing down on her. He pushed her over and she fell on her back. There was no pain. Even her leg didn't hurt any more. He dragged her ten yards further into the wood, the dart she'd been clutching spilling out as her head bumped over roots and earth. Her mewling cries were muted and vague as he pulled her away from sight of the path. Out of sight of prying eyes.

His hands tore at her weather-proof jacket and the running vest beneath. She tried to fight him but her arms were moving at a different speed, too sluggish to be effective. His open hand caught her a glancing blow on the head, but his second punch landed square on her nose and upper lip, mashing soft tissues against her teeth. She fell back, hands to her face, the salt in her own blood tasting amazing. He forced her down roughly, but she kept her hands over her nose until he kicked her in the belly. No pain, just a whooping expulsion of air as the breath was driven from her lungs. Something gave, a feeling like a soggy balloon rupturing inside her. She pulled her legs up, making herself a smaller target, but the fuzziness from the drugs slurred her words of pleading, turned her actions into slow-motion puppetry.

He hadn't spoken a word throughout. The only noise was his rapid breathing through the cycle mask. His eyes, locked on hers, were feral.

Seeing. Not blind.

He ripped off her running pants, the leaves cold and wet on her bare buttocks, before straddling her, his weight crushing, hands ripping, his knees forcing her legs apart. It was then that she knew she was going to die with this man on top of her. It would be his hands on her throat, or a knife in her chest, and all she could think of at that moment was of how she didn't fight enough. Slack would send help and it would arrive in time to find a still-warm corpse. Tears of sorrow and muted fear mingled with the blood in her mouth as she strained feebly to turn her head away from Willis's choking hands.

He sat back then, one hand squeezing her throat, the other clutching the glinting knife as it penetrated her breasts in sharp, stabbing bursts. He paused only to watch the blood run as she fought to ease the pressure on her windpipe. These were not deep wounds meant to kill. That would come later. He was playing with her. A cat with a mouse. But then her mind was drifting, lack of oxygen from one strong, choking hand colluding with the drug that was never meant for human use, pushing her towards unconsciousness.

A shadow behind him drew her flickering eyes. A human shape moving quickly and stealthily for its size. Sharp crack like a stick breaking, Willis stumbling forward over her, half turning. Another crack and another. Then the weight was off her. The sudden light above coned her vision, but she heard noises and yells and oaths. She turned her head, willing her eyes to follow.

Two people were struggling. The cyclist on top, knife still in his hand, held there by the second figure on the floor, reaching up, arms shaking from the strain of keeping that arm and knife away.

She wanted to close her eyes, to giggle at the ridiculousness of it, stopped herself in time. She brought her fingers up to touch the blood on her breasts. Her skin felt strange, unreachable. She turned over, wanting to hide herself, wanting to crawl away...until her eye caught the brilliant yellow tuft of the unspent dart that had fallen from her hand. It lay a yard away, intact, the plastic chamber primed, the sharp needle dull with mud.

Another yell and a grunt of effort from the combatants feet away from her. A voice shouting, desperate, 'Run!'

Despite her confusion, Anna knew she could not run. But she would not lie there, either. She crawled to the dart and picked it up. Sucking and blowing air like a steam train, she remained on her knees, the world swimming about her, and began crawling forwards. The cyclist had his back to her, kneeling over the other figure, limbs trembling with effort.

Moving was taking all her willpower and effort. It would be so easy to lie down, collapse on to the floor. *So easy…*

No! Not now. Not yet.

Another foot, another, the leaves and dirt sliding like slime beneath her, her head hanging. The men were close. The smaller man could see her, his face grimacing with effort, eyes wide with fear and sudden determination. She reached out, and the cyclist, jolted by her touch, turned to look. The cycling mask had slipped, or been torn off, and Anna saw Willis's face. Saw it and knew that all she'd surmised was true in the second before she summoned what was left of her energy and thrust the dart deep into the muscles of his back.

She fell, his foot kicking her away, unable to do any more, vaguely aware of the cyclist on his feet, arching his back, desperate to remove the dart, stumbling down the slope to the path, heading for his bike and not reaching it as the drugs took hold and he stumbled and fell.

The world darkened. Anna slid towards unconsciousness, but never quite reached its soothing shores. After seconds that felt like hours, she focused on a face leaning over her, large and craggy, the eyes full of concern. She concentrated, her own battered brows frowning, confused. She knew that face and yet couldn't name it, because it was the last one she'd ever expected to see at that moment. One hand on the collar of the coat he'd thrown over her; the other still clutching a long black steel baton. He saw her look at it and put it down with an apology.

'Done its job. I was watching your house. You were becoming the obvious target.' He squeezed her fingers and she was grateful for it.

'Thank you,' she said in a small voice.

'No, thank you,' said the craggy face. 'He was a strong bugger. Stronger than me.'

She found a smile of acknowledgement from somewhere, and tried to push it through her cracked and bleeding lips at the man who had promised Emily Risman's parents that he would find her killer. At last, retired Inspector John Wyngate had done just that.

CHAPTER THIRTY

They took Anna's spleen away, fixed her nose and sutured her breasts. And the cheerful surgeon that visited her said they could have done it all without a drop of anaesthetic, there was so much thiafentanil in her system.

Afterwards, after they'd reversed the opiate with naloxone and the ketamine had left her system, pain came in waves. Most of the time she declined the analgesics, preferring to use the aching as penance for her own stupidity. But sometimes she gave in to the soothing comfort of the analgesia pump she controlled with a push-button. A milligram of morphine now and then dulled everything just enough.

Kate and her mother were there when she regained consciousness, though her memory of those early hours were viewed through a grey filter. But when that cleared, it was her sister's hand and her mother's wailing that she registered. When she and her mother were alone together, Anna pretended to sleep so as not to have to listen to the cajoling.

'You'll have to leave the police force now, of course. Someone I spoke to in Tesco said that you could sue them. Besides the physical injuries there's post-traumatic stress…'

When it was only Kate, Anna made her promise not to leave her mother alone with her any more.

Holder and Khosa came to see Anna on the third day after surgery. She was lying on her bed, resting with her head on one side, staring at a print on the wall of the room they'd put her in. One of three prints of nineteenth-century anatomical drawings with all the muscles delineated. The one she was staring at was on the wall opposite the window. It showed a human leg. It was meant to seem elegant and pleasing; a reassurance of how science and technology had progressed. All it made Anna think of was a scene from a shark movie, where a severed leg had drifted silently and slowly to the ocean floor after a ferocious attack.

Holder knocked quietly and he and Khosa crept in.

As if noise could make things worse! Anna smiled, grateful for the distraction. Holder's gaze flitted over her, unsure on where to fixate on her face. She read in his closed expression the shock and horror of her appearance. It would all mend, the doctors said. But for now, every day was Hallowe'en.

'They've cancelled my photo-shoot with *Cosmo* for this week,' she said, her voice nasal from the splints up her nose.

Khosa smiled with relief, but the frown didn't leave her forehead.

They feel responsible, Anna thought. *They shouldn't.*

'They've given us ten minutes, ma'am,' Holder said. 'I didn't know whether we should've come but—'

'I need to know.' Her words emerged muffled because of her swollen tongue. They'd sutured a big laceration inside her mouth, caused by one of Willis's blows. It made it difficult to keep her lips moist.

'We've got Willis in a secure hospital. A few cuts and bruises but Wyngate didn't break his skull.' Holder sounded regretful.

'Has he said much?'

'He hasn't stopped, ma'am,' Khosa said. 'Claims to be full of remorse for the victims and their families. But I think I've caught him trying not to smile when we ask him how he tracked the rape victims.'

'Has it all come together?' Anna shifted in the bed and winced. Khosa reached out a hand but she waved it away.

'Everything. He'd obviously been following you. Saw you at Emily Risman's crime scene when we went to visit. You were right, we were being watched.'

'And Emily?'

'He picked her up at the bus station in Coleford,' Holder nodded. 'You were right there, too. She never caught the bus. The blue car that the witness reported was Willis's father's Granada.'

'With Willis driving?'

Khosa answered this time. 'Yes. His brother, Roger, had taught him to drive when he was fourteen. By then, Roger's eyesight was already fading so he had his little brother chauffeur him. That was how they managed the alibi. As you know, ma'am, Roger was out of the frame because of the hospital appointment and he told the court that he and his brother caught the bus to Gloucester. What they'd actually done was to take their father's car from the lock-up and drive. This cut the journey time in half and gave Charles ample time to get his brother back home and then get to Coleford to meet Emily.'

Anna nodded. Under the sink, to her right, between a metal bracket and the wall, she saw a spider scramble out over a dense, dusty cobweb. It had been her companion for three days, the only movement in the still quiet of the room. It turned now, showing her its large white abdomen before scrambling back to its nest to hide from the cleaners.

'It wasn't Roger Willis's baby she was carrying, was it?'

Khosa shook her head in agreement and a small smile of admiration appeared. 'No. It was Charles's baby. Emily knew it was Charles's because he was the only one that had not used a condom. She was angry with him. He says he panicked when she told him. Panicked and wanted to make her shut up. However, he told Roger that the child was his. Told him that Emily was about to blab, that was why he'd killed her. And best of all the blood tests came back positive, as well they might.'

'I don't understand.'

Holder spoke. 'I didn't either so I spoke to a forensic guy. In 1999, they used only thirteen locus matches in DNA tests, looking for thirteen different markers. The chance that two people will have the same DNA profile at all thirteen loci is infinitesimal. But, in brothers, the chance is much, much greater. They were similar enough, in the Willis case, to not cast a doubt over Willis's paternity. These days the more sophisticated DNA tests would have ruled Roger out. We would have got there eventually by retesting.'

Khosa added, 'It was his brother, he claims, who suggested planting the underwear at Cooper's house. To throw the police off. Neither of them thought for one moment that Cooper would confess. Eventually, Roger Willis simply couldn't live with it. That part is the one thing Willis won't talk about.'

Anna nodded. 'I'm not surprised. Roger Willis acted to protect his little brother, but then had to watch Neville Cooper rot in that prison, and that wouldn't go away. I suspect his guilt erupted each time Cooper's plight was paraded in the press. The year Roger died might have been the time of the first TV programme highlighting Cooper's appeal.'

Holder and Khosa stared at Anna in silence.

'I think Charles Willis drove off the road and into that river deliberately, to silence his brother,' Anna said.

Khosa winced. 'It must have been horrible. All that water rushing around you and not being able to even see.'

It didn't bear thinking about. Anna asked, 'So Willis was committing the rapes while Gail was away at her shop in Cheltenham?'

'It looks that way.' Holder nodded. 'I mean, who would suspect a blind man?'

'Gail. That's why he killed her,' Khosa said. 'Osbourne visited, Willis told us that. Wanted to speak to him about things. He saw the Isuzu, commented on it, thought he'd seen it over near Blakeney a couple of times when he'd been delivering his Cruck barns. Gail finally put two and two together and checked the mileage on the Isuzu. It didn't add up. Charles Willis got to Osbourne as he left. We found traces of the same stuff Willis used on you in the toxicology analysis of Osbourne's remains. He hasn't said much about Gail, but my guess is that it must have been her that tried to phone you that night, ma'am. Maybe she sneaked out and checked the car. Thinking it was safe in the dark until her husband caught her.'

Anna wanted to scream. She'd made mistakes. Sucked in like everyone else by Charles Willis's scheming. He'd even insisted that Gail have the Isuzu to keep her safe in the bad weather.

Sometimes her good memory was nothing but a curse because she could remember exactly what he'd said when they'd talked to him: *'Ever since I read about what the police did, the confession and suppressing evidence, it's made me boil inside.'*

'He's probably laughing at us, is he?' Anna asked, the pain in her face thumping again.

'At the CCRC he is. He says Maddox was a thug, looking for the easy route. But not at you, ma'am. He doesn't laugh when we talk about you.'

'What about his computer?'

'Nothing on the desktop,' Khosa said, 'but there was a thumb drive under some floorboards in the studio. In a section Willis used to store wood for carving, ironically enough. We're digging into his Internet history as we speak.'

They'll find something. Shaw knows they will, Anna thought. *Perhaps a girl in a dress with roses on it...*

A nurse appeared in the doorway armed with a blood pressure monitor and a thermometer.

Holder and Khosa stepped back and moved towards the door. 'We'll come back later, ma'am. We can go over the details. Everyone sends you their regards.'

Anna waved them away with her best attempt at a smile, then turned her face towards the window and the world outside, trying not to think of Neville Cooper and the years he must have spent staring out of the window of his own cell, knowing of his innocence and despairing. She despised Willis for what he had done to her and to the women he had killed and raped. But she hated him for what he'd done to Neville.

Occasionally, she put hate aside and thought of what Charles Willis's damaged mind had been trying to achieve. She tried to find sympathy for the tortured adolescent unable to handle Emily Risman and their unborn child; a child Emily was desperate to get rid of. She tried to grasp what kind of warped mind could adopt his brother's affliction as a perfect camouflage, an affliction which even his own wife had not seen through, and which allowed him to attack women for years with impunity. And she tried to understand the look, the smile, that Khosa said he'd given when apologising to his victims. A smile which, more than anything else, cemented her conviction that Willis had all the cunning hallmarks of a psychopath.

And though she tried hard, running it over and over in her head, Anna failed. There was no understanding such a total lack of empathy.

Recriminations were all well and good. The fact remained that she should have seen it all coming. She thanked God that Wyngate had, if indeed there was a God. It brought a bitter smile. If there was a God, his face had been turned to the wall in all the time Willis had been walking the woods.

The bitter smile on her bruised face gradually faded.

Late that afternoon, Anna got a surprise visitor. Shipwright appeared with a huge bunch of flowers.

He stood awkwardly. She saw him try to smile.

'Sit,' she said.

'Oh, Anna. What have you done to yourself?'

'It's the job.'

'It's the way you do the bloody job, more like. If you won't find a bloke then you need to get a dog. Big bugger with teeth.'

'They all come with teeth.'

'Like I said, let me do the jokes. I've taken a hundred calls. They're queuing up to come and visit you. They want to throw you a party. I know you love parties.'

Anna ignored the banter. 'They?'

'Rainsford, Slack, the whole bloody lot.'

She nodded. 'It's just guilt. They can all come, but not yet. Not just yet.'

'I'll keep them at bay until you give the word. I've told them they can send cards. Here' – he hoisted a bulging plastic bag onto the bed – 'these all came to the squad room.'

'Are you back then, sir?'

Something came over Shipwright's face. Sadness? Regret? Resignation? It was difficult to pinpoint.

'No, I went to pick up my things. I'm not coming back, Anna. I've had a wake-up call. I want to be able to see all my kids as goats in Old Macdonald's sodding farm. Too cool for school, me. I'm calling it a day. And no, before you ask, I won't be getting a hi-vis jacket and helping kids across the road.'

To hide the moisture in her eyes, Anna made a show of peering into the bag. There must have been fifty envelopes.

When she looked up, Shipwright looked suddenly uncomfortable.

'What?' asked Anna.

'Rainsford will kill me, but I know you'll want to know. Forensics on the second body that Shaw dug up for you – it's a male. Mihai Petran, thirty-two, Romanian national. Dropped off the radar in 2004. Wanted for questioning in several sexual assault cases. We thought he'd buggered off back to the salt mines in Turda.'

'How did he die?'

'Bled to death. Evidence of electrocution and mutilation. Has friend Shaw's paws all over it.'

'Don't say "friend",' Anna frowned.

'And, surprise, surprise, his DNA matches the other half of the mixed samples found near Tanya Cromer on the night she was attacked.'

'The mixed sample that contains Shaw's as well?'

Shipwright nodded. 'And so the circle closes. Looks like they were in it together.'

Anna shook her head, suddenly and utterly convinced that Shipwright's surmise was wrong. 'No. I think Shaw might have picked this Petran guy out from his online travels. I wouldn't be surprised if he'd been watching him. I think it may even been possible Shaw had tried to stop him.'

'You mean the night Tanya Cromer was raped, Shaw tried to stop it?'

'It would explain the mixed sample. Shaw grappling with this Petran. Of course, I have no proof.'

Shipwright's expression was half-bemusement, half-horror. 'Bloody hell, Anna. You can certainly pick them.'

'I'm beginning to believe they pick me.'

Shipwright nodded. 'The squad is yours if you want it. Rainsford asked me to tell you.'

'Maybe,' she said. Under any other circumstances, she would have danced a jig. If she tried it now, something might well fall off. Besides, she was in too much pain, not all of it physical.

Shipwright stayed a while longer, but she was glad when he left. She wanted to grieve alone.

Some time later, when she'd stopped snivelling and the nurse had fed her, she opened the cards. Get wells and thank-you notes from Slack and the chief constable of Gloucester. Stupid, bawdy puns from Holder. Balloons and a hand-drawn horse from her niece and nephew. There were dozens of others, but halfway through she opened one that was bigger than the rest. It was a large card with a cartoon of a young woman tearing up an 'L' next to a shiny new car. The greeting said: *Congratulations on Passing Your Test*

Inside was a folded sheet of paper and a photograph; a slightly blurred snapshot of Anna in her running kit outside her house. She frowned and looked at the message in the card. There was one sentence in capitals: *GLAD WE COULD HELP*

He'd signed it:

HS

Anna dropped the card as if it had burst into flames. After a moment, she dared to pick up the folded sheet. There was no letterhead or address, but it was typed and the paper was of good quality. As she read it, she heard all the words in Shaw's voice and accent.

Dear Anna,

I hope this finds you well. Like the card? One of my journalist friends chose it. I didn't think the woman looked much like you, but it captured the moment quite nicely, don't you think?

I hope your injuries aren't too serious. The papers said that you were stable and that they were not life-threatening. You're a survivor, Anna. Like me. Strong and capable. So was the Woodsman, of course. But I knew that you would be a match for him. He needed to be flushed out. I guessed his ego would not tolerate your successes being waved in his face like a red flag. And the Internet's a wonderful thing, Anna. CILF, I thought, would be very effective, if a touch crude. Did you know you went viral? The rest I left up to you and you acquitted yourself magnificently, as I hoped you would.

By now, maybe your gorilla and the labourer will have worked out who I buried on the east side of the chapel in north Wales. He told me his name along with many other things, but I forgot it. You don't remember the name of the poisonous insects you crush. I refer to him only as the Gypsy and I trust you to work out the truth. During our discussions, he told me many of his secrets and drew many maps, sometimes in his own blood. He was a busy man. If you plug him in to your DNA database, I am certain he will light up the board. We will, I'm certain, enjoy many days out when the time is right for more treasure hunts. Take great care, Anna.

Best wishes and until the next playtime,
HS

PS: Your meddler-ex, Lambert, whose filthy mouth needed shutting, is no longer singing his tawdry song. It's difficult enough to breathe through a wired-together jaw, let alone speak.

Anna picked up the snap again. A yellow marker pen had been used to encircle two things on the glossy paper. The first was the front door of her flat, the number grainy but just legible. The second, a blurred smudge of the street name stuck to a low brick wall. It, too, was unreadable, but she guessed that if you ran the tape that this photograph was taken from enough times and froze it at just the right spot, it would have been legible.

God, she'd been so stupid. Her photograph in the newspapers, the CILF tweet. Shaw had designed them to get underneath the Woodsman's skin and offered her up as the Judas goat.

Sometimes, when she woke up in the early hours, or during those curiously quiet periods in hospitals in the late afternoons, when no one stirs, she knew her father was there with her. She saw his silhouette sitting in a chair, watching her, but it was Jane Markham's words she'd hear coming from his mouth. Another one of the grave, poetic warnings she so loved to deliver to her students: *'Remember, we are all capable of acts of terrifying destruction when the tenuous constraints of consciousness snap and the primal impulses ooze and stain the world.'*

Anna had proof enough in the dark recesses of her mind that she'd been tainted by the ooze and was driven by a need to clear it away from herself and those near her. It was why she did what she did.

But at what cost, Anna?

She still let the pain come occasionally. Harnessed it as a reminder of how instrumental Shaw had been in putting her where she was. But had he not also been responsible for helping her to get closer to the Woodsman, pointing her in the direction of finding what he'd been doing for all those years, and helping give all those other women closure?

She knew she'd supped from a poisoned chalice. But she was alive and, somehow, had passed his bloody test.

A LETTER FROM DYLAN

I want to say a huge thank you for choosing to read *The Silent Girls*. If you enjoyed it, and would like to keep up to date with all my latest releases, just sign up at the following link. Your email address will never be shared and you can unsubscribe at any time.

www.bookouture.com/dylan-young

I hope you loved *The Silent Girls* and if you did I would be very grateful if you could write a review. Authors still live and die by word of mouth. Honest reviews by genuine and loyal readers help bring the books to the attention of others. I'd love to hear what you think, and it makes such a difference helping new readers to discover one of my books for the first time.

I love hearing from my readers – you can get in touch on my Facebook page, through Twitter, Goodreads, or my website.

Thanks,
Dylan

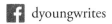 dyoungwrites

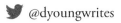 @dyoungwrites

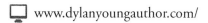 www.dylanyoungauthor.com/

ACKNOWLEDGEMENTS

Thanks go to my family who put up with me when my mind is elsewhere, in dark places where no one else would want to go, but where I have all the fun. And to Jennifer Hunt at Bookouture for giving me the opportunity to share these dark places with the world.

Printed in Great Britain
by Amazon

78074366R00169